The Skinny

Jeff Zwagerman

Black Rose Writing | Texas

ISBN: 978-1-68433-156-7
PUBLISHED BY BLACK ROSE WRITING
www.blackrosewriting.com

Printed in the United States of America
Suggested Retail Price (SRP) $19.95

The Skinny is printed in Book Antiqua

This book is dedicated to my friends Dennis and Nancy. Without their encouragement, I would never have discovered Southwest Florida or the Sanibel Island area. It has been a wild ride for this midwestern born and raised child, but has given me countless adventures and a whole host of new ideas. Thanks you two.

The Skinny

Prologue

Wie zijn billen brandt, moet op de blaren zitten
When you burn your butt, you need to sit on the blisters.
---Dutch Proverb

Fats went by his nickname. He figured no one else, other than his good friend Zander, knew his actual nomenclature. He could hardly remember it himself. It had been so long ago. Roland Sinning really didn't fit his personality, at least that's what he always told himself.

Fats sat with his elbows on the bar and his head resting on his fists. He had done a good job of putting Zander out of his mind. The bar had been busy over the holidays and the ski season, but now March had come and he could see the tail end of it. Fats had lost track of Zander and his new girlfriend. He tried to remember her name, but Audrey was the only thing that came to mind. He knew that wasn't right.

Fran, Fats' ladylove, was sitting on the other side of the bar drinking some lousy coffee. She looked up at Fats meaning to say something about his bad coffee, but she noticed the puzzled look on his face.

"What's the matter with you? This shitty coffee freaking you out?"

Fats ignored the question.

"What was the name of Zander's new romantic companion?"

"His significant other's name is Aubrey. Don't use the word 'was' when referring to her." Fran didn't like it when Fats spoke in past tense. It always signified that he was unhappy with what was happening in the present.

"You know Zander's track record with women. He may already have screwed everything up," Fats said, still resting his head on his fists.

"What's really bothering you?" Fran asked, losing the sarcasm.

"Those two have fallen off the face of the earth."

"And?"

"And I think Zander should have the common decency to at least check in regularly, so we don't have to worry."

"He's a big boy, and he's with a woman he might very well be in love with for a change. Why don't you just let everything work itself out?"

"It's not in my nature, my dear inamorata." Fats was back.

"Don't try to vocabulary me to death. I was an English major in college. I can circumnavigate spirals around your labyrinthine babble."

Fats knew it was the truth. Fran was the only woman he had ever met who understood him. She could cut through all his bullshit and get him back on point before he even realized what she had done.

"You know what is really bothering me?" Fats finally asked.

"Of course I do. We've had this conversation more times than I'd like to remember. I'll tell you what I've always told you, 'Mind your own business.' Sara Jane and her child are of no concern of yours."

She was talking about Zander's girlfriend from his youth and the fact that she was pregnant with his child. Every time Fats heard her name he would wince. It was the reason he never used it. He generally found an appropriate moniker that better fit a woman of her lack of talent and inabilities.

"But he's my friend. If the tables were turned, I would want to know." Fats sounded like a scolded child.

"Grow up. Not everything is under your control. This thing will work itself out without your meddling." Fran emphasized the last word.

Fats realized what she was talking about immediately. If it hadn't been for his meddling, Sara Jane would never have become pregnant with Zander's child. He was the one who sent Mona to follow Sara

Jane and when that went south, he talked Zander into following them to Key West. It seemed like a bad dream, but it didn't go away during his waking hours.

Someone once said, "No good deed ever goes unpunished." Fats knew it was a basic truth. He also knew he just couldn't help himself. He was one of those "rainy day people."

"I'm going to Wal-Mart to get supplies for the bar. Do you need anything?" Fran asked.

"A kind word?"

Fran went around the bar, took his face into her hands and kissed him squarely on the lips.

"The bar opens in an hour. Are you ready for the day?" Fran asked.

"I think so."

"Then get off your dead butt and get to work. Make some fresh coffee, and don't be using the soft water from the bar sink. Go in the back and use the hard water from the tap. Hard water is the key to good coffee." Fran said.

"Why haven't you told me that before?"

"I have. You just refuse to listen." Fran's voice was filled with frustration, but she was smiling.

Fats smiled back. They sounded like an old married couple, and that gave him a warm feeling somewhere down in his gut. He thought that was a strange place for a warm feeling. Most of the time his warm feelings went quite a bit lower. He wondered if he was getting sick.

"Marry me, woman. Let me put you in the midst of all these good things." Fats swung his arm around to indicate the entire bar.

"I'm already here. Don't ask me again. I don't need a scrap of paper to tell me that we are a couple," Fran said and walked briskly out the back door.

Fats watched her leave. He must have asked her to marry him a thousand times. She always turned him down. Once she told him that she didn't want to jinx their relationship. He had no idea what that meant. Something probably happened to her before they met. Fats figured she'd tell him about it when she was ready. In truth, Fats didn't know if he was the marrying type, either.

He went back to his thinking pose with his head on his fists. Many things had happened to him, since he met Zander at Ole's Big Game

Bar in Paxton, Nebraska. Most of them were good, and even the crappy things had made their friendship stronger.

Fats began to think of a time when he was known as Roland Sinning, a name that never fit him. It was a time before Zander. His life had taken many twists and turns. Most would have devastated a weaker person. He wondered if his desire to mend other people's lives came from his inability to reconstruct his own.

1

Billings, Montana-July 1948

Roland Sinning's way of life had begun long before he was born. His father, Coleman Sinning, worked at the oil refinery in Billings, Montana. He came from a long line of oil workers. It was expected that the children of oil people would become oil people as well. Something similar happened in the coalmines of West Virginia and Kentucky. It wasn't a matter of choice, but more to the point, these people were stuck without any other options. Most were uneducated and dropped out before getting close to attending high school. It was difficult and dangerous work

Coleman hated every second of his life. To make things more palatable, he would frequent the bars after work. He didn't care which one it was as long as there was whiskey.

It wasn't long before everything was spinning out of control. He received his second reprimand at work for being drunk on the job. One more incident and he would be fired. Luckily for Coleman, the refinery needed men, or he would have been fired long before the reprimands.

Coleman decided to split his off-work hours between two bars called the Rainbow and the Crystal. He knew the management at both places, and they agreed to limit his drinks to five per night. That was his way of coping with the growing concern of his alcoholism. Of course, if he were in the mood, the five-drink maximum would work in both places. He stayed true to going to only the two bars but went to both almost every night.

It was after a particularly grueling day at work, with the thermometer pushing ninety-five, that Coleman decided on the Crystal to cut the trail dust of the oil refinery. Their air conditioning always felt cooler.

He had just received his first Canadian Club and Coke and had taken about half of it down in one big swallow when he turned on his bar stool to survey the after-work crowd. There was diversity in this bar long before it became a standard with the people who leaned to the left. There were cowboys, Native Americans, bikers, old couples, young singles, street people and everything in between. It was why he liked this bar the best. Coleman didn't know where he fit in the crazy mix of humanity, but he knew he was somewhere in there. He just liked being around people and forgetting about his mundane, unimportant life.

He was still viewing the vast array of people, when his eyes stopped on a group of Native American women huddled around a pitcher of beer at one of the tables. He figured they were from the nearby Crow tribe. His eyes fell on the most beautiful woman he had ever seen. She had high cheekbones, bronze skin, and coal black hair. She was wearing her hair down around her shoulders, and Coleman couldn't take his eyes off her. From time to time she would look up and gaze around the room.

Coleman wanted to meet her in the worst way, but he didn't have the first clue about how to go about it. It was on one her gazes around the room that he gave her a small wave. She caught it immediately and focused on the bar stool where the man had dared to get her attention.

Coleman almost fell off his chair. Her eyes were blue. He had never seen a Native American with anything other than dark brown eyes. It was something unexpected. He liked the unexpected.

She smiled at Coleman and exchanged a demure wave. He raised his drink, pointed toward her, and then pointed at his drink and raised his shoulders. She understood his meaning immediately and nodded. She would let him buy her a drink.

Coleman was unsure of how to proceed. He decided to go over to her table but was surprised to see she had already risen and was moving toward him.

When she approached, Coleman stuck out his hand.

"Hello, my name is Coleman. I couldn't help but notice you at the table. I'd like to buy you a drink." Coleman hoped he didn't sound as nervous as he felt.

The Crow woman smiled broadly and Coleman couldn't help but notice her extremely white teeth. He liked everything about her, and he hadn't even had time to check out her body.

"I would like a drink. We have been drinking beer, but I'm not much of a fan. My name is Enola. Everyone just calls me Nola."

"What can I get you to drink?" Coleman asked, still nervous.

"What are you having?"

"Canadian Club and Coke."

"I'll have the same."

Coleman ordered the drink. He thought about ordering himself a second, but stopped when he realized he still had over half left. He wanted to put himself in the best light for this woman, and it wouldn't do to be slurring his words.

When the drink came, Coleman suggested they take a vacant table. He wanted to have a conversation with this woman and knew it would be difficult with everyone else within earshot.

"Enola is an interesting name. I don't think I've ever heard it before." Coleman hoped his initial attempt at conversation didn't make him sound like a fool. He was twenty-four and hadn't had much luck with women in the past.

"It's pretty common with the Crow. But I don't like it much."

"Why's that?"

"Have you heard of the Enola Gay?"

"No, I don't think I have." He didn't pay much attention to things outside his little sphere of control.

"It was the name of one of the planes that dropped the hydrogen bombs on Japan."

Coleman hadn't realized that the planes had nicknames. History had never held much interest for him, even though this particular event happened just a few years prior.

"I don't think the bomb was named after you." He was groping for something to say, and it sounded terrible coming from his mouth.

"Who knows? Enola mean solitary in the Native American culture," Nola said.

"But weren't there two bombings from the B-29's?"

"You know more than you first let on." Nola seemed impressed.

"I have always been interested in boats and planes. Nicknames haven't been on my radar."

"Well, I do happen to know that Enola Gay was the pilot's mother's name. I needed to find out the background, so I could stand up to the idiots who constantly bring up my name in connection to that horrific assault on the human race."

Coleman nodded his head. He wanted to ask if the bombs ultimately saved many more lives than they took, but he decided silence would probably be the best course of action if he wanted to see where the relationship might lead.

"So, I'll call you Nola. I like that name."

"Words have power and names have power. The Crow tribe believes that the name bestowed upon a child is the indication of the kind of life or a particular ability desired for that child."

"If Enola means solitary, what does Nola mean?" Coleman asked.

"It's Gaelic and means white shoulder, so it doesn't really apply to me."

Coleman looked at her for a few moments.

"Excuse me, but I noticed you have blue eyes which might mean that the Gaelic might have some meaning for you. I don't know what white shoulder really means, however."

"I looked it up once."

"And?"

"Exceptionally pretty." Nola looked down in embarrassment.

"Well, they got that right." Coleman laughed out loud.

Nola couldn't help but laugh with him. She had been curious about this man who wanted to buy her a drink, but now she was beginning to be entertained. She knew he was socially awkward around women, but she felt he had a good heart.

They spent the rest of the evening small talking. Coleman wanted to know more about her but was willing to take it slow. Nola didn't ask any personal questions, so he took his lead from her.

When Nola's table decided to call it a night, Coleman offered to take her home. Nola decided she could trust him and agreed. It gave him more time to just be around the most beautiful woman he had ever seen.

The interesting part of the entire evening was the fact that Coleman had only one drink. When he realized that he hadn't offered Nola another drink, he panicked.

"I'm sorry. I haven't been a very good host. Would you care for another drink?"

"One or two is usually my limit, and I reached that with your whisky and Coke. Besides, it's after one, and the bar will be closing in forty minutes."

"Where did this evening go?"

"It went with the conversation, but I have to work tomorrow so I think I should be getting back."

"I'm sorry to have the evening end. I don't even know where you live."

"I feel rather sheepish. I never told you that I live in Crow Agency. I have an apartment there. It's about fifty-five miles. So, I'm sorry as well."

"Any excuse to spend more time with you is fine with me." Coleman was serious, but he wondered if he sounded like someone with a cheesy pick-up line.

Nola didn't seem to mind and smiled as she got up from the table.

"I think we better go. I've got to be at work by eight, and we won't get to my place until after two. Then you have to come all the way back. I assume you have a job."

Coleman nodded and got up.

"Looks like we've both had a full evening, and it will be a short night. It was nice spending time with White Shoulders."

Nola gave him a push, and Coleman almost fell over the table. It was a position he was familiar with, but usually it was because he had been drinking. He was stone cold sober now, and he hadn't missed the alcohol at all. By the time he had righted himself, Nola was waiting for him at the door.

He led the way and pointed out his wheels. It was a beat-up older pickup.

"I apologize for the truck," Coleman said.

"I've ridden in much worse," was all she said.

Since the speed limit in Montana had always been what ever was reasonable and proper, Coleman decided to drive fifty. It would give him more time with this beauty. He had no idea if this would be the last time, or if she would agree to see him again.

"I didn't ask you what you did for work," Coleman said.

"That's right, you didn't. I didn't ask you what you did, either."

Coleman thought for a moment. "I work for the oil refinery."

"What do you do?"

"Everything they ask me to do."

"Do you find it rewarding?"

"I hate every minute of it."

Nola turned and looked right at him.

"Then why do you stay?"

"What else would I do? It's all I know. It's all my father knew. Before the oil fields were discovered, my grandfather worked in the coal mines and so did his father."

"You're telling me you are stuck?" Nola asked.

"I guess I am."

"I can relate to that. But I think it's for different reasons." Nola said.

"I don't know what you mean."

"Here I am, working on the reservation. Why do think that is?"

"I just assume with your ability to talk to people, that it must be a good job."

"Do you know what I do?"

"No, I don't think you told me."

"I do tours of the Little Bighorn National Monument. I point out the graves of General Custer's men and where they fell on the battlefield to tourists. Then I take those same white folks to the gift shop and sell them trinkets."

Coleman started to laugh but caught himself and looked over at Nola.

"Sorry."

"Nonsense. I'm happy you caught the irony. The government helped send me to college at Montana State University, but the only place I can find work is back on the reservation."

"I'll bet you graduated pretty high on the totem pole." Coleman realized what he had said. "That was insensitive. I apologize."

Nola laughed.

"Good joke. But the joke really is on us both. We're stuck going nowhere for different reasons. Sure, I graduated with honors, but what good is it? No one will take a second look at me because of my heritage."

"I liked what I saw on the very first look."

"You're sweet, but you aren't hiring college-educated Native Americans are you?"

Coleman thought he might not have a chance with this beautiful woman. He was outclassed in so many ways. He never even went to high school. How in the world could she even want to be seen with him? It caused him a great deal of anxiety. He decided to find out immediately where he stood.

"Could I see you again?"

"I would have been disappointed if you hadn't asked," Nola said, easily.

Coleman was taken off-guard. He looked straight ahead and smiled. Then he remembered the ball was in his court.

"When would be a good time for you?"

"A bunch of us go to the Crystal every Friday. So, I can meet you there in a week."

"I could pick you up."

"I don't think I'm ready for that just yet. Let's do it this way and see where it takes us."

Coleman was in no position to argue and nodded in agreement.

Nola directed him to her apartment, and as she was getting out Coleman grabbed her hand.

"We haven't exchanged last names."

"You first," Nola said.

"My full name is Coleman Sinning."

It was Nola's turn to smile.

"It is an unusual last name for sure. I'll bet you get a lot smart remarks."

"More than you'll ever know. How about you?"

"You know my first name. My last name is McGuire."

Coleman's jaw dropped open.

"My father was a trapper and mountain man. I think he might have been Scottish or Irish or maybe a little of both. That's where I got my blue eyes. Maybe that's why I'm different. Solitary may very well be a good definition of my name and my life."

Coleman was about to ask her what she meant, but she pulled her hand back and jumped out of the truck. She slammed the door and was gone.

It was a long ride back to Billings, and Coleman was running the entire evening over and over in his mind.

2

Coleman didn't have a drink the entire week. He spent his time cleaning up the small trailer he called home. He rented a non-descript one-bedroom trailer in a sea of trailers owned by the refinery. The lyric line about "owing your soul to the company store" defined the entire place.

He wasn't a very good housekeeper. In fact, he was terrible. There had never been a reason to keep things neat and tidy. It took the entire week to clean things up so he wouldn't embarrass himself if someone came to visit. With any luck, that someone would be Nola, but he wasn't going to rush anything. Working on his trailer was just fine, because he had time on his hands. He wasn't spending every waking hour at the bars.

It was unusual for Coleman not to wake up with a hangover. It was a new experience and not altogether unpleasant. He decided to be more productive at work and try to change his attitude. He started by arriving early and leaving later than the others. His immediate supervisor became puzzled when Coleman started to volunteer for some of the shittier jobs. Coleman just smiled and went about doing the job he hated.

The week crawled by until finally Friday arrived. It was the only day he didn't stay late. When the five o'clock whistle blew, Coleman was already in his pickup heading to his trailer. He needed to shower and change clothes before heading to the bar to meet Nola. There had been a nagging feeling pulling at him all week. Would she actually show up, or had their first meeting been a ruse? He had seen women play guys in bars all the time. He didn't understand what enjoyment these women got from that kind of thing. It seemed sad somehow. He wondered who was sadder, the guy being played or the woman doing the playing? He just hoped he wasn't being "that guy."

Coleman arrived at the Crystal fifteen minutes before six. Many of the regulars were there, but he didn't see Nola or her group of friends. He took a stool at the bar and ordered his usual drink. He had taken extra care to make sure he wasn't sporting any of the oil from the refinery on his skin. He had spent more time than usual in the shower scrubbing his body until it was almost raw. He shaved for the second time that day. Finally, he splashed a great deal of Old Spice over most of his body. He hadn't wanted the smell of the refinery on him when meeting Nola. He thought he might have overdone the cologne just a little.

The bartender brought over his drink and looked at Coleman.

"Did you fall in a bucket of perfume?"

"Too much?" Coleman asked.

"Maybe if we all lost our sniffers it would be just right." The bartender went off to help another customer just to get away from Coleman.

Coleman got up, went into the men's room and splashed water over his face. He decided to take off his shirt, took a few wet paper towels and tried to remove the scent from the rest of his body. When he finished, he went back out to the bar and sat down. He took a sip of his drink. It tasted different. He wasn't sure he even cared for it. Maybe being off alcohol for the week had changed his taste. He was certain it hadn't changed his taste in Nola however.

Coleman hadn't bothered to look around after he returned from the bathroom. He might have been too self-absorbed. Suddenly, there was a hand on his back. When he turned around, there stood Nola. Her hair was in braids, and she was wearing some kind of tribal costume. Coleman thought she looked like a picture postcard.

"Sorry. I didn't have time to change. The rest of the girls decided not to come to Billings tonight, so I hitched a ride with an old white couple that had been on my tour," Nola said, almost apologizing.

Coleman was astonished. She had made a considerable effort to fulfill a promise. He hoped it would be worth her trouble.

"You look stunning," Coleman said. He stared at her in appreciation.

Nola sat next to him at the bar. "I think I'll just have a beer."

Coleman ordered whatever was on tap.

"Have you had anything to eat?"

"I assumed you would be treating."

Coleman smiled. "What would be of interest to you?"

"I think I would like you to cook for me."

Coleman panicked. "I don't think that would be a very good idea. I'm not much of a cook."

"I don't care. I want to see what you can do with the unexpected."

Coleman thought for a moment. He could grill something. He had a charcoal grill at the trailer. He could do some small potatoes and maybe a vegetable in some foil.

Nola was enjoying seeing the wheels turning. His face had gone from extreme discomfort to a look of serenity, as he was formulating a plan.

"What kind of vegetable would you like?" he asked.

"How about asparagus?"

Coleman made a face. "So, you want smelly urine?"

"Sure. If we both eat it, what would it matter?" Nola enjoyed playing with him. He was sweet but just a bit naïve.

"Okay, if that's what you want. Finish your beer. I'll need to make a stop at a market to pick up a few things."

Nola started to laugh. "You don't have to do that. I'm just messing with you. We can go anywhere you'd like."

"No. I'm going to do dinner for you. It's a good idea. Let's go."

Coleman left half his drink on the bar.

Nola chugged the remainder of her glass of beer.

"Lead on. This might very well be the adventure of a lifetime."

Coleman grabbed her arm, and they left the bar. He picked up the items for dinner at the local market. He put Nola in charge of dessert. She picked out chocolate ice cream, and they were on their way to Coleman's trailer.

"You know this was only an excuse to see where you live, don't you?" Nola asked.

"I hope you have low expectations. It's just a small trailer. I rent it from the company."

"So, you don't have any deep roots to this place," Nola replied, and sat back.

Coleman thought it was a strange comment. He was still trying to decide what she meant when they pulled into his gravel drive.

"Wow. You didn't mention that you lived in a palace."

Coleman just smiled and shook his head. He liked this little smartass.

"Why don't you help out and clean the vegetables while I start the grill?" Coleman asked.

"I thought this was going to be your deal."

"It is, but dinner might be ready a little quicker if someone would help."

"Fine." Nola took the bag of groceries and went into the trailer.

Coleman opened the charcoal and put a mound into the grill he had actually cleaned during the week. He splashed on some charcoal lighter and lit the coals. He waited a few minutes to make sure the edges were turning white. When he was satisfied that the coals were lit, he went into the trailer.

The bag of groceries was sitting on counter next to the sink. He didn't see Nola. He took a few steps into the hallway toward his bedroom, when he heard the shower running. He had all he could do to stop himself from going over and taking a peek. It just wouldn't be appropriate yet.

Coleman went to work cleaning and cutting up the asparagus and potatoes. He put both into separate aluminum foil tents along with a good portion of vegetable oil. He went out and placed them on the grill. When he returned, Nola was standing in the hallway drying her hair with a towel. She had found one of his chambray shirts and was using it as a cover up. It was long enough to cover her lower parts, and she had left the top two buttons open.

Coleman just stared. It was the first time he had been able to see what Nola's body looked like. She wore clothes that showed very little, and Coleman had been so intrigued by her face that he forgot all about the rest of it.

"Sorry about the vegetables. I got distracted by your shower."

"No problem." Coleman was relieved he had decided to clean up the place. His shower had been a disaster. "You look fantastic, by the way."

Coleman could have sworn that her eyes twinkled for a moment.

"I hope you don't mind me wearing your shirt. I needed to get out of that costume."

"Whatever you need. It looks so much better on you anyway."

"Do you have anything to drink in this place?" Nola asked.

"There is beer in the fridge."

"Good. Let's drink." She went to the fridge and found two bottles of Schlitz. "Oh gees, you know this stuff makes you fart don't you?"

"Of course, why do you think I buy it?" Coleman was starting to feel comfortable with Nola and wanted to share in her playful nature.

Nola laughed and opened the bottles.

"I think I'm beginning to like you. Once you lose some of that stiffness, you're not half-bad."

"You keep wearing my shirts, and I'll show you stiffness."

"Maybe I should just take it off." She reached for the buttons.

Coleman grabbed her hand.

"We should probably have dinner before you decide to do a striptease in my trailer."

Then he leaned over and kissed her gently on the lips, and she let him. It was one of those moments that neither had expected, but it seemed natural and just right for the moment.

"I hope you didn't think that was too forward," Coleman said.

"I was wondering how long it would take you." She smiled. "Why don't you put on the steaks, and I'll set the table."

Coleman followed her orders. He seasoned the rib eyes and put them on the grill. He decided to remain outside with the grill to make sure they were done just right. He didn't want anything to burn. Nola said she liked her steak medium to medium rare. That was just the way Coleman liked it also. These steaks were too expensive to ignore.

Nola came out to join Coleman and brought out his beer. She sat on the steps and put the shirttails between her legs to avoid giving any passerby a free show. Coleman thought it was the most provocative thing he had ever seen. He had a hard time keeping his mind on the steaks.

They talked a little about their pasts, and Coleman figured they were about the same age. She might be a year younger after he found out when she had graduated from college. She was right in the ballpark, anyway. A few years, either way, didn't matter much to him.

When the steaks were cooked to his satisfaction, they brought everything in and placed it on the table. Nola put the potatoes in a bowl, and the asparagus went right on the plates. Coleman let Nola choose her steak. One appeared a bit more done than the other, and she chose that one. Coleman liked his a bit rare, so that worked out perfectly. Everything was cooked to perfection, and Nola told Coleman just that.

"I'm impressed with your grilling talents."

"It would be the only talent I have concerning food preparation."

"I'm pretty good. Maybe I should cook for you sometime."

"I would like that."

There was too much food, and neither could finish their steak.

"Looks like we'll have left-overs for tomorrow," Nola said.

Coleman wondered if she meant that she would take some home with her or if she would be staying the night.

His had his answer immediately. Nola got up and sat on Coleman's lap and kissed him. Then she got up, took his hand and led him to the bedroom. She was unbuttoning the shirt she was wearing as they walked. When they reached the bedroom she quickly took off the shirt and threw it over Coleman's face. He had to laugh at her antics.

He pulled off the shirt but was disappointed to see she was already in bed under the covers. He was uncertain about how to proceed.

"Come over here, and take off your clothes."

Coleman turned his back and began removing his shirt.

"No. Stand at the foot of the bed and face me. I want to watch." Nola was clearly enjoying herself.

"I don't think this is quite fair."

"Oh, you poor boy. Here let me help." Nola threw off the covers and stood in front of Coleman.

Coleman could only marvel how beautiful she was without her clothes. Her breasts were full and erect. Her figure was a complete hourglass with full hips and butt. Coleman didn't want to ogle, but he just couldn't help himself.

"Take a picture," Nola said, sounding stern.

"I would if I could, but I don't have a camera. I just need to etch this in my memory."

"Why? Will this just be a one night stand?" Nola was playing again.

"Not if it is up to me."

Nola embraced Coleman. As he ran his hands down her back, she was removing his belt. Soon his pants were down around his ankles, he stepped out of them, and Nola already had his shirt on the floor.

Coleman stood in his socks and underwear. He hoped there were no holes in either.

"Take off those socks. You look stupid."

He did as he was told.

"Do you think you can get out of those boxers without help?" Nola asked, noting the tent that had appeared in the front.

Once again, Coleman followed Nola's directive. He decided to play along and pulled his boxers down just a bit. Then he would pull them up again like a strip teaser. Nola was soon in stitches. He finally pulled them all the way down, flipped them into the air with his toe and caught them in mid-air. He threw them at Nola and she ducked as they hit the lamp next to the bed. The lamp toppled over and broke on the floor.

Nola stopped and looked at Coleman. He hadn't lost his erection, and she decided she liked what she saw.

"I never liked that lamp anyway," Coleman said, and this time he became the aggressor.

There would be no sleep in Coleman's trailer the rest of the night.

3

The coupling lasted until 6:00 the next morning. Between the carnality there was time for conversation. The dialogue didn't last very long when they began, because they were both in their mid-twenties and virile. Younger eighteen and nineteen year-olds might be able to recovered faster. However, what these two lacked in instant recovery time, they made up for in a variety of life experiences. As their time between recoveries became more prolonged, they would both lay back and just talk.

Coleman realized, almost immediately, that it was easier to talk when he was naked in bed with a gorgeous and seductive woman. He decided that making love with a woman lowered his inhibitions. He liked being comfortable enough with someone to share things he normally kept to himself. Nola always seemed to start the more personal conversations.

"Tell me about your childhood," she said, and rolled over to her side.

"It was shitty. You don't want to hear about that."

"I want to know all about you. I want to know what brought you to this very moment."

"Okay. I'll tell you mine, but you'll need to tell me yours. I think your story will be much more interesting than mine," Coleman replied.

Nola thought for a moment.

"Deal," was all she said.

"My father worked at the oil refinery, my mother was a waitress at a little diner and that's where they met. They dated for a while and then got married by the Justice of the Peace. I don't know much about their early years. I don't know if they even loved each other. I think they just got together out of a matter of convenience.

They were drinkers and went out drinking almost every night. People have told me they would take me along, when I was young, and put me on the corner of the bar. I don't remember any of that. When I was older, they just left me home. I was pretty much on my own since I was five."

Nola was nodding her head taking in everything Coleman said.

"So, they named you Coleman. What does the name mean?" Nola asked.

"I looked it up once. I think the English translation meant 'the burner of charcoal.' The Irish version meant 'dove'. Since my family had a history in the coal mines and oil fields, I think the first definition fits."

Nola was quiet and looked at Coleman.

"Maybe the name is a progression. They may both be right."

Coleman didn't have the slightest idea what she was talking about, so he continued with his story.

"The older I got, the more they drank. I can't remember either one of them ever without a beer in front of them. The more they drank, the bigger their fights became. Most people told me they were of epic proportions. I just assumed everyone's parents were like mine."

"Did they ever hit you?" Nola asked.

"They did a few times. But they were usually drunk, and I was quicker than they were."

"A survivor."

"I didn't spend much time at home. After school I would be with friends. Sometimes their parents let me stay for dinner. At least I was able to eat something decent."

"Your parents didn't feed you?"

"They always had food in the house but most of it was junk. Chips and soda were my usual staples. Remember, I didn't know any better at first. Later, when I was old enough to realize how other kid's parent behaved, I got confused. Then I got angry, and I avoided them like the plague. There weren't any resources for kids and families back then. I was on my own."

"When I was twelve, there was an explosion at the refinery. It was probably my dad's fault, since he mostly went to work drunk. Anyway, he was killed instantly. I never felt much. He never was much of a father to me."

"What happened to you and your mom?"

"She quit drinking almost immediately. She kept her job at the diner, but it didn't pay very much, and soon we were pretty much broke. The oil company allowed us to stay in their housing as long as we could come up with the rent. It didn't take long before she made me quit school and get a job at the refinery. I was barely thirteen and doing a man's job, but I made enough for us to stay living in the rental. We did have food, since my mother had quit drinking."

"I can see why you hate your job. It has nothing but bad memories," Nola said.

"Yeah, but that wasn't the worst of it. When I was sixteen, I came home from work and found a note on the kitchen table. My so-called mother had left with someone she had met at the diner. I think they went to California, because she sent me a few letters the first few years, and the letters had a California postmark on the envelopes. She never listed her return address, so I couldn't have written back even if I had wanted. It was the last thing I wanted to do, however. I hated her. Can you imagine being left at that age to fend for yourself?"

"Actually, I can," Nola said. "Do you still have the letters? I would like to read them."

"No, I burned them. I didn't even bother to read the damn things after the first few. I don't know what happened to her, and I really never cared to find out."

"I can't say that I blame you. I noticed you never used your parents' names."

Coleman quietly thought about it.

"I hadn't noticed. I guess I never use names when it comes to discussing them. If I would name them, it would seem to give confirmation that they were a part of my life. They never were."

"Some people should never be parents." Nola looked away.

"That's my story. Now it's your turn," Coleman said, and rolled over to face Nola.

She rolled over on her back. Her breasts stood straight up. She was beautiful and Coleman could hardly contain himself, but he wanted to hear her story. He ran his fingers up and down her rib cage lightly. He would pause where her leg met her hip and let his fingers brush her pubic region before he made his way back up to her breasts. His fingers would barely touch the area between the bottom of her breast and her chest. He could feel the spot where her breasts rose from her flat stomach. It was the most sensual feeling he had ever had with a woman.

Coleman could tell that Nola enjoyed his touch. She trembled ever so slightly when he reached either her North or South Pole.

"I thought you wanted to hear my story. If you keep doing that I can't keep my mind on what to say."

Coleman stopped and let his open hand rest lightly on her stomach.

She began her saga.

"You already know of my parent's lineage. My father had a small claim southwest of Bozeman. He had a little cabin, and they lived in that the first few years. I think they were happy, at least that's what my mother told me. Then she got pregnant. She moved back to the reservation, because the cabin wasn't a place to raise a baby. My father would come back to visit weekly. At first my mother seemed content to stay with me, while my father went prospecting. But when his return to the reservation became more infrequent, I think she panicked. She truly loved that man, and the Crow Nation would never really accept him. She took his last name, but I doubt if they were ever legally married. I was registered with the Crow, and they allowed me to use the McGuire last name.

She had a decision to make. She chose the man over me. I was left with her sister, with the promise, that she would take me back when I was old enough to brave the prospecting lifestyle. My father never came back to the reservation, and my mother came to see me sporadically, at first, and then later, not at all.

My aunt did a good job of raising me, and it was her relentless pursuit of government money that finally sent me to college in Bozeman. I'm sure it took a huge toll on her social life. What Crow man wanted to be seen with someone who had a blue-eyed youngster in tow?

My first year at college, I found a guy who agreed to help me find my parents' cabin if I would go out with him. He seemed nice enough, so I agreed. I was more interested in finding my mother. It took us a long time, but we finally tracked down their claim. The cabin looked like it hadn't been lived in for some time. The mine entrance had rubble from top to bottom. After talking to the nearest neighbor, I found that there had been an explosion and cave-in. The mine was gone, and both my parents were thought to be inside. That was at least three years prior."

"Didn't anyone try to inform you?" Coleman asked.

"The neighbor lived a few miles away on his own claim, and he barely knew who they were. He told me they weren't much for socializing."

"Didn't anyone try to retrieve the bodies?" Coleman asked.

"Nobody cared. I decided that it was a fitting burial site for the two of them. I did have a stone with their names and dates placed at the entrance of the mine. It still is there as far as I know."

"What about the cabin and the mine?"

"I guess I own it now."

"Have you thought about selling?" Coleman was curious.

"No. It never crossed my mind. I suppose I should look into it."

"We could do a road trip sometime when we both have a day off. I would be happy to drive you."

Nola thought about the offer and decided almost immediately that she wanted to move on the sale of the property. It had no real meaning for her. She had never actually lived there, and her parents were dead and gone. She didn't believe in all the sacred burial ground tradition. Once someone died, they were gone: ashes to ashes, dust to dust.

She turned to Coleman. "I would like that."

"By the way, I noticed you never mentioned your parents' names. We must have a great deal in common."

They made love once more.

Neither wanted to leave the bed, but they had to get to work. It was a Saturday, but they both worked six and seven days per week in a two-week cycle. The real trick to finding a mutual time to get to Bozeman would take some advanced planning.

Coleman had to be to work at 7:00, so he showered first. He tried to be as quick as possible. As he was getting out of the shower, Nola brushed past him and took his place. Coleman had all he could do to keep from pulling her to him and returning to the bedroom.

He knew she had to be to work by 8:00, however. He wouldn't have time to take her back to Crow Nation and get to work on time himself. He had an idea, as he got dressed. It was something he had been considering almost the entire night. It would be touchy, since they hadn't known each other for long. He knew he would have to be careful how he presented his idea. He was thinking about everything, when Nola emerged in her Native American dress and pigtails.

"I have cereal if you wanted something to eat before you go.'" Coleman said.

"I never eat breakfast."

"Me either. It seems like a waste of time. I'd rather spend the extra minutes in bed." Coleman wondered if she caught his meaning.

Nola smiled. She knew what he meant.

"I'm ready for you to take me back," Nola said.

"Sit for a minute." Coleman took her hands, and they sat at the table.

"We're both going to be late," Nola said, but she didn't pull her hands from Coleman's.

"That's what I wanted to talk about. I can't take you back and be on time for work, so I want you to take my truck. I can walk. It's only about a half-mile and it's an easy walk."

"I guess I can do that." She smiled. "It will give me an excuse to come back tonight."

It was what Coleman wanted to hear.

"About that. I would like you to move in with me. You could give up your apartment and save some money."

Nola lost her smile.

Coleman figured he had blown his opportunity by rushing into something that should have happened over weeks or months, not days.

Nola's smile returned.

"I would consider it with only one demand."

"What's that?" Coleman asked, feeling a huge weight being lifted from his shoulders.

"Never, ever, ask me to marry you."

4

Nola moved in that Saturday night after work. She loaded Coleman's truck with her belongings and left her apartment key with the manager. He told her that she wouldn't get any money back, even though she had paid for the entire month in advance. Nola told him she didn't care and was happy to leave the fleabag that he called an apartment.

Nola had very few personal items. Most of her things consisted of clothing she used for work. Coleman gave her the closet and single chest of drawers. He moved his clothes into the little space that housed the laundry. He didn't have much either. They both lived Spartan lives.

The summer was speeding by the two of them. They would see each other in the evenings and then be thinking about the other at their jobs. They couldn't wait for work to be over. They seldom went out, opting instead to cook for each other. Most would call it love.

One evening in August, as the two were sitting outside, enjoying the beginning of the change of seasons, Nola made a decision.

"If we're going to Bozeman, I think we should be going soon."

Coleman got up, went to his pickup and returned with a road atlas. He opened it, found Montana and handed it to Nola.

"Plan the route, and let's go," Coleman said.

"I can get some vacation time, but I have to give them a few days' notice," Nola said, thinking out loud.

"Sounds good to me."

"Wait. Do you have vacation time?"

Coleman snorted. "I can take as much time as I want. Of course I won't get paid. There is no vacation on the refinery rig."

"Won't they fire you?" Nola asked.

"Sure. But then they'll hire me back when I return. They need bodies to work the rig. It's dangerous and dirty, and no one in their right mind would agree to ever work there."

"And yet, there you are."

"Exactly. How much vacation can you take?" Coleman asked, excited.

"I can squeak out a week, I think."

"That should be enough," Coleman said, still showing a great deal of excitement in his voice.

"I think you'd better tell me what is going on. I thought we were going to the cabin and make some decisions on that."

"We most certainly will, but I've been thinking about something else lately. And it could very well be a factor concerning your property."

"Are you going to tell me, or are we going to play charades?" Nola asked, enjoying his boyish antics.

"The refinery pays well, because they want to try and keep the people they train for more than just a few months. I've been putting quite a bit of money aside since I started working there. Even more since I've cut down on my drinking." He smiled, hoping Nola wouldn't be alarmed by the confession.

"Someone save me from all these ramblings," Nola said. "Cut to the chase."

"I think I want to get into a business." Coleman stopped and looked at Nola.

"Still not enough information. What do I have to do to pry this idea out of you?"

"Take off your clothes," Coleman joked.

"I might be persuaded if it would get me away from your soliloquy. What kind of business?"

"I was thinking about opening a bar. It's about the only thing I know besides the refinery. I have spent enough time in them. I'm pretty sure I could make it work. I have some ideas about making it someplace unique."

"Where would you want to try this crazy idea?" The question didn't really mirror Nola's true feeling. She was actually warm to the idea.

"That's what I want us to do on this trip. We need to check out places. We would need to be in agreement."

"What would my role be in this business venture?" Nola asked.

"I can be the bartender and run the bar, but I would need someone to help with the business end. I know nothing in that area. I never even went to high school."

Nola's nostrils flared for a moment.

"That means nothing. You have life experiences that make you smarter than most people. I doubt whether most could have survived what you went through and come out as undamaged. Anyone can learn the business side. I'll teach you that part, and you'll teach me how to make drinks and talk to people."

Coleman liked what she said. He liked that she said he was smarter than most people. He doubted it was true, but it was nice to hear. It was the other thing she said that made him feel even better. It meant Nola was accepting his wild dream.

"So, I guess you're in with the idea?"

Nola looked at Coleman for a few seconds. She realized she had just made a commitment while defending Coleman's honor. Where had that come from? She probably had liked the idea from the start, so it shouldn't have been a surprise. But it was a surprise. She didn't usually jump into anything so quickly without some thought and weighing of options. This was the second time in a few months she had made a snap decision. The first was moving in with Coleman, and it was a bit unnerving.

Nola grabbed Coleman's face with both hands.

"We will be equal partners. I expect to use whatever money I get from the sale of the mine and cabin."

"I was counting on it." Coleman smiled, and put his hands gently on her face as well. "If you haven't noticed, I'm in love with you."

"I know," was all Nola could say.

She kissed him fully on the lips. She felt that she loved this man also, but she could never say it. She had never told anyone she loved them, and the words would stick in her throat whenever she thought about saying them. She hadn't even told her aunt that she loved her. That was crazy, because she had given up everything to raise her, and Nola knew she actually did love her. She just couldn't say it.

"Why don't you give the tribe a week's notice, and we'll leave next Saturday early," Coleman said.

Nola heard him talking and nodded in agreement, but her thoughts were miles away. She had needed to be strong and independent and very seldom relied on anyone but herself. Now this man inserted himself into her life, and everything was changing. It seemed all too rapid for her comfort.

Then something snapped in her mind. It was time to throw away her cautiousness. Life was going nowhere for either of them. If they stayed where they were, they would both be miserable. Move on, her thoughts were saying. Her emotions were having a harder time, and the conflict was too much to handle.

She knew she would need to rely on Coleman. It would be easier for someone else to be the decision maker for a change.

Letting someone else make a decision was a decision in itself. The weight she had been feeling had lifted.

"You're in charge. I'll be along for the adventure," Nola said, finally.

"That's fine with me, but we both have to be in agreement where we'll finally settle. A partnership won't survive unless there is total agreement." Coleman was firm.

~

They were on the road the following Saturday by 6:00. Nola had charted the course, and Coleman was happy to have her engaged. They stopped in Bozeman, and Nola showed him the campus. It was a beautiful place, and Coleman thought he would have liked to have the opportunity to attend college. But he was twenty-four without a high school diploma. That part of his life had passed him by some time ago. Although it might have been different with a set of parents who cared, Coleman didn't dwell on it. His life's path and experiences were all he had ever known.

After breakfast at a local restaurant, they headed southwest toward the claim where Nola's parents had lived, worked and died. There was little traffic on the narrow rocky dirt roads, and Coleman thought it was lucky for them. It would be difficult to meet a vehicle on these winding paths. He was happy it hadn't rained recently. The road would be impassible in mud. Even his pickup wouldn't be able to navigate in conditions like that.

After two hours of bouncing around on what was billed as a road, the two came around a side hill and almost ran right into Nola's cabin.

"Wow. I wasn't expecting that," Coleman said, when he finally took his foot off the brake.

"Sorry. I haven't been here in so long that I forgot about the terrain."

"Nothing hurt." Coleman got out of the pickup.

Nola followed Coleman toward the small cabin. She pointed over toward the mine. She stopped short. The mine's entrance was open. Someone had been removing the debris.

"Someone has been here. The mine is open," Nola said.

Just as Nola finished speaking, Coleman caught some movement. A gunnysack covering a window in the cabin moved ever so slightly.

"Hey, you in the cabin, show yourself," Coleman yelled.

Suddenly someone stuck a carbine out of the same window. Coleman grabbed Nola, and the couple dove behind the pickup.

They heard a high-pitched voice.

"You'd better get off my property, or I'll shoot you both."

"It's not your property. This woman owns it, and you are

trespassing," Coleman yelled.

"No. It's my claim, and you'd better get out of here."

"If it's yours, why are you hiding and threatening us with a gun?" Coleman was getting pissed. "We are unarmed by the way. If you want, we can let the law sort this out."

There was silence. Obviously, the trespasser was considering his options. Nola looked at Coleman and just shook her head.

"What kind of mess did we just stumble into?"

"I think if whoever is in the cabin really wanted us dead, we would have been shot when we first got out of the pickup," Coleman said.

They saw the gun that had been hanging out of the window tumble to the ground. Coleman ran over and grabbed it and ran back to the pickup.

"Look at this thing. It's all rusted up. It isn't even functional. It's pretty old."

"All right. Come out of the cabin. Nobody is going to hurt you," Nola said, trying for calm.

The only door opened a crack, and then a young man came out with his hands in the air. He was dressed in a light blue chambray work shirt and a pair of dark pants with suspenders. He had a big round straw hat on his head, and his dark hair fell to his shoulders. Nola thought it looked like a pageboy cut. Everything he wore apparently hadn't seen the wash in quite a while. Nola thought he might be sixteen or seventeen.

"Oh, put your damn hands down. We aren't here to hurt you," Coleman said.

The boy did as he was told. He looked frightened and glanced over toward the cabin.

"Who else is with you?" Nola asked.

"My sister."

"Tell her to come out," Nola said.

"Ruthie, come out here," the boy said simply.

The girl came out timidly. Nola guessed her age at sixteen. She was wearing a long dress made of some kind of simple light blue material. There was what looked like a white cap or bonnet on her head. At least Nola thought it might have been white at one time. It was a dirty gray now. But what caught her eye almost immediately was the dirty white apron she had tied around her waist. Nola could see a thickness at the lower part of her stomach that the girl seemed to be trying to cover up. There was no doubt she was pregnant.

Coleman didn't notice any of those things. He was scratching his head wondering what these two were doing alone on someone else's property.

"I'm Nola and this is Coleman. You are Ruthie, I guess. What's your name, young man?"

"My name is Jeb."

"What are you doing here?" Coleman asked.

"None of your business, English."

Nola started to laugh. The three looked at her.

"Well, bless my tired Crow feet. We've got a couple of Amish on our hands."

5

"Do I look like 'English' to you?" Nola asked the boy named Jeb.

He just shrugged. The girl called Ruthie had finally raised her head looking at Nola.

"You are the most beautiful woman I have ever seen."

"Finally. Someone with the right answers," Nola said, and then laughed.

It broke the tension, and Ruthie smiled. Even Jeb had something tugging at the corner of his mouth.

"It's hot standing out in the sun. Let's go inside." Coleman pointed at the cabin.

It was dark inside but at least ten degrees cooler. After their eyes adjusted, both Nola and Coleman were surprised at the cleanliness of the cabin's interior.

"I was expecting this place to be pretty much in ruins after it sat empty for so long," Nola said, looking around.

"It was pretty bad when we got here. We've fixed it up a bit," Jeb said.

"Pretty livable, I'd say. Better than my damn trailer," Coleman said, trying to follow Nola's lead.

"Let's all sit and hear your story," Nola said.

"What makes you think we're going to tell you anything?" Jeb asked, still trying to act tough.

"Jeb, sit down. Stop being stupid. This is obviously her land," Ruthie said, in control.

Jeb looked stunned and sat down. Nola hid a smile. She was sure Jeb had never been spoken to like that by a woman before. The Amish were known for being a patriarchal sect where women had their place, and the men were at the top of the hierarchy. Nola liked this Ruthie girl's spunk. She had some of her own similar traits.

"Who wants to start?" Nola asked.

"We're from a little town in eastern Iowa called Kalona. Most of us live on farms in the area." Jeb looked away as he spoke.

"You are a long ways from Iowa," Coleman said.

"We left there in May," Jeb replied.

"Why?" Nola asked.

"We were shunned. There was no reason to stay."

"I don't understand. What is shunned?" Coleman asked.

"No one talks to you. It is forbidden, and we couldn't converse or break bread together with anyone in our order." Jeb had disgust in his voice.

"I've never heard of such a thing. How long does that go on?" Nola asked.

"It depends on how the elders feel about the seriousness of breaking the rules of the order."

"How long would you be shunned?" Nola asked.

"Forever."

"What did you do to get such a shitty punishment?" Coleman asked.

Jeb wouldn't answer. He looked away for a time and then looked back to Ruthie. Both Nola and Coleman continued to try and be patient with the couple. It was quiet for an uncomfortably long time. Finally, Ruthie spoke.

"They caught us laying together."

The shock on both Nola and Coleman's face was evident. Neither could find the words to reply.

"It's not like it sounds," Ruthie said. "We aren't brother and sister by blood. Jeb's mother and her baby died in childbirth, and my father fell from the top of a barn during a community barn raising. He died right there. Since these two things happened at almost the same time, the elders approved his father and my mother for marriage. We became a family of convenience. We had many brothers and sisters by that union, but we weren't really related. Jeb had an older brother, but he was angry that his father took my mother, and he left the order."

"That's not how the elders saw it." Jeb had anger in his voice.

"Well, they were wrong." Ruthie was being strong. "Jeb and I grew up together like brother and sister, it is true. There was always something more between us. We didn't know what it was until later. We fell in love, and we spent time together in secret places. When we were discovered, they wanted to excommunicate us and throw us out of the order. Our father asked the elders to shun us instead, and that's what they decided to do."

"It would have been better to just throw us out," Jeb said.

"We lasted almost a year without being able to talk to anyone but each other. It was no way to live. So, we just left and never looked back."

"When did you find out Ruthie was pregnant?" Nola asked.

Ruthie and Jeb looked at each other, and Nola could see they were shocked. Neither of them responded.

"How in the world did you end up here?" Coleman asked, trying to break the tension and his own confusion.

"It's my fault," Jeb said. "There was a circus show up in Iowa City, and we hitched a ride. They needed people to work, and they hired us right away. But it was bad. They worked us like mules, and somewhere in South Dakota, we found out that Ruthie was pregnant. She hid it the best she could, but she got sick and couldn't do all the work they stacked on her. We decided to make a break for it. We had a little money but they didn't pay us very much. We waited until we made Jackson, Wyoming, and then left when they started to put up the tents. I'm sure it made them angry to lose their two slaves, but they were too busy to go after us and by then it was too late. We were gone. We were headed straight up for Bozeman when we stumbled on this place."

"Where did you think you could go without money?"

"My older brother lives in Spokane, Washington. I know if we could get there, he would help us."

"When is the last time you've had contact with him?" Nola asked.

Jeb shrugged his shoulders.

"I don't remember. He used to send letters, and if I got to the mailbox before anyone else I could read what he wrote to me. I'm sure most of his letters got burned."

"What makes you think he's still around Spokane?" Coleman asked.

"I just know it. That's where we're going." Jeb was resolute.

Nola and Coleman exchanged glances.

"That's quite a story. You two have been strong, but Ruthie is pregnant. You've got to get where you are going for her sake."

"Jeb thought that maybe we could find some gold in your mine to help us get to Spokane," Ruthie said.

"You know about mining?" Nola asked.

"He knows nothing. We cleared out all the rubble, and he found nothing." Ruthie had her hands on her hips. "It was a waste of time."

Nola thought about her next question before she spoke.

"What did you do with the remains you found in the mine?"

"There were two sets of bones. We saw the stone at the entrance, so we figured who they were. We buried them next to the mine and put the stone over the grave." Jeb said.

"Thank you," Nola said.

"We were taught to respect the dead," Ruthie said.

"Yeah, we were taught a lot of things. How has that worked for us?" Jeb asked, but it wasn't really a question.

"How long did it take you to clear the debris from the mine?" Coleman asked, trying to change the subject.

"It wasn't as bad as it first looked," Jeb replied. "Most of the rock and dirt was near the front of the entrance. The rest of the mine was clear. That's where we found that old rifle."

Ruthie looked at Nola.

"Your parents' remains were under the rubble. It looked like they might have been trying to get out, when the top of the cave fell on them. I'm sorry."

"It was a long time ago, and we weren't a close family," Nola said.

"Not unlike us," Jeb said, almost under his breath.

"We're all pretty much in the same boat," Coleman answered. "Let's not go down the pity road. Besides, it sounds like you have a plan about what to do next."

"You might just need a little help. You shouldn't be afraid to ask for help. Most people are good and willing to help out when asked," Nola added.

"We weren't raised that way. We were always suspicious of outsiders. Our order always relied on its own," Ruthie explained.

"That was there and then. This is here and now. Let go of the past unless you are planning to return to it," Nola said.

"Never." Jeb yelled.

"Your decision has been made. No sense bringing up the terrible things that happened to you. You can't change anything. You can only move forward and try to make better choices without the same mistakes." Nola was speaking to Jeb and Ruthie, but she was really talking about herself.

"Jeb, why don't we go over to the mine, and you can show me what you have done," Coleman said, moving on.

Jeb jumped up and went to the door.

"I think you'll like what I've done. I've shored up the ceiling and the walls with timbers. I don't think there will ever be another cave-in."

The two went out the door.

Nola called after them. "We'll join you in a minute."

She was sure neither of them heard, because they were having an animated conversation, and they were already halfway to the mine.

Nola took Ruthie's hands in hers.

"Are you okay?"

"I felt pretty sick when I first realized I had a child growing in me.

I'm feeling better now. I'm just nervous about what is going to happen to us. We have a long ways to go to get to Spokane, and you have seen Jeb. He just won't ask for help, but I think we are going to need some real soon."

"Try not to worry about that. We'll think of something. We aren't going to leave you without doing something to get you to where you want to go."

"You are so kind. Thank you." Ruthie smiled. "My name really is Ruth and Jeb's is Jebediah. He said we needed to change to the common name to better fit in. I don't like Ruthie at all. It sounds like I'm a little girl."

"I can see why Jebediah would want to shorten his name. It's not a common name by any means. However, Ruth is common, and I think it is just perfect the way it is. I'll talk to Jeb, and we'll get this straightened out."

Ruth leaned over and gave Nola a hug. Her small bonnet brushed across Nola's face.

Nola took off Ruth's bonnet. "Looks like you could use some new clothing if you want to fit in around here. This stuff has got to go."

"We just didn't have the money for any new clothes. Jeb wanted to steal some things off clotheslines when we were with the circus, but I wouldn't let him. Stealing is wrong."

"I agree. That attitude will get you far. You need to understand what to hold onto from your past and what to let go. Seems like you are on the right path to me. You'll need to share that with Jeb whenever you can."

Ruth smiled coyly. "He does most everything I say if I handle him right."

Nola messed up her hair and threw the cap in the corner.

"Let's go join the boys. I'm interested what you've done with the mine."

They walked out the door and moved toward the mine. Nola noticed that the boys must have gone into the mine. She didn't really want to go inside. Mines always scared her, and the memory of her parents being buried alive put her off.

"Show me where you buried my parents," Nola said to Ruth.

Ruth took her hand, and they walked a number of yards to the left of the mine entrance. Nola saw the headstone she had made and stopped in front of it to read the names. She was surprised that she felt a bit of sadness. She knew that her mother had loved that Irishman. So much so, that she abandoned her own child.

All those things she had had been preaching to Ruth and Jeb hit home. Nola had been holding herself down because of her past. It was exactly what she had been telling everyone else not to do.

The past would not define her. This would be her mantra forward.

She would enter her new life with a renewed sense of urgency. She was about to embark on a new adventure, and it had started right here at the place her parents had lived and died. The adventure was not just about her; it was about the three other people she was with right at the moment.

6

The road back to Bozeman was no better than the road that had brought them to her parents' claim. Ruth and Nola rode in the pickup with Coleman driving. There wasn't enough room for Jeb, so he rode in the back. He sat next to a canvas tarp that covered Coleman and Nola's luggage. It was a dusty ride, and he had to use his shirt as a mask to keep from breathing in the dust.

When they reached Bozeman, Nola directed Coleman to a little storefront that housed Catholic Charities. It was a place she had frequented while attending college. They offered all kinds of services for those in need. Right now they would be taking advantage of their free donated clothing. Ruth and Jeb were in dire need of a change of clothing.

One of the "sisters" was minding the store, and when she saw the condition of Ruth and Jeb's clothing, she smiled sadly.

"Just take what you need. Someday, when you find your way, you'll be able to pay it back." She smiled and left the room.

Nola helped Ruth pick out some things she thought she would need. She was looking for things Ruth could wear when her stomach got bigger. Coleman tried to help Jeb, but he would have none of it.

When they both had a number of items in their arms, the nun

came back with paper bags and helped them pack the clothing in them. Nola thanked her and returned to the pickup. Coleman helped Jeb put the bags under the tarp.

"Now what?" Jeb asked.

"I think we'll ask Nola. Sometimes it's better to let the women make the decisions," Coleman answered.

"I'm not accustomed to doing that."

"Better get used to it. You are not on the farm anymore. If you want your relationship to work, it will need some give and take."

Jeb looked at Coleman like he was from another planet.

Nola and Ruth had been talking.

"I think we should find some place to stay for the night. I'll need to talk to someone about selling the property tomorrow."

"Any suggestions?" Coleman asked.

"There's an old hotel downtown where we can stay pretty reasonably. Hopefully it's still there," Nola said.

"We don't have any money. We can't stay in any hotel," Jeb said, with noticeable disgust in his voice.

"Sometimes you need to take help from people when they offer it," Nola shot back.

Jeb was about to answer back, when Ruth interrupted.

"We are going to stay wherever they invite us. That's the end of it."

Coleman looked at Jeb, raised an eyebrow and smiled. Jeb got the message and shut up. He pretended he didn't like it, but Coleman could see some relief in his face.

The hotel was still in existence, but the owners hadn't done anything to it since Nola had been in college. Some people might have called it a fleabag, but Ruth and Jeb thought it was the greatest thing they had ever seen. Neither had ever stayed in a hotel before, and it seemed decadent to them both.

Coleman booked two rooms on the third floor next to each other. They had beautiful views of the building next to them. It didn't matter; they would only be staying for one night.

Coleman and Jeb brought up their things. Nola was waiting for them at the top of the stairs.

"Ruth is already in the room. She's taking a bath. When she's finished, you take one as well. You don't smell very good, so be sure to use a lot of soap."

Jeb obviously wasn't used to being spoken to like this by a woman.

"You're not my mother."

"No, I'm not. But I think I can kick your scrawny little ass if you don't do what I tell you."

Coleman just raised his eyebrow and smiled once again at Jeb.

Jeb took his paper bags and threw them into their room and followed slamming the door.

"Nice," Coleman said, and laughed.

"He's a handful. I hope Ruth will be able to point him in the right direction."

"He's not used to taking orders from a woman. I don't think he knows what to make of you," Coleman answered.

"Why, because I'm Crow?"

"Well, sure, but also you are a strong woman. The Amish men are always in charge. This is all new to him."

"You'd better talk to him then. If he's going to live in the world, he should know how it works."

"I'm trying. Maybe the subtle approach from me might be the water to your fire." Coleman put his arms around Nola. "Speaking of fire."

"You need to take a bath first. So do I."

"How about we shower together?" Colman asked heading her toward the door.

"This is an old hotel. They don't have showers. Just big old bath tubs."

"Done." Coleman slammed the door.

The tub had clawed feet and was deep. It would be more than enough room for them both. They made love on the bed while it filled.

When they were finished with the bath, Coleman wanted to love it up some more, but Nola was having none of it.

"We just got out of the bath. I don't want to have to run another whole tub to scrub you off me."

That was it. Coleman knew the decision had been made, and he knew it would do no good trying to persuade her otherwise. This was what he was trying to convey to Jeb. Ruth seemed to be trying to understand their new identities, but it would take Jeb longer to understand.

"Let's go get something to eat. I'm sure those two are starving. Go tell them we're leaving," Nola ordered.

"I don't think so. I think it should come from you. Jeb seems to react quickly when you speak. Maybe you could use this opportunity to tone things down. You know, like a vinegar and honey thing." Coleman decided that Nola shouldn't think that she was totally in charge. Give and take always seemed to be a better arrangement in his mind.

Nola went out into the hallway and knocked softly on their door.

"Would you two be ready for some dinner?"

The door opened immediately. "We thought you'd never ask," Ruth said, smiling.

Nola couldn't believe her eyes. The couple had been transformed. No more dirt or grime, just two smiling teenagers ready for some food.

"You two look amazing," Nola said.

"The pants are a bit tight, but they'll do," Jeb answered.

Jeb hadn't changed his clothing all that much. He still wore dark pants but they reached the floor, and there were no suspenders. He had on a white shirt, but it was opened at the neck and he had rolled up the sleeves to the elbow. He was quite handsome Nola thought.

"Just one thing, Jeb. We've got to cut that hair. Coleman, get me my scissors." She pushed Jeb into their bathroom.

After much protest and grumbling, Nola had cut his hair above the ears.

"There. Now you look like a typical American guy."

Ruth was smiling. "Jeb, I've never seen you with short hair. You look like the man I want to marry."

Ruth went over and pulled Jeb up from the toilet seat where Nola had placed him to cut his hair.

"I will always be proud to be with you no matter how long or short your hair."

"What if I lose it all?"

"Then I'll kiss you on the top of your bald head every night and every morning."

Ruth had a dress with a hemline that went just above her knee. Nola thought that it might have been the most skin she had ever exposed. It also sported an empire waist that did a great job of hiding her stomach bump but highlighting her breast line. Everyone in the room noticed. Ruth had assets no one had noticed in her Amish garb. Jeb noticed also.

"Take a picture, and let's go eat," Ruth said, and pulled Jeb along by the hand.

Coleman just shook his head and followed the three down the steps and out of the hotel. He wondered how they managed to stumble into this can of worms. He had no idea how they were going to reconcile what would happen with these two. It appeared Nola had something in mind, and she would share it when she was ready. He was fine with it as long as it didn't take too long.

Coleman had decided to look around for the right environment for his bar. His idea was to check out a number of locations, mostly to placate Nola. But if they wasted too much time, he would need to go to the area he thought would offer the most promise.

He was still deep in thought when he heard his name.

"Are you going to get in the pickup and drive? We're all hungry here," Nola said, chastising him.

"Where to?" Coleman asked, as he slid into the driver's seat.

"I know a restaurant just a little north of town. The prices are fair and they have good food. At least that's how I remember it."

The place still was in business, and after a hearty meal of steak and potatoes, the foursome was filled up. There was plenty of conversation fueled by Nola's questions about the Amish ways. She shared some of the Crow customs when she thought they seemed similar.

Finally Coleman interrupted.

"What is the plan for tomorrow?"

The conversation ended abruptly.

"That was rude, Coleman," Nola said, and she sounded angry.

"Ruth and I will be heading out to look for my brother in Spokane," Jeb said.

"How are you going to get there? You have no money. Ruth is pregnant so you need to start thinking about her for a change. She can't go hitching all over the country," Nola said, changing her focus back to the two teens.

Coleman suppressed a smile. Nola was definitely in charge when it came to these two. That's what he had wanted in the first place, and it just took a little prodding to get everyone pointed toward some sort of agreement. He really didn't care how it ended; he just knew it was time to do something.

Ruth didn't say anything and Jeb lowered his head. Nola saw her opening and went right into it.

"Tomorrow, we're going to see about selling my property. Then we're going to Missoula and put you on a bus for Spokane. Do you happen to have an address for your brother?"

Jeb fished a little beat-up tin Sucrets lozenge box from his front pocket. He opened it carefully and took out a scrap of paper. It looked like the return address torn from an envelope. He handed it to Nola. The first name was Fredrick, and she noticed there was no last name written. The address was written in full.

"Maybe if I knew your last name, we could try to find him in the phone book."

"We never use our last name in our letters. It's too common," Jeb said.

"I don't know what that even means. What's your last name?" Nola was short.

"My father said our relatives in Germany called themselves Muller, but the community and elders call us Miller."

"Well, it's a start. Even if we can't find him in the phone book, the address looks promising."

"He won't have a phone," Jeb said resolutely.

"I thought you said he left the faith. Maybe he found the phone a useful tool," Nola said.

Jeb smiled. "It's not that. He's just too cheap to pay for a phone."

The comment, coming from Jeb, broke the tension. Nola even laughed out loud.

"I think we've all had enough excitement for one day," Coleman said. "Let's go back to the hotel and get some sleep. It sounds like Nola has a big day planned for all of us."

Nola pretended to give him a dirty look. Coleman didn't really care. He was happy. He and Nola would be heading north from Missoula after they dropped off Ruth and Jeb. That had been his plan all along.

7

They checked out of the hotel by 7:00 the next day. After breakfast at the diner, Coleman drove to a bank where Nola thought she could find someone to help sell her property. The bank didn't open until 9:00, and that only served to peeve Coleman. He was anxious to get on the road. He parked in the bank's lot and decided to wait the half-hour.

Nola saw a second-hand shop down the street a block-and-a-half. She took Ruth in tow and left the two men to themselves. Coleman wondered what she was planning to buy. He was sure it would be something for the young couple. She just couldn't help herself. He hoped she wouldn't spend all their cash before they got back to Billings. They still had a lot of area to cover.

It was almost 9:00, when they saw the women returning with what looked like a suitcase. It looked pretty beat-up but still functional. Nola showed them the treasure. It was a worn brown leather bag with two belts with clasps on either side of the handle. Coleman thought it was a very expensive piece of luggage in its day, but its day had pretty much set with last night's sun.

"You can't believe how little they charged me for this bag," Nola said.

"They probably just wanted to get rid of it. Selling it to you would raise the net worth of their entire shop," Coleman replied.

"Ha. You are so funny. These two need a suitcase to put their things into. They can't be traveling with paper bags."

"Can't argue with that. The bank is open. Let's go."

"You all stay here. I'll take care of this." Nola was in charge once again.

Coleman wasn't sure how he felt about it.

It was a small local bank that Nola had used when she was in college. They had always been friendly, and she felt comfortable returning. The tellers were getting ready for the day and paid little attention to her. She walked right past them and into the office of the president. He was busy with some paperwork and didn't look up.

Nola cleared her throat and then spoke.

"I was wondering if you could help me."

He looked up from his work and eyed Nola before dropping his eyes back to his work.

"Well?"

"I want to sell property that my parents owned south of Bozeman. Can you help me with that?" Nola asked, feeling somewhat dismissed by his attitude.

"Tell me about it," the banker said, still not looking at her.

"It's a cabin and a mine on a number of acres. I don't really know how many."

The banker seemed a bit more interested and looked up.

"Oh, I see. It probably isn't worth much. Property out that way isn't selling very well. Prices are down. I've got a meeting to go to right now, so I can't talk to you about it at present."

"What should I do? I've never dealt with anything like this before."

He thought for a moment and then pointed over to a little cubicle next to the teller cages. There was someone sitting behind a desk in the small space.

"Go talk to my assistant. He can take your information, and we can see what we can do to help you. I wouldn't get my hopes up, however." The banker gave her a dismissive glance, as he brushed past her in an effort to get out of his office as quickly as possible.

Nola had no time to ask any more questions, as she watched him exit the bank through the front door. She walked over to the assistant's desk.

He was a pleasant young man and smiled at Nola as she entered his little domain.

"How may we be of service?" he asked, as pleasantly as possible. He motioned for Nola to sit.

"I have some property that I want to sell. It was my parents' homestead. They are both dead," Nola said, matter-of-factly.

"Sorry to hear that. What kind of place is it? My name is Bruce, by the way."

Nola explained the property as best she could and noticed that Bruce's eyes had narrowed near the end of her description.

"The guy in the office didn't give me much hope in selling it," Nola said, looking for a response.

Bruce sat back in his chair for a few moments. It looked like he was trying to decide what to say next. Finally, he leaned as close a possible toward Nola's chair and spoke quietly. It was almost a whisper as if he didn't want anyone else to hear what he had to say.

"Don't listen to him. He's an asshole. He doesn't care about any of the customers unless they have something he wants. Let me tell you, he wants your property."

"But he didn't seem interested in it at all."

"That's what he does. He's been buying everything he can get his hands on out that way."

"Why? What's going on?"

"I don't really know. It might be some development coming in, or maybe they've found something in the area. There are a lot of mines out that way. Who really knows? I am just telling you not to deal with him. He'll lie and swindle you out of the money that's due you." Bruce was forceful.

Nola was impressed.

"Then I want to deal with you. Will you help me?"

"Certainly. But we're going to have to do this secretly. We will have to do everything by phone or at a neutral location. If he finds out, he'll fire me."

"Maybe that wouldn't be such a bad thing. You shouldn't be working for someone like that anyway."

"I agree, but until I find something else, I'm stuck."

"I trust you. What do we do now?" Nola asked.

"Let me do some checking. There are people looking for property like yours. If I can't find anyone, we could always do a land auction. That way if someone really wanted it, they would have to pay up. You need to give me some details, and I'll do the research."

Nola gave Bruce all the necessary information, and he gave her his phone number.

"It's going to take a little time to get this all done legally," Bruce said, almost apologizing.

"We're on sort of a vacation, so there isn't really a rush," Nola said.

"Call me at the end of the week at the number I gave you, and I'll let you know what I've found. Remember; don't come back to the bank. I'll make up a story that you must have had second thoughts. You never stopped to talk to me." Bruce winked at her.

Nola left the bank feeling better than when she had entered. The three waiting for her in the pickup saw her smile, and it raised everyone's spirits immediately. Nola explained what had happened in detail, as they sat on the pickup's endgate. Nobody said anything. Coleman was trying to figure out what should come next.

Jeb broke the silence.

"What are you planning to do with us?" he asked Nola, because she had proven she was in charge.

The question took her off guard.

"I hadn't gotten that far," she said, apologizing.

Coleman saw his chance. "I have a suggestion."

Nola, Jeb and Ruth looked at him for some follow-up. Not hearing anything forthcoming, Nola spoke.

"Well, are you going to tell us, or is this to be your little secret?"

"I think we should take your original suggestion and head over Missoula way. We can buy a bus ticket for Ruth and Jeb and get them to their brother in Spokane just like you suggested," Coleman said.

"I think you have more on your mind than you are sharing. I'll get the rest out of you when we get these two on their way."

Coleman didn't find the need to say anything more. He put the truck into gear and shifted through the four-speed. Soon they were heading up US highway 10 toward Butte and finally Missoula.

They stopped in Butte for an early lunch, and Nola used the pay phone to call the Missoula bus terminal.

"They've got a bus leaving for Spokane this afternoon at 2:30. We're still over an hour-and-a-half out, but we should make it just fine if we don't waste a lot of time."

They grabbed their food and were on the way. It was a scenic drive, and everyone was still enjoying an upbeat spirit.

They made the bus terminal in plenty of time. Coleman paid for the tickets, while Nola said her goodbyes. She was back in the pickup wiping her eyes, when Coleman handed Ruth and Jeb their tickets in a small folder. Tucked inside were two twenties that Coleman had slipped in as he walked over.

"Good luck to you both. Hopefully life will be a little easier for you down the line. God knows you could use it."

"I hope He knows," Jeb said, meaning Coleman's reference to God. "Someday I will pay you back for the good things you have done for Ruth and me."

"Everyone needs a little help now and again. Just remember that, and we'll be even."

"Where would Ruth and I be able to find you if we were to look for you down the line?"

"Can't really say for sure. I'm thinking we will end up in a little town north of here called Whitefish. We're going to run a bar up there."

"That's strange. Nola never mentioned anything like that to me," Ruth said.

"She doesn't know yet. She only knows that we're looking for a place. I looked at different areas, and I think that it might hold the most promise for the future."

Both Ruth and Jeb shook Coleman's hand and then turned and walked into the seating area to wait for the bus. Coleman took the opportunity to make it back to his pickup. By the time he got into the driver's seat, Nola had recovered from feeling bad for the two travelers on their way to Spokane.

"That was really nice of you to pay for their tickets."

"How else were they going to get to Spokane? They don't have any money."

"I think they might now," Nola replied.

"I am good for something, is what you're saying?"

"I wouldn't go that far. We missed quite a bit of Montana coming all this way."

"All part of the plan my dear."

"I suppose you'd better tell me about this harebrained plan of yours." Nola tried to sound angry, but she just couldn't.

Coleman started to explain what he had in his mind from the very beginning. Every phrase made him more excited.

"There's a town north of here on Route 93 called Kalispell. Just little north of that is a place called Whitefish."

"Never heard of either place. Do you think it is wise to invest in something that far off the beaten trail?"

"Whitefish is the gateway to Glacier National Park. It's a place of immense beauty during the summer. More and more people are vacationing by car, and they will come to see the park. We will have a built-in tourist business. If we make it more of a tourist-type bar, we will do well."

"What about the long cold winters? That's almost in Canada if I remember right."

"I thought you never heard of it?"

"I never heard of Whitefish. Everyone's heard of Glacier. It's a sacred place to many of the Indian Nations. Don't change the subject. What about the winter months?"

"There's a place called Big Mountain just north and a little west of

Whitefish. It's going to be a big ski resort someday. We will have plenty of people coming in looking to warm up after a long day of skiing in the cold."

Nola sat back trying to digest everything Coleman had just told her. It was a lot to consider. Finally, she was ready to share.

"I'll have to admit, the place sounds like it has possibilities. I only hope you're right about the tourists coming to participate. Without them, I'm afraid it would be a bust."

"We will have to work at it, but I think together we'll be successful," Coleman said, and looked over at Nola.

She sat back to consider. She liked what Coleman had just shared about being together.

"Let's go," was all she said.

8

The first thing Nola noticed, as they drove into Whitefish, was that they could see Big Mountain. It was quite a view. It was nothing like the Crow Reservation or the ugliness of the Billings refineries. There were mountains and lakes surrounding the entire community. If there were a nicer place on the face of the earth, Nola couldn't believe it existed.

She was somewhat perplexed, when she noticed the size of the town.

"What's the population of Whitefish?" she asked Coleman.

"It's just a little over one thousand, I think."

"It's a pretty place, but how are we going to make a living in a town so small?"

"That's the total of permanent residents. It swells to double and triple with tourists both in the summer and winter. That's what I've been told, at least."

"Who told you that?" Nola wanted to know.

"Hey, I've done my homework. I'm not one to enter into anything blindly. Their motto is "Montana's Outdoor Playground." The ski runs get the people in the winter. The "Going to the Sun Road" in the Glacier Park gets the summer folk. That would be our target base."

"What now?" Nola didn't quite believe Coleman's explanation.

"We'll need to check out the community and see if there is any property that will suit our purpose. If we find something, then we'll have to find a bank who will back us."

"I thought you had money."

"I do, but I doubt very much that I have enough to buy a building and be able to start a business. All that takes capital. We may need some financing for the real estate part."

"I hate borrowing money. Debt always scares me," Nola said.

Coleman stopped the truck and pulled into a spot on the main street. It looked like a little outfitter's store right in front of them. He turned to Nola.

"What the world do we have to lose? What's the worst thing that could happen?"

Nola shrugged her shoulders. "We could go broke and lose everything."

"How would that be any worse than what we are doing right now? If we never take a chance on something, we'll never know if we could be successful," Coleman said, softly.

"I know. It's just terribly frightening to me."

"Me too. I believe that because we are afraid of failure, we'll be successful. We will work until it becomes a reality."

Nola put her hand on Coleman's cheek and held it there.

"Then I suppose we should get on with it. Where do we start?"

"I think we could walk around and check with some existing businesses. Maybe they could point us to some properties that would work. We could start with this little outfitter place in front of us." Coleman was already opening the door.

Nola followed along. She decided to let Coleman take the lead on everything. She had no idea what she was doing and had no idea what questions to ask. Coleman sought out the owner, while Nola looked around the business.

She was amazed at all the items people needed for their treks into the wilderness. There were things for campers, fisherman, hunters and even mountain climbers. Nola had no idea what drove people to climb mountains. It must be the constant high and adrenaline rush knowing you could die with just one little misstep.

She was still lost in thought, when Coleman came to get her. He took her by the hand, and together they went back to the truck.

Nola could see something was bothering Coleman. She decided to try and be more helpful.

"I saw a bar up the street. Maybe we could go and ask them for some information."

Coleman couldn't help but smile. "I don't think announcing to someone who would be our competition that we are thinking about starting up a bar would serve us very well."

"Not my best idea for sure." Nola smiled back.

Coleman's demeanor became serious once more. Nola noticed immediately.

"What's wrong?"

He was silent for some time. Finally, he turned toward Nola.

"The owner of the outfitter was helpful, but he said something that really bothers me."

"What is it? Just come out with it. I'm not much for twenty questions," Nola said.

"He asked me if you were a Flathead or a Blackfoot Indian."

"What's that got to do with anything?" Nola was hot.

"Well, it seems there's a number of racists around here. They don't want Indians around their town especially if they are Flathead or Blackfoot. They want them to stay on the reservation."

"I'm neither, I'm Crow." It was a simple answer. "What was his suggestion when you told him I was with you?"

"He liked our idea of a cowboy and Indian bar. He thought it would be a good draw for tourists."

"But?"

"But he suggested that I do the negotiating until we got established, since we don't know who we are dealing with. He thought you should remain out of sight." Coleman paused, and looked to see how Nola would react.

She thought about what he had said for a moment.

"It's not something totally unexpected, is it? I've dealt with things like this all my life."

"He gave me the name of a bank who would work with us. He said the owner is married to a Native American and doesn't discriminate."

Nola nodded.

"Let's go see him right now." Nola was determined.

Coleman smiled and put the pickup into reverse. He knew that Nola's sense of right and wrong had been challenged, and that was the best motivator he could have hoped for.

An hour later the couple walked out of the bank with a list of properties that the banker had given them. He liked their idea and hoped they would use the bank for any of their financial transactions. Coleman felt relieved, and Nola had asked all the right questions. Coleman could tell the banker was impressed with her. He was impressed with her as well. She never ceased to amaze him.

They checked out each place on the list, and in the end, they both agreed on an old Icehouse at the end of the street. Before refrigerators became part of the American households, companies used to store ice in big brick buildings for use in the summer months. Coleman didn't know what the name of the company had been, because the sign painted on the bricks just read "ICE." The walls were thick, and it appeared to have been insulated quite well for the time period. There was a faded sign on the door that listed a phone number and an address of the seller. They decided to find the owner and talk face to face.

After they found the address, Nola suggested she remain in the pickup until Coleman could determine if the owner was bigoted. Coleman knew it would be for the best, but he didn't have to like it.

It was an old house and looked like it hadn't had much care over the years. The front porch was sagging to the left and didn't look like it would hold his weight. Coleman looked around and saw a side door adjacent to a shed that at one time served as a garage of some sort.

Coleman knocked on the door and waited. He thought he could

hear a chair scraping on the floor somewhere inside. He waited patiently until finally the door opened just a crack.

"Who is it?" A tiny voice asked from inside.

"Ma'am, my name is Coleman Sinning. I'm here about the property you have for sale."

"You must mean the old Icehouse?"

"That's the one. Do you still have it for sale?"

The door opened further, and Coleman could see a little old lady struggling to open the door. He thought she couldn't be a day younger than ninety. He had no idea how all this was going to work, because he had never been good with old people. It wasn't that he disliked them; it was just that he had never been around any old folks. He didn't know how to talk to them.

"My goodness, where are my manners? Come in. Come in. I don't get many guests these days."

Coleman followed the old woman into the house. It was at a snail's pace and seemed to take forever. Finally, they reached the kitchen, and the old woman fell into her chair. Coleman sat across from her. It appeared she needed to catch her breath, so Coleman waited before speaking to her. When she seemed rested and had looked Coleman over from head to foot, she decided to speak.

"So, you're here to inquire about the old Icehouse?"

"That's correct, and I was wondering if it was still for sale?"

"It's been so long since anyone asked about it, I almost forgot I still had it. Of course it's for sale. That's why I have the sign on the door. I'll make you a good deal, but you'll have to tell me what you're planning to do with it."

Coleman was instantly alarmed.

"Well, I had hoped to make it into a saloon that would draw in some tourist trade."

The old lady sat back. Coleman wondered if he had just kissed any deal goodbye. Then the old lady laughed.

"That would be a nice bit of irony, wouldn't it?"

"I'm not following," Coleman replied.

"Well, young man, it was an Icehouse, and now you want to sell drinks out of it. It still will be an Icehouse after a fashion."

"I guess I never thought of it that way, but you are right."

"Of course I am. I'm old, so I'm always right. I'll be ninety-six next month and still live at home. I'm not senile either, so don't get any notion about trying to stiff me on the property."

Coleman had to smile at the feisty old woman. "I wouldn't dream of taking advantage of you, but I'll try to cut the best deal I can."

"Wouldn't have it any other way. That's business. What's your name again?'

"Coleman Sinning from Billings."

"Well, Coleman Sinning from Billings, my name is Bella Beeman."

"Pretty name. Is Bella short for something?"

"Isabel I think. It's been so long ago, that I can't quite remember. Everyone always called me Bella."

"Bella it is."

"I like you Coleman Sinning."

"And I like you as well, Bella Beeman." Coleman found he did actually like the old lady. She was easy to talk to, and he could tell she was lonely. He decided to be upfront with her from the very beginning.

"I wouldn't be buying this place myself. I have a partner who will be joining me."

"Where is this partner?" Bella asked.

"Well, she's out in the pickup."

"So, it's a she, you say?"

"Yes." Coleman stopped. He didn't know how he should label Nola. She wasn't his wife, but he thought she might be someday. She would be his partner. He would need to ask Nola how they should introduce each other.

"So, what is she to you?"

"Pardon?"

"Well, is she your wife, girlfriend, sister or what?"

"I would call her my girlfriend, but you would need to ask her how she sees it."

"Bring her in then. Don't let her sit out in the vehicle all by herself. What's wrong with you?"

"I need to be honest with you. She's is part Crow Indian."

Bella sat back in her chair again. Once again Coleman wondered if he had overstayed his welcome.

"What's the mix?"

"She thinks her father was Irish or Scottish. He was a miner in the day, and he and her mother were both killed in a cave-in."

"I'll wager you thought that would make a difference in our negotiations, didn't you?"

"I didn't know. I wanted to test the waters."

"If people were honest around here, I think you'd find that all the natives have some Indian blood coursing through their veins. We're all tolerant of each other. It's these transplants that come from other parts of the country to settle here that cause the problems. What's her name?"

"Enola, but she goes by Nola."

"You go out and get her, and bring her to me. Tell her that I won't hold it against her that her father was Irish."

Coleman knew he would be listening to her entire story before they would even get down to business. He knew he needed Nola for moral support and patience. He went out to the pickup to invite her into Bella's home. He was afraid it was going to be a long evening. He wished they had found a hotel before he stopped.

Coleman explained things to Nola in an abridged version and just before they reached the door, Bella stuck out her head.

"Go get your things. You'll be staying with me tonight. There isn't a hotel worth a damn in this town."

"But…" Coleman tried to respond.

"Not another word about it." Bella was firm.

"You are so kind," Nola responded. Coleman knew she always had the right thing to say.

"Nonsense, my dear. You have very pretty blue eyes. From your father I'm thinking. Come in, and tell me all about yourself."

Coleman decided to take his time and let the women get to know each other. The conversation was getting too tedious to suit him anyway. Maybe if he stayed away long enough, Nola would have the whole deal wrapped up.

He could only hope.

9

Coleman brought in the bags and was directed to put them into a second story bedroom. When he returned to the kitchen, the women were talking like old friends.

"Bella would like to make dinner for us this evening," Nola said.

"Why don't we go out to some nice place for dinner? It will be my treat," Coleman said, but knew he was wrong when he saw Nola's eyes.

"The hell you say. I'm too old to go tottering out for dinner in the evening. I haven't cooked for anyone in a long time, so that's what's going to happen." Bella was firm.

"We've been making a list for you to fill at the grocery," Nola smiled, and handed the list over to Coleman.

"You'd better get going if you want something to eat while it's still today," Bella said, and then turned to Nola to continue some conversation that Coleman had interrupted.

Coleman did as instructed. He wasn't in a rush to get back, hoping to give Nola some time to bond with Bella. It appeared they were going to have some Italian dish from the list he had to fill. Coleman took a little drive around the community and decided that this was the place for them. He was anxious to make the deal with Bella and get started on their new adventure.

Bella had other plans. When he returned with the groceries in hand, Bella told him to go back and find some white wine that she had forgotten to list. Coleman did as he was told once more. He didn't buy one bottle, because he thought three might be better. It might serve to loosen Bella's purse strings a bit.

When he got back to Bella's, she handed him the daily paper, and told him to go into the parlor and not get in the way. Bella and Nola went into the kitchen to prepare the meal.

When dinner was over, Coleman opened a bottle of sherry and gave everyone a healthy pour. He settled back into his chair to begin discussing the sale of the Icehouse. Bella once again disappointed him.

"We won't be talking business after this big meal and too much wine. None of us will be thinking clearly," Bella stated.

Coleman sat back in his chair showing some frustration.

"I think it's a good idea," Nola said, looking at Coleman.

"We will speak of everything after breakfast tomorrow. You will need to be at the table precisely at 7:00." Bella was in charge.

Coleman decided to relinquish.

"You two sit and enjoy the sherry. I'll clear the dishes."

"Ah, spoken like a true gentleman," Bella said.

Coleman cleared the table and decided to wash and dry the dishes. The women spoke of things he probably wouldn't have understood anyway. He stacked everything on the counter, because he didn't have a clue where anything went. He was finishing the last pan when the women walked in with their sherry glasses. They handed them to Coleman.

"I'll help you put away the dishes," Nola offered.

"Thank you dear. It's getting harder for me to reach the higher shelves in the cupboard. I think I may be shrinking."

Coleman thought she might be right. She was such a petite little woman, but he knew from her demeanor that she had been quite a formidable character in her day.

They sat around the kitchen table when everything was put back into its place. The women talked and Coleman listened. He knew his place. Bella told her story about how the Icehouse was handed down from her husband's family over the years. It had been a great source of income until the refrigerator became a staple in everyone's home.

"What did you do after that?" Nola asked.

"Well dear, it wasn't until the early forties that the refrigerator replaced the ice box. I was in my eighties then. My husband had passed about ten years before that, so I just retired and closed up the business. The place has just sat empty for years."

"How's the structure's integrity?" Coleman asked.

Bella shot him a look that could have killed the average man.

"No business until after breakfast." Bella was pretending to be angry.

"Understood," Coleman said, smiling.

Bella was having fun with him, but he knew it was much more. She had been alone and needed human contact. She was lonely and wanted to feel vibrant again. Coleman wouldn't do anything to take that away from her. He was thinking about what else he could do for this interesting woman, when she made an announcement.

"My word, it's after 10:00. I haven't been up this late for as long as I can remember. You two are a bad influence on me. It's time for bed. See you at 7:00 in the morning." Bella got up and turned off the lights.

It was Nola and Coleman's invitation to get their behinds up the stairs and in bed. As they climbed the steep stairs, Bella called after them.

"If the bed squeaks don't worry about it. I was young once too."

Coleman thought it might be an invitation to some sexual encounter with Nola. She was having none of it, however. Coleman tried to fall asleep while still being aroused. He acted like he was upset, but in reality he was quite entertained by the events of the entire evening.

The bed was small, and it did squeak when he turned over. Coleman decided to have a little fun with it. He turned over a few times making the bed sound like it was in rhythm. When he made some moaning sounds, Nola slugged him. He quit immediately. Some people couldn't take a joke.

The next morning they were both up by 6:00 and ready by 6:30, so they sat on the bed and talked.

"What were you and Bella discussing yesterday?" Coleman asked, quietly so not to be overheard.

"Bella has a plan for us," Nola said.

"What is it?"

"It's for her to say. She didn't really tell me. Although, she did ask some questions to make me think I know where she is going."

"So, if I ask, you'll just tell me to wait for her response."

"You've got it. Let's go down and see if we can be of some help."

When they descended the steep steps, they could smell bacon. When the kitchen door opened, they could see that Bella had the table set and was pouring the coffee.

"A few minutes early. I like that quality in people. I think we will be able to do business."

Coleman was heartened.

"Do you want me to strip the bed and wash the sheets for you?" Nola asked.

"Absolutely not. I've got someone who comes in to do that for me. Besides, you don't know how long you'll be staying with me."

Neither had thought much about what was coming next, and they hadn't considered staying on with Bella. It wasn't an unpleasant thought, however.

"Sit down please. Everything is ready," Bella said, and turned away to put breakfast on the table.

It was a huge breakfast. Much more than either Nola or Coleman were used to eating. There were eggs and bacon, toast with three flavors of jam, pancakes, fried potatoes, orange juice, and coffee. There was enough food for ten people, and Bella kept shoveling it out until neither could eat another bite. She, on the other hand, ate like a small bird.

"Stop. I can't put another thing in my mouth," Nola said, and groaned.

"No more food. But I will take a refill on the coffee. Everything was done to perfection. You are a great cook, Bella," Coleman said, heaping on the praise.

Bella was beaming.

"Breakfast was always my favorite meal, but when you get old you just can't eat very much."

"Maybe you should try making a little less," Nola said, smiling at Bella.

"Just can't help myself. I'm one of those people stuck in time."

Coleman thought about what she said. He had never considered that getting older meant that your circle of influence would keep getting smaller and smaller. But here it was staring him right in the face. Bella's ninety plus years had isolated her from the outside world. She was living her memories, because life had pretty much passed on by. It just made his resolve that much stronger to try and make this new adventure work for them.

"I'll clear the table," Coleman said, and started to get up.

"Sit. It's time for business. Here's what's going to happen. You are going to pay me 10,000 dollars for the property and the Icehouse."

Coleman almost choked on a sip of his coffee. The property wasn't worth that much. He was thinking about half that would be a fair price. It was no wonder she hadn't sold it before now. He was about ready to make a counter, when she spoke back up.

"The price is non-negotiable. But here's what I will do for you. You buy the property on contract from me with no interest charged. I'll expect no payment the first year. Then, I'll expect 500 dollars every six months until it is paid off. If you need some working capital, I will make you a loan up to 10,000 dollars and not charge you interest on that either. If I die before it is paid off, the debt is forgiven. I'll have the lawyer draw up the papers if this is acceptable to you."

"Acceptable? Hell, this is crazy. We would be complete fools to pass this up." Coleman's voice was an octave higher than normal.

"You are smarter than you look," Bella said, and then looked over to Nola.

Nola just shrugged her shoulders. Coleman knew these two had hatched up the whole plan the day before, and they wanted to see his reaction. He didn't disappoint either of them.

"I could just come over and kiss you," Coleman said, to Bella.

"What's stopping you, big boy?"

Coleman went over and actually kissed her on the lips.

"Who-whee. I'll bet I haven't been kissed in almost 20 years. I remember it being somewhat more satisfying back in the day, though. I think you need to put some work into it so Nola has something to look forward to."

Coleman smiled. He realized Bella must have been quite something in her day.

"Where do we go from here?" Coleman needed to know.

"Well, I would think you'd want to go out and check the property you are almost ready to purchase."

"I was thinking the same thing," Coleman said.

Bella reached into her apron pocket and brought out a set of keys.

"These are the keys to the place. I've forgotten which is which, but one opens the front door, one opens the overhead door, and one opens the second story door. Have at it."

"I don't know how to thank you," Coleman said.

"Well, for starters, you can shake my hand signifying that we have a deal."

Coleman grabbed her hand and shook it until she pulled away.

"Back in the day, a handshake was all that was needed in a business transaction. Now you need a wheelbarrow full of paperwork. I don't like it at all, but that's the way it is. I liked it when things were simpler." Bella seemed to lose herself in some past memory.

"I'm afraid that it is just the world we live in today. It will only get worse, I think." Nola said, sharing her feelings.

"That's why I live here in the past. It is more than enough for me."

"Is it ever too much?" Nola asked.

Coleman had no idea what she was talking about.

"Sometimes. But then I meet people like you, and it is better."

"Thank you," Nola answered.

"Let's get this kitchen cleaned up and go look at the property," Coleman said.

"Nonsense. I need something to do with my time. You two go out and look it over. I'll expect you for dinner this evening and not a minute before 5:00 for cocktails," Bella barked.

"Do you want me to pick up some groceries?" Coleman asked.

"Heavens no. I'm well stocked with everything we'll need."

"Then why did you have me go get groceries last...?" Coleman stopped. He knew damn well it was to get him out of the house so the two could talk. He wondered what other plans they had hatched together.

"Would you like to go with us to look at the Icehouse?" Nola asked.

Bella considered the offer for a moment.

"No, I would rather keep the memories of the place when it was a thriving business. I believe it would be too sad for me to see it in the condition it is in today."

Coleman and Nola remained quiet. Then Bella spoke again.

"But I want to see the place when you are finished fixing it up. I expect to be your first customer."

"It would be compliments of the house," Coleman answered.

"Well, certainly. I would expect no less," Bella said, and pushed them out the door.

10

Coleman pulled the pickup in front of the overhead door of the Icehouse. He jumped out of the vehicle and fumbled with the keys. He was excited and dropped them on the ground twice. He found the key that fit the lock, but when he tried to turn the key it wouldn't budge. The lock had rusted tight. Coleman worked with it a bit, until he decided to use Liquid Wrench to prevent him from breaking the key off in the lock. He had some ideas concerning the door, but that would need to be further down the road.

Nola had also exited the pickup and was walking around the building. When she returned, she took the keys from Coleman.

"Let's look inside."

Coleman hoped the front door wasn't in the same shape as the overhead, or they might end up breaking in. That wouldn't look good to the locals. The only proof he had that he was going to own the building were the keys. He didn't want to have to waste time explaining and then ultimately involving Bella. Knowing her, she would deny any knowledge of their dealings just as a joke.

His fears were unfounded, however. When he turned the corner, the front door was already open and Nola was inside. Coleman grabbed a flashlight and followed her inside.

The first thing he noticed was that the walls were at least two feet thick. He assumed it had been to help keep the ice from melting during the summer months. Coleman was encouraged when he saw three or four bare light bulbs hanging from the 20-foot ceiling. He tried the light switch near the door and nothing happened. The electricity had probably been shut off years ago. There was no furnace, and that didn't surprise Coleman in the least. Who would need heat when selling ice? The floor was made up of cobblestones and was in surprisingly good shape. There were no windows, which Coleman thought would be a good thing for his bar business. Bars didn't need windows, although they did need good ventilation.

Nola was at the foot of the wooden staircase that led to the second story. Coleman was surprised that the building had a second floor. It sparked his interest, but he was concerned that the staircase might be safe.

"Nola, don't climb those stairs until we decide if they are safe. They're old and may be rotten. I don't want you falling through before you get to the top."

Nola stopped and waited for Coleman to determine if the steps were safe to climb. When Coleman put his weight on the bottom step, it broke in half. The second step creaked when he put his weight on it, but it held. Slowly, he ascended each step by putting his weight on the upper step while keeping his other foot on the previous step. Finally, he reached the top and turned to tell Nola it would be safe to come up. He was surprised to see she had been following him up the staircase.

"Well, that was kind of stupid," he said, trying to sound stern. "What if this whole thing had given way? We would both have been in a predicament."

Nola just laughed. "I figured if they held your fat ass, they could handle my weight."

Coleman decided not to argue with her logic, so he turned to explore the second floor. The first room was small and looked like it had been an office area. There were two old file cabinets stuck into a corner and not much else.

Nola opened the single door at the opposite corner and went inside. Coleman followed her with the flashlight. It looked like it might have been living quarters a few generations prior. There was no furniture, but an old cast iron cook stove stood against the far wall. Coleman went over to examine it.

"This must have served both as a heat source and cooking facility," Coleman said.

"Everything is so old. It's going to take a lot of work to get this looking the way we will want it." Nola sounded a little frustrated.

"Do you think we're up to the task?"

"Well, of course I do. I guess I was just expecting more."

"We're getting a pretty good deal here. I've got enough money saved up, so I don't think we'll even have to borrow anything from Bella."

"Don't forget about the money from the sale of my property," Nola said, quickly.

"We can't rely on that, since it hasn't sold as far as we know. That could be our rainy day fund if and when it sells."

Nola nodded in agreement. Coleman looked at her for a moment. He wanted her to be a full partner in their venture, but he was concerned about taking her money. He didn't really know why that was, but there was something nagging at him. He put it out of his mind.

"I think we need to go back to the pickup and put some kind of plan into action. The quicker we get started on this the better." Coleman was already leading the way down the steps.

This time Nola waited until he was almost down until making her decent. There was really no reason to tempt fate unnecessarily. Coleman smiled at her change of heart.

They put their ideas down in a notebook that Nola had in her bag. They discussed the electricity, heating, plumbing, water and sewer. There would be ample parking around the building so that was something they didn't have to worry about. Coleman knew that the first thing he would need was a carpenter to fix the inside of the building. He would need someone he could rely upon to work on plans. Coleman's background in the refinery had given him skills to do the electrical work and the plumbing. It would save them quite a bit of money.

After almost two hours of initial brainstorming, Nola was tired.

"What do we do now?"

"We need to talk to Bella and get some names for the carpenter work," Coleman said.

"Let's not bother her until dinner. Remember what she said. She didn't want to see us until then."

Coleman remembered. "What would you like to do in the meantime?"

Coleman was on a mission, and he wanted to attack the project immediately. That was the way he did things, but he knew that he had to consider what Nola wanted as well.

"Let's get some lunch and then explore the area. I don't know much about what this place has to offer. We should know those things if we are going to cater to tourists," Nola said.

The logic was sound. They spent the rest of the afternoon exploring. They had lunch in Kalispell and looked the town over. Nola wondered if it might have been a better choice for a bar, since it was bigger and had more shopping. Coleman reminded her about their long-range goals, and that seemed to satisfy her.

They were both awestruck when they took the "Going To The Sun Road" in Glacier National Park. They drove all the way to St. Mary, and then turned around and drove back, stopping frequently to hike on a glacier, or watch mountain goats climb steep ridges. The park was pristine, and Nola could see that it would be quite a draw for people coming by way of Whitefish. Suddenly, her whole demeanor changed.

"This is going to be a great adventure, Coleman. You were right all along."

"What, you had doubts?"

"Of course, it is you after all." Nola sat back in the seat and smiled.

Coleman was pleased. "I'm happy that this is something you want to share with me."

"Let's get started. Drive to Bella's and let's get some names for contractors."

Colman sped up the pickup, and by midafternoon they had some names from Bella. She wasn't even irritated that they had come back to her place before dinner.

Coleman talked to the carpenter that was Bella's first choice. He was agreeable to look over the property, after he found out that Bella had recommended him. Nola was careful not to include herself in any preliminary negotiations. It would be hard to know who was trustworthy.

The contractor said he could draw up some plans, and he might have them ready in a few weeks. That would give Coleman and Nola time to go back to Billings and Crow Agency to tie up loose ends. They could also stop at Bozeman on their way and check on Nola's property.

Coleman went to the local hardware store and gave the proprietor a list of items he would need for plumbing and the electrical work. The owner was excited hearing about the possibility of a new business in Whitefish. He told Coleman everything needed would be on hand; even the kitchen sink. The bathroom sinks and stools would need to be ordered from his supply company. Coleman picked out what he needed and gave the guy some money for a down payment. Things were falling in place.

Both Coleman and Nola were feeling pretty good about how things were shaping up. They got back to Bella's a few minutes before 5:00. Bella had made a tuna and noodles hot dish, and the three finished off the entire double boiler.

"I thought I might have some leftovers for lunch tomorrow, but it appears you two were quite hungry this evening," Bella said, with a smile.

"Pigs," is what you ought to say," Nola responded.

"Oh no. I enjoy it when folks like what I prepare. I don't have much to look forward to these days. Don't take that away from me."

"We're going to be leaving tomorrow," Coleman said, while

shoveling in a last forkful.

"You can't leave. What about the Icehouse?" Bella sounded panicked.

"It's just for a short time," Nola said, soothingly. "We've got some things to take care of back in Billings. The new bar is a go, but we'll need your help with something."

"What would that be?"

"We don't have a name for it yet. Since it's your old business, you should give us some suggestions to help us come up with an appropriate name."

"I see." Bella was already thinking.

"We'll be back in a week or less. So, you have some time to think about it."

"That's fine, dear. Now let's retire to the sitting room for a glass of sherry."

Both Nola and Coleman had a big day and were beyond tired. They would have liked to go to bed, but they didn't want to disappoint Bella.

Coleman got three small aperitif glasses and filled them with the thick red liquid. It warmed them all the way down. It was relaxing, and Coleman wanted to just enjoy the drink. Bella, however, wanted all the details of what they had accomplished during the day. Coleman let Nola do most of the talking. He was concentrating on their trip back to Billings to get the rest of their things. He knew it would be difficult for Nola to leave her job at Crow Nation, but he also knew she was committed to this new business venture. He would go with her for moral support when she made their new decisions known to those in the tribe that mattered.

They talked until 9:00, and after three glasses of the wine, they were all tired. They told Bella not to make breakfast the next morning, because they would be leaving early. Coleman said he wanted to be on the road by 6:00.

When they got up, they could hear Bella rattling pans and silverware down in the kitchen. When they were ready to leave, she called them in. She had made omelets and had poured coffee.

Everything was waiting for them on the table.

"I swear, I've never seen someone your age with so much energy. You put me to shame," Coleman said, shaking his head.

"What's your point? Sit down and eat." Bella was in control.

They did as she commanded.

"Now Bella, don't go up and change the sheets. We'll be back soon enough, and there's no sense going to any more trouble."

Bella smiled broadly. "You're coming back, and you are staying with me?"

"Only if you want us. I'm afraid our loft won't be ready for some time."

"Stay as long as you like. Just don't tell me how to take care of my guests."

Nola decided to give up while she was still in control of her own destiny. She was afraid this ninety-plus woman would consume them both if they let her.

11

Coleman and Nola's trip back to Billings was filled with conversation about their new business. They talked about how they would lay out the bar and where they would put the bathrooms. Coleman thought they needed pool tables, and Nola said that kind of stuff was up to him. She just wanted to decorate. Coleman reminded her that this was going to be a bar and not some tearoom.

"What do you take me for? I know this is going to be a bar, but if we are going to cater to tourists it has to have some kind of theme."

"Maybe we should decide on a name before we get ahead of ourselves," Coleman offered.

"I've been thinking about that. We should keep the name Icehouse. We could repaint the old sign on the side of the building and put something touristy underneath."

"Like what?"

"Don't know. I haven't thought that far ahead."

"It might be a good idea, but remember, we asked Bella for her thoughts on the name," Coleman said.

"She will like the idea of keeping the Icehouse name. She can help with the other ideas."

"Let's just be careful not to disappoint her or worse, piss her off."

Coleman smiled.

"Oh no. I never would want to be on her bad side."

The conversation about the bar ended as they approached Bozeman.

"Let's not stop now," Nola said. "I would rather check the status of the land sale on our way back to Whitefish."

"That's fine with me. It might give the guy more time to find someone to buy the place." Coleman speeded up and blew right through Bozeman.

~

They decided to go to Crow Agency first. Nola wanted to give notice that she would not be returning. That would be the easy part. It would be difficult to tell her aunt that she was leaving.

"You never told me your aunt's name," Coleman said.

"Her name is Moon Flower."

"That's a nice name," Coleman said, trying to make conversation.

"Nobody calls her that, at least nobody in the family. We all call her Flo."

"What should I call her then?" Coleman asked.

"I don't know. You may not have to call her anything. I don't know if she would even recognize you as a human being."

"That's harsh. I can be quite charming when I want."

"When are you going to start?" Nola responded, but there was just a bit of smile on her face. Coleman noticed.

They pulled into the parking lot of the welcome center. He shut off the engine and turned to Nola.

"Don't let them give you any shit. If you need me to run interference just say the word."

"I can handle myself. You just stay in the pickup." Nola opened the door and entered the building.

Coleman turned the ignition key to acc. and turned up the radio. It was some country station. Country was about all that was played on the radio in Montana. He knew a few of the songs, and he halfway liked Johnny Cash. What he was listening to was some Tex Ritter song. He was humming along trying to match the tempo, when Nola reappeared. She walked over and found her place back in the passenger's seat.

"Everything okay?" Coleman asked.

"Sure."

"Didn't they say anything?"

"Like what?"

"I don't know. How about 'we're sorry to see you go' or 'you need to give more notice' or even 'you're fired.'"

Nola smiled and looked over at Coleman.

"You don't know much about us. That's not our way."

"What? You mean the Indian way?"

"Exactly. We don't wear our emotions for everyone to see like you white eyes." Nola laughed.

"Well, what did your boss say?" Coleman asked.

"Nothing. He just nodded his head."

"What does that mean?"

"It pretty much meant that I was dismissed."

"Crazy way of treating employees if you ask me."

"No one asked you. Besides, it's not much different than your boss firing you for asking for vacation and then hiring you back on your return." Nola looked at Coleman.

"So, how do you know if you were doing a good job or if they valued your employment?"

"If they didn't like what I was doing they would tell me. Either you do the job or you don't."

Coleman just shook his head.

"I guess I don't understand your ways. I always knew when I was doing a good job because they would tell me. They would give encouragement and then more money."

"You whites always need a pat on the back. Not so with us."

"But..."

"Enough of this. Take me to see Flo," Nola said.

The conversation was over.

Coleman started the pickup and followed Nola's directions to Flo's house. It was an old trailer but the place was neat and looked homey enough. Coleman decided to go with Nola and talk to her aunt. When he opened his door, Nola stopped him.

"You stay in the pickup. This is something I have to do for myself."

"I understand. I'll go back to Billings and visit with my boss. He should know that I won't be coming back."

"You'd better not plan on picking me up until tomorrow. This is going to take some time I'm afraid."

"Because of me?" Coleman asked.

"Well, of course." Nola slammed the pickup door and was gone.

"No sense mincing words," Coleman said to himself.

He drove back to Billings, slowly. He had no place to go other than his trailer to load up his things. He stopped in the middle of that thought. It wasn't his things. It was their things. He had to change his way of thinking about the relationship. They were going to be partners now. He had to reason everything through the eyes of two. It would take some effort on his part, but he was sure he could follow through because he wanted it. He wanted it badly.

His former boss gave him the following day to clear out his trailer. There was a waiting list, and Coleman no longer mattered.

Coleman thought that maybe the two races weren't so far apart in behavior after all.

~

Coleman spent a sleepless night just tossing and turning in his trailer. He had gotten used to having someone by his side, and he wasn't comfortable without Nola. He woke up and had a bowl of cereal. The milk was just about to turn, so he tossed it down the sink after he had eaten. The refrigerator had a few items in it, and he decided to leave whatever food was left. The next tenant might appreciate it.

It was a cloudy day. It matched Coleman's feelings. He had this cloud hanging over him, and he didn't know why. Things were finally going his way, and he should have been elated in spite of the weather.

He decided to start packing up their things into the pickup. There really wasn't that much. They both had some clothing and a few personal items. Most of the furnishings and furniture belonged to the company. By noon, he had pretty much gone through everything and there were more items in the garbage than there was in the pickup. He put the keys to the front door on the counter and walked out for the last time. There was no sadness about leaving. Most of his sadness had been while he lived there.

He got into the pickup and remembered his grill. He decided that he had left enough for the next guy. The grill wasn't in the best of shape, but it still had a year or two left in it. He turned it upside down and got rid of the remaining ash and tossed it into the back of the pickup.

It was time to find Nola and leave this place forever.

~

It wasn't going well for Nola. Moon Flower wasn't happy. Unlike Nola's boss, she wasn't afraid to show it. She didn't like the fact that Nola was leaving the area, and she didn't like the fact that she was leaving with a white man. That was two strikes against Nola.

Finally, Nola had to be firm. She was leaving. They could part of good terms, or they could be angry at each other. It was a two-way street, and Nola could be just as stubborn as her aunt.

Flo begrudgingly relented, and things finally started warming up. They had spent the better part of the evening and the following morning trying to be kind to each other.

When Coleman drove up, Nola turned to her aunt.

"Coleman will be coming to the door, and I want you to treat him with respect."

Her aunt just looked at Nola.

"I mean what I say. I'm with this man, and we are going to Whitefish to start a business."

It was Moon Flower who nodded. Flo had disappeared.

"Too many Blackfeet that way to suit me."

Coleman knocked on the door. Nola answered it and put her hand out to stop him before he entered. She turned and looked over at her aunt. She nodded, and Coleman was allowed into the trailer. Flo didn't bother to get up from her chair. Although it was warm in the trailer, the atmosphere was icy.

Nola was the first to speak.

"This is Coleman. He's the one I was talking to you about."

Flo said nothing but looked at Coleman and appeared to be sizing him up.

"Hello. Nola tells me your name is Moon Flower. I don't think I've ever heard anything more beautiful. It's a great name." Coleman tried to be as sincere as possible. He thought about extending his hand but thought better of it. It might be considered too forward a move. Coleman felt like he was walking on eggshells and didn't quite know how to proceed.

Flo motioned for him to sit down. Coleman did so immediately, and Nola sat on a footstool next to her aunt.

"Why don't you explain our plans," Nola said.

Coleman had something he was passionate about and went into great detail about their plans for the Icehouse. Nola smiled, as he spoke to her aunt. Coleman was sincere and that came out immediately. She knew Flo like sincerity.

Flo listened intently to all of Coleman's explanation without any emotion. Coleman was having a hard time reading what she was thinking. When he finally finished with his exposé, he decided to speak to Flo about their relationship.

"I want you to know how much I cherish your niece. Maybe I should call her your daughter, because you've been more of a mother to her all these years. I know she feels the same way. I will always treat her with the respect she deserves, and I'll be there for her as long as she wants me."

Nola looked down. Coleman thought he might have embarrassed her.

"I know that Nola would like your blessing on this venture of ours. It is important to her to have you in her life. I love your daughter. But if I thought for a moment that I would be the reason to destroy your relationship, I just couldn't live with that. Nola can be headstrong, and I believe that is what attracted me to her. If this is going to hurt you and Nola then just say the word, and I'll leave." Coleman hung his head.

It was quiet in the trailer. Coleman could hear the clock ticking on the wall. He was thinking that maybe this was his dismissal. His heart sunk knowing he would be losing Nola.

Then, Flo put her hands over his. Coleman looked her in the eyes. All his fears just melted away.

"Thank you, Moon Flower," Coleman said hoarsely.

Nola got up immediately.

"Time to go." She took Coleman's hand, and they exited the trailer immediately.

Coleman just followed still in a daze over what just happened.

Just as they were about to get into the pickup, the trailer opened and the old woman said, "Flo."

She closed the door.

Coleman sat for some time in the driver's seat just wondering what just had happened. Nola's aunt had said only one word during their whole time with her.

"Is what just happened what I think just happened?"

"Flo gave you her blessing."

"But how do you know that?"

"You know it, or you wouldn't have thanked her."

Coleman just nodded in agreement.

"Besides, I think you may be the first and only white person she has ever touched."

12

Coleman and Nola talked about Flo on their way to Bozeman. Coleman found out that she was in her late eighties. He was surprised. She didn't look like she was past the sixties.

"She's the smartest woman I know," Nola said.

"Does she speak much?" Coleman wondered out loud.

"She has no need. Her wisdom is well known in the tribe. It's probably why she is still alive."

"I don't know what you mean," Coleman said.

"She was born in the 1860's. You know what happened during that time frame in American history."

"I never thought of that. It wasn't a very good time for Native Americans."

"But she was able to live through all the genocide, because she became wise beyond her years."

Coleman was silent. There were many things to consider. He realized what an effort it had been for Flo to accept the fact that he was taking Nola away. She probably thought it was some harebrained scheme, and Nola would be hurt eventually.

"What are you thinking?" Nola asked.

"Your aunt, Moon Flower. I'm thinking that she is quite a

woman."

"I still can't believe she accepted you. She obviously has come a long way." Nola smiled.

"Well, don't discount my way with women. Not everyone has the gift."

Nola rolled her eyes. By the time they were finished discussing Moon Flower, the Bozeman outskirts came to view.

"What's the plan?" Coleman asked.

"Find a phone. I need to call the bank and talk to Bruce."

Coleman remembered seeing a phone booth a block from the bank. He parked right in front of it, and Nola bounced out of the pickup immediately. Coleman watched her in an animated conversation. Nola wasn't smiling, but she didn't look upset either.

The conversation lasted only a few minutes and soon Nola was sitting back next to Coleman in the truck.

"What's the verdict?" Coleman asked.

"He's going to meet us at the diner at 12:30."

"So?"

"So what?" Nola was playing him.

"What is this, twenty questions?"

Nola relented.

"Sounds like we may have some kind of deal, but he didn't want to talk over the phone."

"That's promising. It's 11:00. What do you want to do until then?"

"Let's take a quick drive to see my property. It may be the last time."

"We can't stay long if you want to make your 12:30 appointment," Coleman said.

"Quit talking and let's go."

The trip back to the mine and homestead was quiet. Coleman decided to let Nola get lost in her thoughts, and it gave him time to think about everything he had to do to get the bar in Whitefish off the ground.

The homestead site was just the way they left it. Coleman parked the pickup next to the cabin, and Nola went to the area alongside the mine where the two Amish teens had buried her parents' remains. She found a few wildflowers and placed them on the stone.

By the time Coleman joined her at the gravesite, she was ready to leave. Nola turned around and walked back to the pickup. All Coleman could do was follow.

Halfway to the pickup Coleman noticed a cloud of dust coming from the opposite direction.

"Nola, check that out. Looks like someone's in a big hurry."

Nola stopped and looked in the direction of the dust. They both waited to see where it would lead. When it finally came into view, they could see it was an old flatbed truck, and it was heading right for them.

Nola put her arm through Coleman's, and they both waited to see what was happening. The truck made a sliding stop, and the man inside emerged holding a shotgun. When he came through the dust, they could see he was aiming it at them.

Coleman took Nola's arms and raised them along with his own.

"Easy mister. We don't mean anyone any harm. She's just looking at her property." Coleman gestured toward Nola.

The man squinted and then lowered the gun.

"You're the people I talked to a while back."

Coleman recognized him as the distant neighbor they had spoken to about Nola's parents.

"What's going on?" Coleman asked, as they lowered their arms.

"I'm sorry if I frightened either of you. We're all just a little jumpy around here as of late."

"Sounds serious. Let's get out of the sun, and you can tell us all about it," Coleman said.

They walked over to the cabin and sat on the edge of the porch. The man pushed his sweat-soaked ten-gallon hat back from his forehead.

"We've got a banker putting a lot of pressure on us. He wants to buy our property and now is threatening to dam up the creek. If he cuts off our water supply, we're all dead."

"Can he do that?" Nola asked.

"Who's going to stop him if he owns the land?"

"You have rights. You can let the courts get involved," Coleman said.

"Who has money for that? We're just getting by the way it is. I might even think about selling, but he's just offering pennies on the dollar. I won't let the somnabitch have the satisfaction. Tell me you didn't sell to him."

"Not ever." Nola was firm.

"We're supposed to meet with a guy named Bruce at 12:30 to talk about the sale of the property," Coleman said.

The man scratched his head.

"He's a straight shooter. That makes me feel a little better. Nobody knows why his asshole boss is so intent on getting his hands on our land."

"Mineral rights?" Coleman asked.

"Could be. We can't figure it out."

"Maybe Bruce knows something. We need to get going," Nola said.

"I'm very sorry for all this trouble."

"Nonsense. You have every right to be angry. Just not at us." Nola smiled.

"What were you going to do if the banker showed up here?" Coleman asked.

The man pointed to his shotgun leaning against the porch.

"What do you think? But he's yellow. He doesn't have the guts to face us."

Nola pointed over toward where her parents were buried.

"Looks like a good place to put someone's remains if you ask me."

She turned around and walked toward the pickup and got in. Coleman watched her go and then grabbed the rancher's hand and shook it.

"Good luck to you. I hope everything works out." He turned to go and then thought better of it. "Do you have a phone?"

"No, but my neighbor does. We use it sometimes."

The rancher gave him the phone number from memory.

"If I know Nola, she's already trying to come up with some scheme to get the banker out here, so you need to be ready. I would speak to your neighbor about the possibility of a phone call coming." Coleman pointed at the shotgun. "That thing isn't much good from a distance. You might hit someone you're not even aiming at. Got anything else?"

The rancher smiled. He finally was tracking.

"I've got a 30/30 with a scope that I use for antelope."

"Are you any good?"

"Shoot the eye out of a squirrel at a hundred yards."

"Get it ready. You may have your chance sooner than you think."

The rancher almost ran to his truck. Coleman figured he was on a mission.

Coleman went back to the pickup and wrote down the phone number the rancher had given him. He didn't mind being involved as long as it wasn't directly.

"We've got a lot to talk about with Bruce," Coleman said.

She nodded. They were both in agreement.

~

They arrived at the diner just a little after 12:30. Bruce was sitting in a booth waiting. Nola and Coleman slid in opposite him.

"Sorry we're late," Nola said.

"I just got here myself, so no harm done." Bruce seemed tired.

The waitress passed out menus and asked what they wanted to drink. Bruce ordered coffee black. Nola and Coleman wanted water.

"Is there any good news for me?" Nola asked.

Bruce smiled.

"I've done the background on your property, and it looks like your parents actually owned about 75 acres. It's hard to actually tell because of the terrain, but that's what's listed at the courthouse. It looks like they owned the property free and clear. I couldn't find any liens against it, so I think it looks pretty good for you."

"Okay. Is there interest from any buyers?" Nola asked.

"I believe there is. Land prices are low right now. Most of the area is going for about thirty an acre," Bruce answered.

Nola did a quick calculation in her head.

"That's two thousand and twenty-five dollars," she said, with disappointment creeping into her voice.

"Yes. That's the bad news. The good news is that I think I can get you a hundred per acre."

"Seventy-five hundred is way better than twenty-two five," Coleman answered. "I'd say sell it."

Nola wasn't jumping on anything until she had more information.

"The first thing we need to get straight is that I won't sell to your boss no matter what."

"He wouldn't pay that kind of money. He'd want to steal it first," Bruce said.

"I'm getting that message loud and clear. Who would be willing to pay that much?"

Bruce looked down for a moment and then up into Nola's eyes.

"How about me?"

Nola looked at Coleman and then back at Bruce.

"What's the gimmick?"

"Nothing like that. I'm offering you more than it's worth because I think down the road it will make me money. I don't know how yet, but I know that if the president of the bank wants the land, it will be a sure thing."

"Do you have that kind of money just laying around?" Nola asked.

"No. But I'm working with someone who does. In fact, if we can work this deal, I may quit my job and go to work for him."

Coleman sat back.

"What is this guy's business?"

"I can't tell you. He needs to remain anonymous. He doesn't want anyone to know that we would partner together."

"What would be the terms?" Coleman asked.

"It would be a cash deal. Nola would sign a quitclaim deed and we would handle the rest. You'd have your money by tomorrow if you want."

Nola hadn't commented for some time. She was lost in thought.

"Nola, what do you think?" Coleman asked.

She spoke to Bruce ignoring Coleman's question.

"We just came back from the property and ran into a neighbor who's mighty upset with your boss. It seems he threatened to dam up the creek on the property he owns if the others didn't sell."

"I've heard." Bruce sat back.

"So, you see that I don't want my land to fall into his hands no matter what the cost," Nola said.

"You don't have to worry about that. I've been visiting with a few of the ranchers out that way, trying to get them to stick together. I offered your land to them as well, but they are all just getting by. There is no extra money to buy anything even at the going rate. That's why I decided to do the deal myself."

Coleman looked at Nola, and she looked back. Then she focused back on Bruce.

"Here's what I think. We do the deal, but you don't quit your job."

"Why would I want to continue to work for someone like him?"

"I don't think you would have to work for him very much longer. Let me ask you this. Are you next in line to be the president of the bank?"

"That would be the pecking order unless the board of directors would bring in someone from the outside."

"What are the chances of that?"

Bruce thought for a moment.

"I'd say 80/20 in my favor. But I don't see him resigning. He's got it too good."

"Bruce, you are an honest man, and you would be a breath of fresh air in that bank. You don't need to be involved with what is probably going to happen. Your hands need to be clean."

"I don't understand."

"You will in time. Right now, go back to work and put the sale of my land in motion. I'll take care of the rest."

Bruce slid out of the booth, but before he could leave, Nola reached across and grabbed his hand.

"I'll be coming into the bank in about 30 minutes. Pay no attention to me when I walk through. Got it?"

Bruce nodded and left the diner with a puzzled look on his face.

Coleman turned and smiled broadly.

"What in the world is going on in that pretty little head of yours?"

Nola smiled back.

"Watch and learn," was all she said.

13

Coleman and Nola decided on meat loaf for lunch. Apparently, their discussion had flustered Bruce so badly that he forgot it was lunchtime. It was just as well. Nola had a plan, and she wanted it executed as quickly as possible.

Coleman paid the bill when they finished, and they went back to the same pay phone at Nola's request.

"Give me that number the neighbor gave to you earlier."

Coleman complied, wondering what was really going on. He liked the intrigue and was trying to figure out her actions. He thought he might have an idea, but he knew he'd better wait until Nola was ready to tell him.

It was a quick call, and Nola was back in the pickup smiling.

"Okay, spill it." Coleman was trying to sound gruff.

"I called the neighbor's neighbor. Gees, I wish we had asked for some names. I feel like these people deserve some kind of recognition beside the title of neighbor."

"Go on."

"He will relay the message I gave."

"Which was?'

"Get the 30/30 ready and in place."

Coleman wasn't really surprised, but now the game had changed. This was going to be for keeps, and they had to tread lightly.

Nola opened the door to the pickup.

"You stay here. I want to go into the bank by myself. The less faces noticed in the bank the better," Nola said.

She slammed the door and made the block walk to the bank. She wasn't in a hurry. Coleman figured she was rehearsing what she was going to say. He sat back, and since there wasn't much else to do, he just worried about his bar.

Nola paused outside the front door. This had to be done quickly and without much fanfare. She peered into the bank through the door. She could see the president in his office, and he was alone. She had to make her move.

Bruce was sitting at his desk and noticed Nola enter the bank. He had been expecting her and went about his business without any recognition. Nola moved briskly past the teller's windows and went right into the office. She closed the door softly.

"I have my property for sale, and I believe you want it," Nola blurted.

The banker jumped just a little. He hadn't heard Nola come into his office.

"Oh right, you were the one in here some time ago."

Nola nodded.

"Your land isn't worth much, but if you want to sell I might have some interest." He sat back in his chair.

"What are you offering?" Nola asked.

"Without actually looking at it, maybe five dollars an acre."

Nola saw her chance immediately.

"You know it is worth more than that. Maybe you'd better have a look at it."

"I suppose I could take a look." He pretended to check his calendar. "How about next week Tuesday?"

"No. It needs to be today, or there will be no sale. We are moving on, and I want this all behind me."

"Give me a half-hour to finish up a few things here. Since I don't really know my way around that area, I'll need you to drive. You can pick me up around back. My car is parked right next to the back door. You can wait for me there."

Nola knew he was lying. He knew exactly where her property was located. He just didn't want anyone out that way recognizing his car. The neighbor's assessment of his yellowness was correct.

"We'll be ready," Nola said.

"Just a minute. What do you mean by "we'll?"

"My boyfriend and me. It's his pickup and I wouldn't go out there with you by myself. It wouldn't be proper."

The banker smiled. Nola didn't like the look of his smile. She turned and quietly left the bank. No one paid attention to her exit.

Coleman and Nola waited patiently behind the bank, until the banker finally came out. Nola motioned for him to get in the passenger door, as she slid over next to Coleman.

The banker did most of the talking. He spoke about the history of the area. Nola thought he was probably the most boring person she had ever met. Coleman played along and asked a few questions to just keep him talking.

The pickup was kicking up quite a bit of dust. It was fine when they were moving, but when they slowed down or came to a stop, the cab would fill with dust. The banker didn't like it. He wasn't used to getting dirty, at least not in the physical sense, anyway.

When they arrived, Coleman parked in front of the cabin. The banker got out of the pickup and brushed off his clothes. He looked out over the property. Coleman and Nola got out of his door. They decided to keep some space between them and their passenger.

"The cabin isn't worth much." The banker was pretending to talk to himself but loud enough for both Coleman and Nola to hear.

"Let's take a look at the mine," Coleman suggested, and he led the way.

When they approached the mine, Coleman could see a shallow hole next to the place where Nola's parents rested. Nola and Coleman exchanged glances. It appeared the neighbor had been busy digging a burial site.

"What's this?" the banker asked.

"No idea," Nola answered. "It looks like someone was digging for something."

"Goddamned squatters. The country is full of them." He stepped up and peered into the hole.

Suddenly a shot rang out. The banker stood in place as a fine mist of red filled the air. Everything seemed to go into slow motion. Nola looked over and saw the back of the banker's head explode into nothing. He fell backward. The rancher had been right about his ability with a rifle. The banker's left eye was gone but otherwise his face was intact. It seemed strange to Nola that a small hole in in the front of his face could do so much damage to the back of his head.

Coleman took Nola's arm and pulled her toward the pickup. He could tell she was in shock. He was sure that she had never been witness to a murder especially one this violent. She was rubbing her arms trying to remove the blood spatter.

"Let's go Nola. We've got to get out of here."

"We can't just leave him here like that," Nola said in a hollow voice.

"Someone will take care of this. We need to get back to town and be seen. You've got to go back to the bank and pretend to have set up a meeting with him." Coleman motioned toward the corpse lying next to the hole in the ground.

Nola nodded.

"But I can't go like this." She showed Coleman her arms spattered with the banker's blood.

"We'll stop at the creek, and I'll clean you up. It's not as bad as it looks. It missed most of your clothes. Just your arms and face."

As they were leaving in the pickup, Coleman saw the rancher and another man walk over to the body. There was no rifle but both had shovels and neither wasted any time. By the time the pickup went over the hill, Coleman could see dust coming from the gravesite.

When they came to the creek that ran parallel to the side of the road, Coleman stopped the pickup. He took out his handkerchief and dipped it into the creek. Nola hadn't moved from the pickup, so he opened her door and went to work. First he cleaned up the few drops of blood on her blouse. It was a dark brown so the blood didn't show much. He was glad she hadn't worn white.

After many trips back and forth to the creek, Coleman felt he had done a good job. He was sure no one could tell she had been covered in blood. She had more blood on her than he first noticed. There was some other stuff as well, but he decided not to let Nola in on that fact. He finally had Nola get out of the pickup and did a once-over. He turned her around and was satisfied that she would not attract any attention. Her clothing would be dry by the time they reached town.

All the way back, Coleman talked Nola down. She was responding to his questions, and he felt she was back to normal when they parked in front of the bank. It was a bit before 3:00, and the employees were moving around. Coleman could see they were ready to close for the day.

"Nola, you need to go into the bank and do what we talked about."

Nola breathed deeply and put her hand on the door handle.

"Are you up to doing this?" Coleman asked.

She nodded.

"Maybe I should go in. This has to look real. If you can't do it, let me know."

"No, I have to do this. It wouldn't look right for you to be there. They haven't seen you before."

Nola pulled on the door handle and slid out of the pickup. She breathed deeply again and then marched to the front door and entered the bank.

She walked toward the banker's office and peered inside.

"Can I help you with something?"

Nola turned around and looked right at Bruce. She felt relieved, and decided to speak up so some of the other employees would hear.

"I had an appointment at 3:00 with your president. Is he around?"

"I haven't seen him for a few hours but his car is out back, so he couldn't have gone far. We're about ready to close, but I will be here for a while if you'd like to wait." Bruce was unclear what was actually happening, but he was willing to play along.

"I don't think so. I wanted to sell him my property, but we are leaving. I'm afraid it will be his loss."

"If he comes back soon, can I reach you somewhere?"

"We'll be at the diner down the street for about an hour. After that, we'll be gone."

"I'll see what I can do," Bruce said, as he ushered her to the front door.

Nola went outside, and Bruce locked the door behind her. He gave her a wink before he turned around. Nola went back to the pickup.

"How did it go?" Coleman asked.

"Brilliantly, if I do say so myself."

"What's next?"

"Back to the diner. I think Bruce will be paying us a visit soon."

"I'm thinking we should have bought stock in that diner with all the time we've been spending there."

Nola smiled, and Coleman started the pickup and headed back to the diner.

They both ordered hamburgers. Coleman suggested they should eat because they would be heading back to Whitefish soon, and there wouldn't be time to pull off to eat.

They had just finished their food and right on the hour deadline, Bruce walked into the diner. He had a portfolio in his hands.

He sat down and without a word, opened the satchel and handed Nola a cashier's check.

"You'll need to sign these documents and the transaction will be complete." Bruce was being very business-like.

Nola looked at the documents and then began signing. Coleman took each page when she was finished and gave it a once over to be sure everything was in order.

Nola put the check into her bag.

"Do you want to know what's going on?"

"I believe the less you tell me the better off I will be. I've never been very theatrical, so I don't know how good I'd be at charades."

"Things should start getting better for folks around here with you running the ship."

Bruce handed his card to Nola.

"Give me a call sometime down the line. I'm sure you'll be wondering how all this is going to turn out."

"I would be interested in why my land was so important," Nola said.

"Me too." Bruce stood and shook both Nola's and Coleman's hand.

Nola stood and gave him a hug.

"Thanks for all your help."

"I should be the one thanking you, but that would mean I know something of what happened today and I don't." Bruce smiled and left the diner quickly.

Coleman and Nola were on the road shortly after Bruce left the diner. Coleman had already put the day's events behind him. He was thinking only of their new business venture.

It would take Nola more time to process what had happened.

14

They pulled into Whitefish before darkness had set in. They were both exhausted, but Coleman wanted to swing by their soon-to-be bar. They were both surprised to see heavy equipment parked next to the Icehouse. It was late and there was no one around, so they headed back to Bella's to find out what was happening.

Bella was sitting in her rocker on her wrap-around porch when Coleman and Nola pulled into the driveway. She motioned to them to join her. The evening was extremely warm, and the humidity was almost unbearable. However, Bella was dressed for winter.

"Welcome back. Feels like there might be some storms in the air," Bella said.

"How can you stand to be wrapped up in all that clothing?" Coleman asked.

"When you are as old as me, being cold is a fact of life. I think I should have relocated to Florida, before I got so ancient."

Nola sat on a wicker chair next to Bella. Coleman stretched out on the floor trying to make his back feel better. It always tightened up when he was confined to a vehicle on long trips. He thought it might be some old injury acting up from his job at the refinery.

"What's going on at the Icehouse? We saw some equipment out

front." Coleman spoke from his reclined position.

"Oh, I hope you don't mind. I got the ball rolling with the city while you were gone. They stubbed in the sewer yesterday and will finish the water line tomorrow. The power company is supposed to show up tomorrow and put in your service. I'm happy you're back, so you can show them where you want it."

Coleman was impressed.

"Thank you Bella. You just saved me days of trying to line all this stuff up. How did you get them to move so quickly?"

"People know me around here," was all Bella would say.

Coleman figured she had a great deal of influence in the Whitefish community. He and Nola were fortunate to stumble onto this windfall.

"Sounds like I'll have a busy day tomorrow. I'm exhausted, so I'm going to bed."

"I'm going to stay up and talk to Bella. I'm too keyed up to go to bed right now," Nola said.

"I'll be getting up early, so don't go to the trouble of making breakfast for me," Coleman said to Bella.

"Breakfast is at six. Don't be late." There was just a hint of a smile on Bella's lips.

Coleman shrugged and shook his head. He knew it was futile arguing with Bella. He went to bed.

Bella and Nola sat and looked out toward the street for a time not saying anything. Finally, Bella turned to Nola and looked at her.

"Why don't you tell me what's bothering you dear?"

"I don't know where to start."

"Why don't you begin with the part that is most haunting you right now. I'm too old to listen to stories that don't have some thrill connected to them."

Nola told her the whole story about her property. Bella was interested and didn't bother to interrupt her until she was finished.

"That was quite an adventure. Reminds me of some of the times in my youth. Thanks for sharing."

Nola stared at Bella.

"My heart is heavy. A man lost his life, and I was right in the middle of it."

"You shouldn't concern yourself with such things."

"How can I not?" Bella was conflicted.

"You didn't pull the trigger did you?"

"No, but I was instrumental in bringing him to the property knowing full well what would happen."

"He was a bad man. The world is better without him in it. I'd say you did a necessary service for mankind. Now you need to put that out of your mind and get on with your life here in Whitefish."

"But what if this comes back to haunt us?"

"Sounds like you took all the necessary precautions. I wouldn't worry about things like that. Worry never solves anything. You cross bridges as you come to them and make decisions at that time. Anything else serves no purpose whatsoever." Bella sat back in her chair.

Nola realized that she felt better. Bella had a way of putting things in perspective. She was a no-nonsense person, and in many ways Nola was just like her. She decided to take Bella's advice.

"Thanks Bella. I needed to talk to someone besides Coleman."

"Men are so pragmatic. They put things behind them easier than us women."

"You don't seem to have much trouble in that arena."

"Years of practice, my dear. I'm happy to say that I've wrestled with regret and have won out over it."

Nola didn't realize it at the time, but their conversation would serve to shape the rest of her life.

~

Coleman woke up at 5:30 and got dressed. He thought Nola was still sleeping, so he tried not to wake her. Just as he was about to leave she sat up in their bed.

"I'm going to stay in bed for a while. There isn't much for me to do at the Icehouse right now."

"Good luck with that. I think Bella will have you down for breakfast before too long." He smiled, and left the room.

Nola fell back down. She was dog-tired, but knew Coleman was probably right. She would stay in bed until summoned. Bella was in charge, and it wouldn't do any good to try and buck her. Nola smiled and fell back asleep.

Breakfast was ready when Coleman went down to the kitchen. He explained that Nola was sleeping in.

"No problem. I'll give her a half-hour," Bella said.

Coleman smiled and ate what Bella put in front of him. She was quite a woman. He would have liked to have known her when she was young. He thought she would have been quite a handful.

"I've been thinking about the name of your new bar," Bella said, changing the subject.

"Nola and I both want to keep the name Icehouse."

"That's good news. It was what I was thinking. I've hired a painter to redo the sign. I thought that it wouldn't be enough, however."

"What do you mean?"

"You've got to make it so the tourists want to come. It can't just be a local bar. You'd go broke just catering to the locals."

Coleman was interested.

"I imagine you have some suggestions." He knew her suggestions would be more of a command.

Bella got up and hobbled over to a cupboard and gave a sheet of paper to Coleman.

"See what you think of this."

Coleman looked the paper over. Bella had written The Icehouse Saloon. Coleman liked the word saloon. It gave the place more of an old-time feel. Under that, Bella had written: A Place For Cowboys, Indians And Anyone In Between. Always Family Friendly.

Coleman didn't know about the Family Friendly part, but it seemed to fit the bill.

"Are you sure you want to put Family Friendly on a bar?"

"It is going to be the future. Mark my words. If I thought you could handle it, I would suggest either a restaurant or grill as well. Maybe that will come later. You'll need pool tables, pinball, darts and anything else that would appeal to young people and kids."

Coleman hadn't really thought much about his marketing strategy. He could see Bella's was a sound one. He wanted to attract the tourist trade, but he would also need to think of things to appeal to the locals during the off-season.

"You've convinced me, Bella. This looks like a great idea."

"Good. The painter is coming today. I already gave him the instructions. By the way, since this was my idea, I'm paying for it. Just make sure you have enough spotlights on it when everything is finished. Remember that you don't have windows, so this will be the only advertising people will actually see."

Coleman thought he might have some ideas concerning advertising down the road but decided not to share anything with Bella until the time was right. His mind was still working as he left the table and headed to the Icehouse.

Bella watched him go. She hadn't had this much fun in quite a while. She waited until 6:30, and then took a pot and metal spoon, and went to the foot of the stairway. She beat the pot loudly.

"Nola, get up. Your breakfast needs to be eaten right now." She beat the pot again.

Nola sat straight up and threw off the sheet. She headed right down to breakfast in her nightgown. It wouldn't be very smart to keep Bella waiting.

~

Coleman drove up to the Icehouse and parked away from the heavy equipment. The front door was open, and he could hear someone working inside. The place was illuminated with portable lighting, and Coleman was amazed at what had been accomplished. The actual bar was taking shape, and the walls had been lined with rough- sawn boards. The entire place smelled like new wood.

Coleman walked over to the carpenter and shook his hand. "You are doing a great job. I can't believe how far you've come since I left."

"My brother-in-law has been helping me out whenever he can. He works nights for the police department, so he can use a little more money. I hope you don't mind."

"Absolutely not. The quicker we can finish all this, the faster I can open the place."

Coleman walked around and tried to decide how he was going to finish the plumbing and electrical work. He realized he might have bitten off more than he could chew. In fact, he knew he did. He had some skills in those areas, but he had no tools or equipment. He needed help.

He walked back over to the carpenter and decided to lay his cards on the table.

"I think I might be the biggest idiot around. I'm not going to be able to do all this work myself. Do you have some suggestions on who I could hire for the electrical and the plumbing?"

The carpenter smiled.

"I think all you have to do is talk to Bella. She's got all the connections you'll ever need."

Coleman hated the thought of having to go back to Bella. He had wanted to do this on his own. She had done so much for them.

"I think she's just waiting for you to ask," the carpenter said.

"How do you know that?"

"Well, she comes down every day to see what's going on."

"I should have known," Coleman said, smiling.

"As long as I have you here, we need to talk about the upstairs residence."

"What about it?"

"Well, you have this long staircase that needs to be replaced, and I'm not sure you want stairs to your residence accessible from the bar."

"I hadn't thought of that, but you are right."

"Here's what I thought we could do if you are in agreement. We should tear down the staircase and close off the existing door. There is good access from the loading area that we are closing off from the bar anyway. I assume you are going to use that for storage."

Coleman nodded.

"Let's put an access door behind the bar out of the way somewhere and build a more accessible staircase with a few levels so it's not so steep getting to your loft. That solves quite a few problems."

"Let's do it. It's a great idea. I hadn't thought of all the problems an exposed staircase could cause. Thanks."

"I'll start on it just as soon as I finish the bar. You'll need to get the electrical finished before I box everything in. This will give me something to work on while you figure out the plumbing and electric."

Coleman walked out of the Icehouse without looking at what the city had done with the sewer and water. He needed to talk to Bella. He knew she could pull the necessary strings and get the people he needed. He would have to be content being the general contractor in this new venture.

As Coleman's pickup drove into the driveway, he could see Bella and Nola back on the porch. It looked like they hadn't moved from the night before. Coleman looked like a whipped pup.

"I wondered how long it would take before you came back to see me," Bella said.

"Do you know everything?" Coleman sounded exasperated.

"Pretty much. I've been around a long time. You'd better learn something in all those years, or what's the purpose?"

"I need a plumber and an electrician."

"I know. They are waiting to hear from me. They'll be there this afternoon or tomorrow morning depending on their schedule."

Bella got up to use the phone.

"You'd better get your behind back over there and lay out the plans for them. They aren't going to want to waste any time. You go with him Nola. The carpenter needs your advice as well."

Bella went into the house. Coleman and Nola took the opportunity to get away as quickly as possible.

15

The work on the Icehouse progressed quickly. Nola wondered how all the people coming and going didn't get in each other's way.

The painter had done an outstanding job on the signage, and since it was the only outside job, the electrician had completed the spotlights first. Nola and Coleman turned the lights on one evening just to see how it looked, and they were both impressed.

The plumber and the electrician completed their work quickly. They had their crews working exclusively on the bar, and in two weeks everything was in place. The carpenter was putting the finishing touches on the bar area and was finishing the trim in their upstairs living quarters.

Coleman was pleased with how everything turned out. Their loft had two bedrooms and a nice-sized kitchen. The living room area was quite spacious and would be just perfect for the two of them and any guests they might have. He wondered if Bella would be able to drag herself up the flight of stairs.

Coleman finished painting the loft, and was descending the staircase, when he realized everything was quiet. Everyone had finished and the place was deserted. It was just Nola and him, and he didn't know where she was.

He threw his paintbrush and empty paint bucket in the trash bin outside the garage door. He was finished as well. His pickup was parked out back so he knew Nola hadn't left. When he went to inspect the new front door, he saw Nola sitting smack dab in the middle of the parking lot.

"What's wrong, Nola?" Coleman sounded concerned.

Nola patted the ground next to her indicating that Coleman should join her.

Coleman sat and put his arm around Nola.

"Second thoughts?"

Nola looked at him but shook her head.

"Not for a moment. I just have a hard time thinking that this is all ours. I'm trying to let it wash over me before someone comes and takes it all away."

"Is this some Native American premonition?"

"My people have had a lot of things taken away from them."

Coleman nodded.

"But not this time. This is really ours."

Nola put her head on his shoulder, and Coleman could feel her weeping silently. They sat that way, until Nola was ready to move on.

~

Nola and Bella went to Kalispell to find the items she needed for the loft. They started with furniture and went from there. Coleman had Bell Telephone install a phone in the Icehouse, and he was busy contacting alcohol distributors. He wanted to open the place as quickly as possible. He knew opening in September would actually be between seasons, and it would be helpful for them to start slow until they got the hang of running the business.

Bella helped organize the kitchen, putting to rest the question of whether she would be able to navigate the staircase. She seemed generally excited for the couple and their new digs. She did mention a number of times that she wasn't happy about losing her boarders, however.

The three of them worked tirelessly getting the bar ready for the grand opening. They settled on the third Saturday in September. Coleman knew he could be ready, and they would advertise in the local papers.

Bella sat down at one of the tables and motioned for the two to join her.

"You know, I called in quite a few favors to get this place up and running."

"We know," Nola said.

"Well, I was thinking that maybe we could have a private party on that Friday for everyone who had a stake in making the Icehouse possible."

"That's a wonderful idea, Bella." Coleman was on board immediately.

"I'll take care of contacting everyone, so all you have to do is make sure everyone has a good time." Bella was enjoying herself.

"We'll have a ribbon cutting, and you will cut the ribbon," Coleman said.

"Nonsense. This is your place and your idea. That would be bad luck. I'll tell you what Mr. Coleman. You can pour me the first drink. That will be enough for me."

"Done." Coleman was elated.

"Now, I need to go home. I'm all tuckered out. You two are a couple of slave drivers."

Nola didn't even care that she used the term slave. She knew what was in her heart.

"I'll take her back home. You finish up here," she told Coleman.

On the way to the pickup, Nola grabbed Bella's hand.

"I know what you are doing, and I thank you."

"What would that be, dear?"

"You are inviting people to help try and make this a success. People know if you are behind something, they will support it as well."

"Well, of course. That's no secret. Cater to these folks and they will support you come hell or high water. That's been my experience anyway. Now just take me home."

~

The Friday rolled around faster than Coleman or Nola had really anticipated. They were ready but nervous. People started arriving at 7:00 p.m. Bella had been busy. There were many more faces than either Nola or Coleman could recognize. For a while they wondered if the whole town was going to show up.

Bella took them aside before the evening began.

"There will be no charge for any of the guests this evening. Everything will be on me. You need to keep that a secret, however. I want everyone to think this evening is compliments of the two of you."

"I don't think we can do that," Nola said.

"What? Not charge the people or keep it a secret?" Bella asked, with just a bit of sharpness in her voice.

"This should be on us, not you."

Coleman almost choked at hearing Nola's words.

Bella laughed out loud.

"Nonsense, you can't afford that. Let me do what I do best. No one has to know anything. Trust me on this. It will do more to promote your business than anything else we could do."

"I just don't think it's fair to you. That's all." Nola knew she had lost the battle.

"You let me worry about fairness. I'm old, and there is nothing fair about that. I should be able to do whatever I please. I've earned it."

"Thank you, Bella. We could not have done this without your generosity and help," Coleman said.

"I know. Now let's stop getting maudlin and get ready for a wild and wonderful evening. What kind of beer have you got? I'm mighty thirsty."

The evening exploded and stayed that way until the last guest left at 11:00. Bella had vanished much earlier. Coleman and Nola had all they could do to keep up with everyone's thirst. They sat at a table filled with various glasses and beer bottles. They were both exhausted.

"That was amazing. I've never been so tired. It doesn't get much better than that." Coleman dropped his chin to his chest. "I suppose we'd better clean this place up. We open tomorrow at noon."

Nola put her arm around him.

"We can do that tomorrow. There's something else we need to do right now."

"What's that?"

"Another grand opening of sorts. This one will be upstairs."

Suddenly Coleman didn't feel at all tired.

16

Saturday was another huge success. Many of the same people from the night before were paying customers this time around. It was midnight before they could lock the front door. People were having fun, and they were not the typical late night bar crowd that Coleman had known in Billings.

"We need to work hard and try to keep this kind of clientele," Nola said.

"I was just thinking the same thing," Coleman said.

"How about hiring some muscle?"

"You mean a bouncer?"

"Whatever you call it. I can't see us trying to handle motorcycle greasers by ourselves."

Coleman thought about it.

"I guess you're right. We should talk to Bella. I want to make sure the tourists aren't scared away."

"Let's go on over and see her tomorrow," Nola said.

"Okay but we should clean the place up tonight. There won't be enough time to get everything completed before we open tomorrow otherwise."

Nola just looked at him.

"Tomorrow is Sunday."

Coleman had been so wrapped up with everything that he had forgotten what day it was. He didn't know if it was a state law or a community ordinance. It really didn't matter much. They had to be closed on Sundays. It would be a welcome relief for him down the road. Right now, it seemed like a wasted day where he could be making money.

"We'll get ready for Monday in the morning. I'll call Bella while you do most of the work," Bella teased.

Coleman knew she was teasing. He had never seen a woman work as hard as Nola. He would never tell her as much, but he believed she ran circles around him.

They climbed the staircase to their new quarters above the bar. They undressed and fell into bed. If there were any thoughts about a sexual encounter, it was lost to instant sleep.

Nola woke up a little after nine and noticed Coleman was already up and gone. She went out to the kitchen and saw he had eaten some cereal. She found a bowl and poured in some of her own. She didn't bother with the milk. She was used to eating things dry. They didn't have much choice when she was young on the reservation, and it seemed she developed a taste for things dry and simple.

She went down to the bar in her nightgown to look for Coleman. He was mopping the floor and didn't notice her come into the room. Nola took a seat on a barstool at the end of the bar and watched Coleman work. She realized that he was a good man. She knew she didn't deserve him, and she hoped she wouldn't break his heart down the line.

She cleared her throat.

"What's a girl got to do to get a drink around here?"

Coleman almost dropped his mop.

"Scare the shit out of me, why don't you?"

"That would be almost impossible. You are way too full of it."

"Can't argue. What can I fix you this morning, young lady?" Coleman moved to the back of the bar.

"Tomato juice, straight up."

"Sounds good. I think I'll join you." He found two glasses and filled them with tomato juice. "Would you like ice?"

"I think I'll take it neat."

"Wise choice. More drink and less dilution. That would be just the opposite of what we want to serve our customers."

Nola smiled and pointed to the phone. Coleman put it next to her on the bar. It was an old Bakelite black rotary phone that Ma Bell supplied to her customers. She dialed Bella's number and talked to her while Coleman finished his mopping duties. He was rolling the mop and bucket into the back, when Nola completed her call.

"Bella wants us there at noon for lunch," Nola said.

"Good. I was hoping she would ask. It's just lucky I was able to complete most of the work while you were getting your beauty sleep."

"By design."

"Well, you can restock the bar and coolers while I check the parking lot."

"Sorry, I've got to get ready. You'll have to handle it by yourself." Nola headed for the door and was climbing the stairs to the loft before Coleman could even respond.

He just smiled. He had already stocked the bar and the only thing left was to check the parking lot for trash and police any cigarette butts the patrons might have left.

When he finished with the parking lot, he decided to wash their drink glasses. Everything was in its place and that made Coleman happy. He liked order, and it always felt good when he felt he had a handle on the daily disarray.

Coleman was satisfied that he was ready for Monday and went back up to their loft. He could hear Nola in the shower. They had decided not to bother with a bathtub. It took too much space in the bathroom, and they were both shower people anyway. Coleman liked it, because there was much less expense. He wanted to make money and get the business paid off as soon as possible. Bella didn't seem to care much about a timeline, but Coleman wanted all his ducks in a row. He hated owing people anything.

Just as he was considering joining Nola in the shower, the water stopped and she emerged wrapped in a towel.

"Are you finished down in the bar?"

Coleman nodded.

"Oh, how sad that I wasn't able to help you."

Coleman nodded again.

"Well, I have a little task that I'd like you to complete. That is, if you are up to it." Nola dropped the towel.

Coleman was up to it.

~

Bella's noon meal was huge. It would be breakfast, lunch and dinner for both Coleman and Nola. One of her neighbors had brought her a mess of brown trout he had caught in one of the streams that emptied into Whitefish Lake. Bella had baked it with some secret spices that she shared with no one. It was marvelous, and Coleman couldn't seem to get enough. Bella supplemented the fish with the last of her produce from her garden. There were green and yellow beans in some kind of butter sauce, sliced tomatoes, with salt and pepper, fried potatoes and applesauce. Coleman had never really found the taste for applesauce, but he took a little of it just to be polite. He didn't want to hurt Bella's feelings.

Just as he thought he couldn't pack in one more bite, Bella stood up and went into her pantry. She came out after a few minutes with three large plates.

"It's rhubarb pie. Last of the rhubarb for the season I'm afraid. It's not as flavorful as I would have liked, but with the ice cream on top, it will do."

Coleman looked at Nola, and she could see he was almost to his maximum input. Her eyes twinkled.

"Oh, it's one of Coleman's favorites. Give him the biggest piece."

"Well, I'm happy to hear it. This has got to be eaten while it's warm." She went back into the pantry with one of the plates and came back with half the pie on it.

Coleman thought she had put half a gallon of ice cream on the top as well. He gave Nola a dirty look. He knew he had to eat it, and he knew he was going to be miserable.

After Sunday dinner, Coleman excused himself to go lay on the couch in the living room. He made little gurgling noises in between his frequent moaning. Nola helped Bella clear the table, and soon they were enjoying talking over washing and drying the dishes.

"We've decided to hire someone to help with crowd control. We'd need them on the weekends when things are busier," Nola said, while drying dishes with a flour sack towel.

"That might be a wise decision. You don't want the place turning into a boxing ring. Unless, of course, that's the kind of place that would make money." Bella was a sly one.

Nola wasn't taking the bait.

"You know that we want the place to be family friendly. So we would like to keep a lid on the bar."

"Montana ain't the Bible belt, and people overlook a lot more things than they do in the Midwest, but there still has to be some decorum."

"Sure does. We were wondering if you had any ideas on someone who might be good in a bouncer position?" Nola asked.

"What are you looking for in this position?"

"Well, we don't want a thug. We would like someone who is friendly and can talk to people. However, if the situation would call for it, he would have to be able to remove someone without hesitation."

Bella paused and looked out the window. "I've got it. You want Freddy Fassbinder."

"We do? Why is that?" Nola asked.

"He's a local boy. He hires out as a jack-of-all trades. I've used him a lot. He is a huge person. Used to play football I believe."

"Not so smart?" Nola asked.

"Falling into that kind of thought?"

"What thought is that?"

"Well, that anyone who plays football is dumb?"

Nola hadn't thought about what she had said. She just confirmed in herself what she disliked in most people when they talked about her people. Either they were lazy or drunks.

Bella could see her discomfort immediately.

"Presuppositions are always dangerous don't you think?"

"I know they are. I'm no better than those people I dislike for doing the very same thing."

"Don't be so hard on yourself. We all need to guard against those things."

"Why don't you tell me about him?"

"Freddy is one of the smartest people I know. He's a shy one at first, and doesn't make friends that easily, but he knows what he's doing. He's well read, and he knows geography like the back of his hand."

"He must travel a lot."

"Not at all. Freddy is content to just stay in Whitefish making a humble living working for people and doing the jobs they don't want to do."

"He sounds like a big teddy bear."

"In many ways he is, but he doesn't let people run all over him either. I think he probably possesses the exact qualities you are looking for."

"How do we find him?" Nola asked, suddenly quite interested.

"Let me contact him. What time do you open on Monday?"

"We think we're going to start opening at 10:30."

Bella seemed puzzled. Nola decided to explain.

"We were thinking about offering some food over lunch. I thought we could do hamburgers and hot dogs just to see if it would be worthwhile. I think some people might have a beer with it but we have soft drinks as well. It may make us a little money if it all works out."

"I think it is a splendid idea. I'll have Freddy come in and talk to you both on Monday at 10:30. He will be your first customer, so make sure you do a good job of cooking for him."

"Oh, I'm not doing the cooking. I'll be taking the orders, Coleman will be the cook." Nola smiled.

"Does he know that?"

"Not yet. But he will."

They both laughed at Coleman's expense. It didn't really matter since he was still doing the moaning in the living room.

"You realize, Bella, that we could have never opened the Icehouse without your help. I've thought about it, and we would have fallen flat on our faces if you hadn't been involved."

"You've given me a great reason to be involved in the community again. It's something that had been missing for quite a while. I needed to have purpose, and you two gave me just what I needed. Well, actually more than I needed." Bella drained the water from the sink.

Nola folded the towel and placed it on the towel bar along side of the sink cabinet. Then she turned and gave Bella a huge hug. It took Bella off guard for a moment. Then she hugged Nola back.

"You are a breath of fresh air, Bella Beeman."

"I know," was all Bella said.

17

Sunday had been a bust for Coleman. He had eaten too much and he was miserable the entire day. He had to take a handful of antacids before he could even fall asleep. Even then, he tossed and turned most of the night. He really didn't fall asleep soundly until five in the morning.

Nola got up quietly around eight and let him sleep. She worked around the loft trying to stay as quiet as possible. She knew Coleman hadn't slept much, and she wanted to give him a few more hours.

Finally, at 9:45 she woke him.

"Planning to sleep the entire day?" She asked.

Coleman was groggy.

"What time is it?"

"It's almost 10:00."

"What the hell?" He jumped out of bed and couldn't get his head working to tell his body what to do.

Nola laughed.

"Relax. There's plenty of time. Everything is ready to go, and we don't open until 10:30. I'll go down and open up. You just take your time and screw your head on right."

"Thanks. I'm never going to eat that much ever again."

"Likely story." Nola left the room and went down to the bar.

Coleman went to the bathroom and jumped in the shower.

Nola was wiping off tables when she heard a knock on the door. It was 10:20 and she hadn't unlocked the door. She turned the bolt and pushed open the door a little just to show whomever that it was open. Then she turned around and walked toward the bar. Nothing happened. No one came into the bar. Nola thought it was strange but she figured whoever had knocked must have left when they found the door locked.

She was just about to check the stock in the back room when she heard a knock on the door again. Nola wondered what was going on. It was way too early for kids to play practical jokes. Besides, they were in school anyway. Nola marched right over to the door and pushed hard. The door caught the knocker right on the forehead. He staggered back a step and then started rubbing the spot on his head.

"Oh, I'm so terribly sorry. Are you hurt?" Nola asked.

"Miss Beeman said you wanted to talk to me."

"You must be Freddy. Please come in." Nola could see a welt starting to form on his forehead.

"Thank you."

"Let me get you some ice for that head of yours. Maybe we can keep the swelling down." Nola went behind the bar and got some ice from the machine, wrapped it in a bar towel and gave it to Freddy.

"It's not so bad. I've had worse," Freddy said, as he placed the towel to his forehead.

"Why didn't you just come in when I opened the door?"

"I didn't know if I was too early."

Nola liked people who made their appointments early. It showed dedication. She looked Freddy over and noticed, for the first time, that he was a huge man. He wasn't tall but he was square, and his arms looked like fence posts. Nola was thinking he might be just the thing they were looking for when Coleman came down.

He stopped and looked at Nola with wide eyes.

"Nola, you've got to stop beating on our customers."

"You are so very funny," Nola said. "This is Freddy. Bella sent him."

"I figured as much." Coleman walked over, took his hand and shook it.

"What happened to you?"

Freddy looked at Nola.

"I guess I walked into your door. Everything's just a little fuzzy."

Nola knew right at that moment that she would be hiring Freddy.

"Can I talk to you in the back?" Nola asked Coleman.

"Well, maybe after we talk to Freddy."

"No, we need to talk now."

Coleman followed Nola to the back. After a few moments, Nola and Coleman came back to the table where Freddy was sitting and sat down.

"We were considering hiring someone part time as a bouncer, but we've changed our minds," Nola said.

"I understand," Freddy said, and began to stand up.

"Please sit. We've got another offer."

Freddy sat back down and removed the towel from his face and put it on the table.

"We would like to hire you to work here full time."

Freddy looked around. "Are you sure that's a good idea? You just opened the doors. Are you sure you can afford it?"

"We thought that maybe you could start at 4:00 each day. It would give you time to do your other job during the day and work here in the afternoon and evenings. We couldn't pay you much. Maybe minimum to start and see how things go from there."

Freddy nodded. "What would I be doing?"

Coleman took the opportunity to say something before Nola took over.

"I've been a little nervous about having an actual visible bouncer. It's doesn't look good for a place that wants to project a family image. We would like you to bartend and do whatever needs to be done. Of course, we would also like you to take care of any problem patrons."

"I know just about everybody around here. You won't have many problems with the locals. Once you establish the atmosphere you're looking for, people will conform or they will go elsewhere looking for trouble."

"That's what we thought but we need someone like you to help us through all of that. I've seen too many bars turn into places where fighting follows the drunken bar flies. We don't want this to be one of those places."

"Understood." Freddy stood. "I'll be here at four."

Coleman and Nola stood as well.

"Are you sure you don't want to take some time to get things in order before you report for work here?" Nola asked.

"I've been looking for something just a bit more routine. Being a handy man is feast or famine. This is just what I've been thinking about. No time like the present to get started."

"So we're agreed? We'll pay minimum wage at first with the chance of more when we see how the business goes. Of course, you keep all tips," Coleman said.

"Whatever you decide will be fine with me. Miss Beeman said you are stand-up people." Freddy exited the door and was gone.

"Looks like we fell with our butts in the butter when we hooked up with Bella." Coleman made the observation, and Nola could only agree.

Nola walked over to the bar and picked up her purse. She slung it over her shoulder and moved toward the door.

"Where are you headed?" Coleman asked.

"Going over to the newspaper to run an ad. People need to know that we're going to start fixing hamburgers and hot dogs for noon lunch."

"We are? When did we decide that?"

"Over at Bella's when you ate enough to last an entire week."

"Was I in on the conversation?"

"Unimportant." She turned to leave and then looked back. "Oh, and by the way, you're the cook."

Coleman smiled as she left the bar. He knew he was a better cook than Nola, but he would have to make sure to rub her nose in the decision from time to time.

~

Freddy worked out better than either Nola or Coleman could have imagined. He was always prompt and willing to learn new things. They had the extra-added bonus of his knack for fixing things. Freddy became their personal handyman. They raised his hourly rate by a dollar within a month's time.

It didn't take long for Coleman to ask him to come in at 11:00 each day. The lunch thing had become quite popular with the locals because the food was good and reasonably priced. Nola said it was cheap, and people liked cheap.

Freddy seemed happy in his new employment. More than once, he mentioned that it was quite pleasant not having to look for work. Sometimes he said he felt like people in the past had just felt sorry for him and gave him something to do. He didn't like that at all. Now, if someone needed his help, they had to make arrangements. Freddy thought that it was nice to be wanted.

The Icehouse was a success. Coleman and Nola put in some hellish hours. Neither could fathom how they could have managed without Freddy's help. They had decided, early on, only to be in the food business at lunch. It was just too busy to try and have Coleman cooking during the evening hours. They would have to add a functioning kitchen and more help, and they just weren't ready to take that plunge.

Coleman and Freddy worked the bar, and Nola took orders from the tables. They had their own niches and covered them well. Their first real test came right before Christmas.

Nola had been decorating the bar with Christmas decorations, and the place looked quite festive. She was finishing the Christmas tree in the corner near a fake fireplace that Coleman had set up. It was the Thursday before Christmas, and things were a little slow because of the upcoming holiday.

Some guys from the after-work crowd were unwinding at the bar with a few beers, before they went home to the wife and kids. Coleman had gone to the market for some of the items that they supplied on the bar. They tried to have dishes of peanuts, hard-boiled eggs and various potato chips available for their patrons.

Freddy was busy checking the stock and filling empty spaces with the appropriate alcohol. No one was paying much attention, when the front door opened and three strangers walked in. They looked around and found three spots at the end of the bar away from the others.

Freddy's radar went off immediately. He didn't like the looks of these guys and decided to keep his eyes on them. He waited for a moment, before he went over to see what they wanted. He pretended to be adjusting the kegs in the cooler under the bar.

"Hey, barkeep. We need a drink over here."

"Be with you in a minute, guys."

One of the other three was looking around at the décor.

"What is this place, a bar or a church basement?"

The other two snorted.

Freddy made sure his baseball bat was where he kept it, before he sidled over to the three.

"What can I get you?" He almost said "gentlemen," but he knew they weren't.

One of the men had a wandering eye, and Freddy couldn't tell if he was looking at him or at the back wall.

"Why don't you get me that squaw over there."

"That's the owner. I think you'd better keep that kind of talk to yourself."

"Or what? You gonna take on all three of us?"

"If I have to. But I'd rather not. We run a nice clean place here, and if you want to stay and have a drink you are welcome. You just need to show a little respect, that's all."

"Fuck you and your nice clean place." He grabbed a dish of eggs and threw it at Freddy just missing his left ear.

"Not an athlete I see." Freddy turned and walked over to where he had put his baseball bat.

"You boys won't be drinking here this evening, I'm afraid,'" Freddy said, as he pulled up the baseball bat and rested it on his shoulder. "We don't allow that sort of language in this family place."

Freddy was probably as comfortable swinging a bat as he was once playing lineman in high school football. His size alone should have given all three some pause, but they believed there was strength in their numbers.

"Why don't you leave this bar while you still can walk. We'll all be happier with that outcome." Freddy only wanted to put a little scare into the three. He had no intention of hurting anyone.

All three jumped off their barstools in unison. One by one each pulled out a bowie knife from their coats. Freddy knew that they were after more than just drinks. His intention of doing no harm had just changed.

"Let me tell you want's going to happen now. You are going to open that register, put the money in a bag and hand it to me," the tall guy said.

Freddy decided the tallest guy with the biggest knife must be the leader, so he would direct his attention to him. He looked at the half-dozen guys sitting at the bar. They were unsure of what to do.

"Hey, why don't you guys take a seat over by the Christmas tree? It might get a little messy here soon, and I wouldn't want you to get your clothes all bloody."

The comment took the three by surprise. They weren't used to being challenged while they worked over their mark.

Freddy came out from behind the bar swinging his bat at some phantom ball. He stopped just short of the three men. He could reach them with his bat, but they would have a hard time thrusting their knives at him without moving forward. At present, they didn't seem all that motivated.

"What's it going to be? You walk out of here on your own, or someone carries you out. It's your choice."

When the three looked at each other, Freddy knew they had made their decision and would be rushing him together. He decided to make the preemptive strike. The three guys didn't realize that the bartender was as quick as he was. Freddy sidestepped the first man and in the same motion swung his bat hard hitting him in the knife hand. The first man screamed and fell on his knees holding his wrist so his hand wouldn't fall off just before he passed out.

The other two were stunned for a moment and it was just long enough for Freddy to swing and hit the second guy right in the melon. He was unconscious before he hit the ground.

The leader seemed undaunted by Freddy's ballet moves. He raised his knife and moved around Freddy, until they had changed positions. Freddy knew his element of surprise had been used up, but he still was comfortable with his bat against the thin man's knife.

"I'm going to gut you like a deer being field dressed."

The guy was quite sure of himself, and that gave Freddy some pause. He might be better with the knife than he had anticipated.

Freddy saw some movement coming from behind the guy with the big knife. The leader must have sensed it as well. As he was turning his head to see what was going on, a chair came crashing down right on top of his head. The knife went flying across the floor, and the leader went down to his knees in slow motion.

Freddy gave him a little push with his foot, and he joined his other two unconscious friends on the floor.

Nola still had the chair in her hand and was gasping, trying to take air into her lungs. Freddy didn't know if she had expended too much energy, or if she was just so excited beaning the guy that she could hardly breathe.

18

Everyone stared at the three men on the barroom floor. Freddy was the first to speak.

"Are you okay, Nola?"

She looked at him.

"I am now. How about you?"

"Never better. I suppose someone should call the police."

"That should be me," Nola said.

"I think it would probably be better. I have a bit of a history with the sheriff."

The other men near the Christmas tree decided to make their getaway and stood up to leave.

Freddy stopped them.

"Nobody is going anywhere until we get this straightened out with the cops. You are all witnesses." Freddy smiled to put them at ease.

"Drinks are on the house until we get this cleaned up," Nola said.

The men weren't in such a rush to leave after all. Nola went over to phone and started dialing the police department. Freddy collected the three knives and put them on the bar. A few of the patrons helped him tape up their arms and legs with some masking tape left over from painting the interior of the bar.

Whitefish wasn't a big place, and the police actually arrived in a few minutes. Nola figured that not much happened in the community, so this was going to be big news. The police would want to be right in the middle of it.

The sheriff came into the bar followed by two deputies. He barked out a few orders to his deputies.

"John, take the guys at the bar over to a table and get their story."

"Duane, stand at the door and keep out the looky-loos."

Both men did as they were told. The sheriff walked over to Nola and looked her over.

"I'm Sheriff John Durst." He looked at the three men on the floor. Two of the three were starting to stir.

"Are you with these men?" Durst looked right into Nola's eyes.

Nola was angry.

"Why would you ask me that? Is it because I'm Indian?"

Durst took out a notepad.

"Tribe?"

"Excuse me?"

"I asked you what tribe you're from." Durst clipped his words.

"What has that got to do with any of this?"

Durst ignored her question.

"Blackfoot or Flathead?"

"My name is Nola. I'm one of the owners of the Icehouse. I'm neither Blackfoot nor Flathead. My people are Crow, if you must know. I don't know why that's germane to what happened here."

"You're a long way from the reservation. I may have to hold you until I can contact Billings. Until then, your account of what happened here is meaningless."

Nola just stared at Durst with her icy blue eyes.

Durst moved to the bar and noticed Freddy for the first time.

"Well, well, well, look who we have here. Got a new job, I see. I wonder how that happened?" Durst was angry.

"You don't pull all the strings around here. Looks like I snuck this one right by you," Freddy said, trying to get under Durst's skin.

Durst had made it his life's ambition to freeze Freddy out. Anytime Freddy found a job, Durst would put pressure on his employer to have him fired. There was no love lost between either of them. Freddy was so easygoing that he just took what Durst dished out. It was probably why the only thing he did for so long was odd jobs and handyman work.

"Not for long. You're wrapped up in something here, and I'm going to get to the bottom of it. It should very well cost you this job." Durst looked at his notebook.

"Don't you want to hear what happened?" Freddy asked.

"Freddy stopped these three men on the floor from robbing us." Nola was pissed.

"Well, I may have stopped two of them but Nola probably saved my life by beaning the thin man over there with a chair." Freddy smiled, and winked at Nola.

"I'll get the real story from John when he's finished interviewing the locals. You both may be charged with assault." He flipped his notebook closed and walked over to the three men lying on the floor.

Just as he was reaching for his radio to call for the fire department, the front door opened and in rushed Coleman. He dropped his bag of groceries on the floor.

"What the hell is going on around here?"

Durst whipped around.

"Duane, I thought I told you to keep people out of here."

"I tried, but he said he was an owner," Duane said.

"I don't give a shit if he's the governor. Get him out of here."

Duane pushed Coleman back out the door. When they got outside, Duane gave him an extra push, and Coleman went sprawling onto the gravel. His left hand broke his fall and he skinned his palm.

Coleman stood and balled his fists, meaning to take this deputy out. Duane was quicker and had his pistol out and pointed right at Coleman's chest.

"You'd better think about it, mister. You seem to be outgunned."

Coleman didn't like the odds. He wanted to get back inside, but it didn't look like that was about to happen any time soon. He had to come up with another plan. He turned around and walked toward his pickup.

Coleman knew what had to be done. He got into the pickup and left the Icehouse parking lot on two wheels. Duane watched him go and went back to his post guarding the front door. He smiled at showing this guy who had the power.

John finished giving the local account of what happened to Durst. Durst told the men to go home. When a few of them objected, he had John push them all out of the door.

Freddy didn't like what he was seeing. It was just he and Nola stuck in the bar with Durst. He didn't like the odds. The three men had recovered enough to sit up. The fire department's first responders had arrived, and Durst cut off the tape from their legs.

"Can you boys walk?"

They nodded, and Durst helped them up. The two firefighters took the three to the truck.

"John, go with them and keep an eye out. We don't want to lose any witnesses before I have a chance to interview them." John walked out with the three men and the two firefighters.

Durst turned his attention back to Nola and Freddy.

"You must be the Indian that's mentioned outside," Durst said to Nola.

She said nothing.

"So, do you want to hear what happened from our perspective?" Freddy asked.

"Not really. I don't want to hear a damn thing from you."

"Just listen to Nola. She watched the entire thing unfold. She even got to participate." Freddy smiled.

"How can I believe anything from scum like her? They're all drunks and liars."

Nola's eyes flashed, and Freddy was quick to head her off. He knew Durst was baiting them both and wanted them to do something so he could charge them.

"You're speaking to a friend of mine. I believe you owe her an apology."

"Fat chance. I speak only the truth."

"You've never spoken the truth. Your entire life has been one big lie after another," Freddy said, trying to get Durst to react.

He didn't have to wait long at all. Durst reached and pulled out a flashlight from his belt. In one fluid motion he swung and cracked Freddy on his head right above his eyebrow.

Freddy was a big guy, but the action took him off guard. He staggered backward against the back bar. The cut was bleeding profusely. Freddy's head was dripping with blood. Nola shrieked and moved behind the bar to help him.

Durst took a swing at Nola when she passed him. Nola was too quick, however. She ducked and the flashlight came out of Durst's hand and went skidding across the floor. Durst cursed and went over to retrieve it.

Nola had a towel and was holding it to Freddy's head trying to stop the bleeding. When Freddy came out of the fog, he took the towel from Nola and kept it pressed against the wound.

"You two will be charged with resisting arrest. I'll be taking you both down to the station to book you. Looks like you'll be spending some time in our lovely jail. It's so beautiful this time of year. Christmas and all, you know."

Nola could not believe an asshole like this ever got to be a sheriff. She found a plastic bag and put some ice in it and handed it to Freddy. He handed her the towel and she threw it in the sink.

Suddenly there was some commotion outside the front door. They could hear Duane's muffled voice, and then it was quiet. The door opened, and in walked Bella followed by Coleman.

"My, my, my. It appears we've had some excitement here this evening. Is it safe to enter?" Bella asked.

"You shouldn't be here, Miss Beeman," Durst said, but his tone of voice had changed considerably from a few moments ago.

"I shouldn't be in my own building? Why is that, sheriff?" Bella's tone had an edge to it.

"This is an ongoing investigation. I was just about to book these two for resisting arrest."

"Is that right? Well, from what I hear from a reliable source, it seems to be a simple robbery gone badly. You may be reading more into this than you should."

"Who's this reliable source of yours?"

"Coleman, please go get the gentlemen that were here this evening," Bella said. "They are just outside. They never left. It seems they aren't comfortable with your brand of justice."

Coleman came back into the bar with the locals the sheriff had kicked out of the bar a few minutes earlier. They were smiling at what seemed like a sudden turn of events.

"You can't interfere with a police investigation, Miss Beeman." Durst didn't sound like he even believed what he just said.

"You watch me. We've had enough of your brand of justice around here. Too many of us have turned a blind eye because you just were teetering on that fine line. Today you finally crossed it."

Durst was concerned. He decided to go on the offensive.

"People look up to you, Bella Beeman. However, I'm the sheriff, and I say what's going to happen around here."

Bella ignored the outburst and turned to Freddy.

"How'd you get that cut on your forehead, Freddy?"

Freddy pointed to Durst.

Bella turned toward Durst. "I'd call that assault. Wouldn't you, Sheriff Durst?"

"It's what I call it that carries the weight around here. I say he was trying to elude arrest."

Bella took a step toward Durst. He raised his flashlight out of instinct.

"Are you going to strike me as well, Mr. Durst?"

Durst dropped the flashlight and fumbled with it until he could return it to his belt.

"That might have been your wisest move of the entire day," Bella said. "Now let's all have a seat until the mayor gets here."

"Why would the mayor come here?" Durst asked, concerned.

"I believe he's coming here to relieve you of your duties, Mr. Durst."

"He can't do that."

"Oh, but he can and will. You work at the pleasure of the city of Whitefish. Right now, there doesn't seem to be much pleasure in your employment."

"You don't have anyone else who can do this job."

"I believe almost anyone could do this job a great deal better than you and with more success. In fact, I think we might have the best candidate standing right behind the bar."

Everyone was trying to process what Bella had just said, when the mayor walked in. Coleman smiled. It was the guy who owned the hardware store. He had become good friends with the man. This was starting to work out better than he could have imagined.

19

The mayor stepped into the Icehouse and walked over to Durst.

"Sheriff Durst, I am relieving you of your duties beginning immediately. Please give me your badge and weapon."

Durst just stood dumfounded. He couldn't believe how the events of the past hour had turned and bit him right in the ass.

"You can't do that," he sputtered.

"You were promoted to sheriff at our discretion, and now you are terminated at our discretion," the mayor said, and held out his hand for the badge and the service revolver.

Durst fumbled with both the badge and gun and finally handed them over. The sometime mayor and hardware man looked at the items and handed them over to Bella. Then he turned his attention back to Durst.

"In one hour, I'm going to call the county attorney. I'm going to request an inquiry into your tenure as sheriff. That won't turn out very good for you. It may even gain you some time in prison unless…" He stopped.

"Unless what?" Durst's voice cracked.

"Unless you clear out. By that, I mean you'll clear out your things from the PD, and then you'll leave town. I'll be watching, and if you aren't completely away from this community, I'll get the ball rolling. Trust me on this."

Durst turned around and walked out of the Icehouse. Everyone watched him go. There was applause as the door closed.

The mayor grinned. "I've been wanting to do that for a long time."

Bella placed the badge and handgun on the bar and pushed it toward Freddy.

"What do you say, Freddy? Are you ready to become the new sheriff?"

Freddy looked helplessly over toward Nola and Coleman. Coleman smiled and put his arm around Nola.

"I think I can speak for Nola and me. You'd be foolish not to consider this. We can't pay you what you're worth. This would be a real career opportunity for you. The community could use someone who's fair and doesn't have other agendas."

"What he said," Nola answered.

"I've never thought much about law enforcement," Freddy said.

"This community is going to grow, and we could use an honorable person in your position. You've been held down long enough. It's time for you meet your destiny," Bella said.

"Well, I suppose I could always give it a try. If I didn't think I was doing the job, I could always resign."

"Can't see that happening. Mr. Mayor, let's swear this new sheriff into office," Bella said.

"We will need to do this officially at the next council meeting, but I can do the unofficial swearing in right now to make this all legal."

He went through an abbreviated version of the swearing-in process, because he couldn't remember all the words. When he was finished, he shook Freddy's hand.

"Welcome aboard. Now I've got to get back to the hardware store. You can keep your two deputies, or you can fire them and hire someone new. That is up to you." The mayor turned and left the building.

"What are we going to do about the deputies?" Bella asked.

Freddy looked at her and knew her well enough to know the question was a test.

"I know both those guys. They are pretty decent people. They were just following orders from Durst. There is something to say for employees who are loyal and follow orders. If they want to stay on and take orders from somebody like me, they are more than welcome."

"Good answer," Bella said and turned to leave. "I'll need a ride home."

One of the locals jumped up and followed Bella out the door. Freddy fitted the holster through his belt and then placed the .38 into it. He fumbled with the badge until Nola took it from him and affixed it to his shirt just above his right breast pocket.

"You look official now," Nola said, and went around to the back of the bar where Freddy was standing.

She pushed him around to the front of the bar and sat him down on a barstool.

"You don't work here anymore, but you are always welcome here."

"Thanks," was all Freddy could say.

"We really mean that, Freddy," Coleman said. "We want you to come in regularly. A police presence is welcome in a place like this. It keeps out that element that normal people want to avoid. We want normal people in here."

"Your first drink will always be on us," Nola added.

"Well, let's not go crazy here." Coleman tried to look stern, but everyone knew he was having fun. "Thanks you two, but you know I couldn't accept that. I'll pay for whatever I order here, and you'll see quite a bit of me."

"We should have a celebratory drink on the house." Coleman started to reach for glasses.

The remaining locals joined in, and everyone seemed in a festive mood.

"I'll just take club soda with a lime," Freddy said. "Can't drink when I'm on duty."

Nola and Coleman set up everyone with their drink of choice, and when everyone was settled, Nola raised her glass.

"To Freddy and the best sheriff Whitefish will ever have."

There were quite a few "hear hears" before the glasses were drained. Freddy thanked everyone and stood up to leave.

"Sit down, sir," Nola said. "We need to know the backstory between you and Durst before you have permission to leave."

Freddy smiled.

"I think you've been spending too much time with Miss Beeman. You're starting to sound quite a bit like her."

"Is that a bad thing?" Nola asked.

Almost everyone in unison shouted a resounding "NO."

Freddy sat back down at the bar and began his story about his relationship with John Durst.

"We didn't really know each other until high school. We played football together, and we got along until we were seniors. His father was the football coach, and he worked with John for most of his life. He groomed him to be the quarterback, and when we became seniors, he took over that position. I was always a big guy and was used on the offensive line. I was big but always quick, and I enjoyed the position."

"What happened to make things go sour between you two?" Coleman asked.

"Durst was a genuine asshole. He pranced around like he was the entire team, and we were all just there to do what he said. He was really nasty to the underclassmen and berated them right on the field during some of our games. I told him to go easy and help them learn without being such a dick. After that, he decided we were enemies. When you think about it, it was really stupid. His offensive line was the only thing that kept him from getting killed."

Coleman was weighing every word. He loved sports, and this story obviously had some special meaning.

"How did you get back at him?"

"We couldn't really do much. His was dad was head coach and all. But things kept getting worse and worse, and coach wouldn't say anything to John. Things weren't good on the team. A few of the guys just quit after becoming the targets of his constant berating. We had a good team, but we started losing games that we should have won. Things got even worst after that, so we had a team meeting one night after practice without coach or John. Everyone was down, and we needed to find a way to come back from all of it. That's when I made the suggestion." Freddy stopped and took a swallow from his glass of club soda.

"Don't stop now. This sounds like the good part," Coleman said.

Freddy looked down and then spoke.

"Not a highlight in my life. I suggested we teach him a lesson. We played Missoula on that Friday night. They had a good team, but we could beat them if we played well."

"What did you do, throw the game?" Coleman asked.

"No. We played our hearts out, and we were ahead just before the half. We had the ball and almost ready to score. That's when the entire offensive line just stopped blocking. What's worse, we told their line when we were going to do it. They rushed the quarterback and he went down, hard."

Freddy stopped to collect the rest of his thoughts.

"We just wanted to show him he wasn't the only member of the team. We weren't planning on him getting hurt."

"But he did?" Nola asked.

Freddy nodded.

"They broke his ankle. He was out for the rest of the season."

"So what happened?" Coleman was growing impatient.

"Coach put in the backup QB who probably should have been the quarterback to start with. We ended up winning the game and didn't have a loss the rest of the season. The next year, after I graduated, that guy led them to play in the state championship."

"That couldn't have gone over very well with Durst," Coleman said.

"You could only imagine. He blamed me for everything. Coach never said anything, but our relationship was strained after that. I always thought it was funny that he couldn't see what his own son was doing to the team. He tried to place blame on anything and everything that really had nothing to do with the real problem."

"Sounds like Durst had everything coming to him," Nola said.

"It doesn't make what we did right. If I had to do it all over again, I wouldn't. It wasn't right, and John never got over it. I've had to live with it all these years, and I've paid the price."

"He was a bully. He needed the lesson," Nola said.

"But it wasn't constructive. We ended his football career, and he remained a bully. Sometimes when you're young, you don't make the best decisions."

"You've been paying for it all these years. He was the one who couldn't let go. You turned the other cheek far too much in my opinion," Nola said.

"Thanks. He and his dad did what they could to make sure I didn't get any meaningful employment for many years. Miss Beeman helped to change that for me. Now this." He looked down at his badge and shook his head. "Maybe things are actually turning around for me after all."

Coleman finished his beer.

"What a great story. Now it's time to open for business." He went out the front door to remove the yellow police tape from the area.

The rest of the locals finished their drinks and left. It was lunchtime, and the Icehouse would be busy with people wondering what had happened. Freddy stood and placed his hand on Nola's arm.

"You are special. Bella could see that, and so can I. Coleman loves you, but you will leave him someday. Make him happy until that day. He's a good man, and he deserves to be happy for as long as he can." Freddy left quickly.

Freddy's words shook Nola. She just looked at the door confused. It would be just one of four life-changing events.

~

Nola put Freddy's words out of her mind and concentrated on the business. She and Coleman worked tirelessly, and they were successful. Their bank account was growing much faster than either of them had even hoped.

Things were going smoothly, and it didn't hurt that they had the sheriff as a good friend. His frequent presence at the Icehouse had the desired outcome. People came in with their families. The kids played pinball, darts, and pool while the adults had their favorite beverage and something to eat. Coleman and Nola decided to expand their menu and hire someone to take over the kitchen duties.

They had to make changes in the kitchen to accommodate equipment that a cook would need to put out meals. That was way beyond Coleman's pay grade, and he was thankful to come out from the kitchen.

They had asked Bella about someone she thought might be a good kitchen employee. Bella answered by saying she would think about it. It shouldn't have been a surprise to anyone that she came to work after the kitchen had been remodeled.

Nola and Coleman tried to talk her out of it, but she said she was having the time of her life. She did give them a few names for someone to come in during the evening, but she wanted to take care of the noon meals as long as she could.

No one was complaining. Her cooking was superb, and she would come up with specials everyday. They decided early on they would have daily specials in addition to the hamburgers and hot dogs. It served to keep things simple and not overly tax Bella.

The real problem was trying to convince Bella to keep things scaled down so they could see a profit. She seemed to think every day was Thanksgiving, and it took quite a few meetings before she agreed to try and be a bit more frugal with her meal preparation.

Days came and went and just melted into each other. Life had become almost too perfect. Nola should have probably realized from experience that life's perfect moments could not last.

The Skinny

It was about that time that the second life-changing event came out of nowhere. It shouldn't have been such a complete surprise. They were both adults and old enough to know how things worked.

Pregnancy shouldn't have been the huge bombshell it turned out to be for Nola or Coleman.

Part 2

20

Whitefish, Montana-July 1951

Roland Sinning was born to Coleman Sinning and Enola McGuire, the cowboy and the Indian, without much fanfare. Nola had chosen not to speak about her pregnancy with anyone, and that included Coleman. When he had shared his concern with Bella, she told him to ignore it. Nola would come around. It just took some women longer to adjust.

Coleman wasn't quite so sure. After Roland was born, Nola seemed to warm up just a bit. She was a good mother and saw to his every need, but Coleman thought the bond just wasn't really there.

Roland was a skinny little thing. He resembled Coleman, although he had Nola's blue eyes and high cheekbones. He had an easygoing personality right from the beginning. He slept most of the night right from the hospital. Nola had to wake him from time to time just to make sure he was getting enough to eat from her full breasts.

Coleman tried to give Nola more time to be with Roland in their loft. Nola didn't seem to want to spend time alone with him, however. She would take him back down to the bar and put him in a box on the bar. Coleman didn't really think the bar was the best environment for his son day in and day out, but he was afraid to bring up the subject with Nola.

Roland became sort of the bar's mascot. People would come over and play with him. Soon enough they were calling him "Skinny." Skinny was one of those children content to take everything in. He would lie for hours not making a peep and just look around at the people in the bar. Nola asked Coleman once if he thought Roland was all there. The comment concerned Coleman immediately.

Bella seemed to come to the rescue after that. She would come in to prepare the noon special and take Roland into the kitchen with her. She talked to him constantly, and Roland responded to her with his babble and smiles. Some weekends she would actually take him home with her. Coleman and Nola would pick him up on Sundays, after they had had dinner with Bella.

This went on for the first five years of Roland's life. It was a delicate balance, and as Nola's motherly attention waned, Coleman's fatherly duties increased. He taught him how to shoot pool when business at the Icehouse was slow. Roland had to stand and move a chair around to play, but that didn't stop him. He took to pool immediately, and the locals enjoyed playing with him and schooling him on the finer points of the game.

The local school didn't have kindergarten, so Roland started first grade when he turned six. He was a good student. Things came easy for him. Coleman figured that it was from his mother's gene pool.

After school, Roland would rush home and hope to play pool with someone hanging out at the Icehouse. By the time he no longer needed the chair to play, he was pushing nine. He was beating most of the people at the pool table, and Coleman thought it might be time to give him some responsibility at the bar. He wanted him to realize that life was more than just shooting pool.

It was around that time, that the third life-changing event happened for Nola. Bella had been slowing down, but she didn't want to give up working in the kitchen. Nola was concerned. After all, she was in her nineties. Who comes to work every day when they're that age? When she tried to confront Bella, she was promptly dismissed.

It was Christmas vacation for Roland, and he was doing his chores at the bar before it opened. He was hoping to find someone for a game of pool when he finished. Bella was busy in the kitchen, and Roland was busy bringing her items from the cooler to save her some steps.

Bella seemed quiet. That was unusual, because she was quite fond of teasing Roland.

"Are you feeling okay?" Roland asked.

"I should be asking the skinny kid that," Bella shot back. "You look like a prisoner-of-war."

Roland smiled and went back to the cooler for some items. When he returned, Bella was on the floor. Both Coleman and Nola heard a loud wail come from the kitchen. They both ran over quickly and found Roland holding Bella in his arms.

Coleman moved quickly to Roland and gently lifted Bella from Roland's arms. He rushed out of the Icehouse and Nola drove his pickup to the hospital with Bella in his arms. Roland jumped into the back. No one worried about leaving the Icehouse unattended.

Coleman knew she was already dead. He couldn't bring himself to say anything to either of them. He figured it would be better if the doctor told them both. He wasn't good at handling bad news, and this was as bad as it could get.

Roland cried when the doctor told them that Bella died of a heart attack. He tried to hug his mother, but she just stood limply without returning his hug. Coleman thought Nola might be ready to collapse herself. He went over and hugged both Nola and Roland. Roland buried his head on his shoulder and sobbed. Nola was stoic.

"We should go back to the Icehouse. There is no one there. I'll need to call in the cook to handle the noon lunch. I hope she's not taken on something else, or you'll have to work the kitchen."

Coleman assumed she was talking to him but she seemed to be speaking from another dimension.

"We can close up for today. This is a lot for everyone to process."

"Nonsense, it's not what Bella would want. People are going to need to have someplace to come to talk about all this," Nola said.

"Mom, this is Bella." Roland was devastated.

"You need to buck it up, Skinny. You are not a baby any longer."

Both Coleman and Roland were more shocked than surprised. Neither had ever heard her call Roland "Skinny" before. She showed no emotion and went to the pickup and sat in the passenger seat. Coleman was somewhat surprised that she didn't decide to take over and drive. He didn't know if she was trying to be strong or if something had changed with Bella's passing. He hoped for the former, but down deep, he knew it was the latter.

~

Bella had made all her arrangements at some previous date. The funeral was held at the Icehouse. People came out in droves, and there just wasn't enough room for everyone. They stood in the parking lot listening and shivering to the service over a PA that the funeral home had rigged up.

Bella had stopped going to church when her husband died. She hadn't been very religious. She told Nola that she didn't think anyone needed to go to church to be a good person. It fit with Nola's philosophies as well.

There was no body to view, because she had been cremated. It was shocking to many of the funeral attendees. It wasn't something very typical at the time. Nola knew that Bella was far from typical, so she thought it was a perfect choice. Her urn would be buried on top of her husband's grave.

Roland was confused by Bella's death. It was the first time he had lost someone close to him. Coleman had tried to have a discussion with him, but he wasn't very good at it. Nola was more distant than before. What little warmth she had shown Roland before was now non-existent. Roland was confused by his mother's behavior. The more he tried to speak with her, the more agitated she became. Finally, he just quit trying.

Bella's passing was a huge loss to the community. Coleman knew that her influence was far reaching, but he didn't realize how many lives she had touched. People came into the Icehouse through

Christmas and the New Year just to talk about Bella and what she had done for their families.

Coleman and Roland would share stories. Coleman would explain how the Icehouse was theirs only because of Bella. Nola would find things to do during these conversations, so she wouldn't have to participate. Coleman was concerned with her behavior. Roland, on the other hand, had already written her off. He had the feeling she was blaming him for something that wasn't his fault. He didn't want to be blamed for something he didn't do. His perception had been correct, however. Nola had never verbalized her feelings, but her pregnancy and Roland's birth had changed things for the worse in her life. Either she didn't care, or she didn't know how her behavior had affected her only child.

Nola handled negative things in her life by becoming more reclusive. Coleman handled it by immersing himself in the bar business. He would come up with promotional ideas to get people in the doors. It gave him something to keep him busy while he tried to bring Nola back to some kind of reality.

Roland, the skinny kid, had decided to become the best pool player in the area. He practiced every chance he got. Soon he was the local champ. He would challenge some unsuspecting patron into games for money. These visitors would see a chance to school this kid and win a buck or two. Little did they know.

About that time a Hollywood movie, based on the book called *The Hustler* by the author Walter Tevis, was making the rounds. Jackie Gleason played a character named Minnesota Fats. Jackie Gleason won best supporting actor for his role and the movie was a huge hit. The locals started calling Roland by the name of the Jackie Gleason character. He decided to go see what all the fuss was about, and he ended up seeing the movie six times. He loved it, and he loved being called Fats. It was so much better than being called Skinny.

The locals all knew enough not to play Fats for money. So his hustling had to start and end with some unsuspecting visitor to the bar. Fats became adept at the art of hustling and knew when to let the mark win and when to lower the boom. Neither Coleman nor Nola would allow him to visit other bars out of town to expand his abilities. They watched him closely, and when Coleman thought he was crossing the line, he'd put a stop to his antics. His growing up in the Icehouse would serve him well later in his life, and his father's constant vigil would help to keep him much more conventional.

~

Coleman had grown increasingly concerned about Nola's behavior. He had no one to talk to since Bella's death. One day he thought about something in their past and felt it was a good time to change Nola's focus.

"Do you remember the banker from Bozeman that bought your parents' land?"

Nola had been wiping down the bar, and she sat on a bar stool after Coleman asked the question.

"I hadn't thought about him for a long time."

"I wonder how he came out on the land?" Coleman asked.

Nola seemed interested.

"He gave me his card. I think it's somewhere in my bag. If I can find it, I think I'll give him a call."

"Sounds like a good idea," Coleman said, playing his own card.

Nola dug around in her purse until she came up with the card. She went right to the phone and dialed the number. Someone at the bank asked how she could direct her call, and she said that she wanted to speak with Bruce, president of the bank.

"Please hold," the woman said.

A few seconds later she heard the phone click.

"This is Bruce. How may I help you?"

"Bruce, this is Nola. We sold you some land my parents owned a few years back."

The line went silent.

"Oh, I remember. How are you? I didn't think I would ever hear from you again."

"We're fine. Coleman and I own a bar in Whitefish, and we are doing a great business."

"That's very good to hear."

"So, tell me what's going on with the land. Did the old bank president ever return?" Of course she knew the answer to the second question, but she knew she had to play it close.

"No, they never found him. People think he was killed by one of the many people who hated him."

"No love lost there I'm thinking."

"You would be right."

"How about the land? Did you ever find out why he wanted to buy it?"

"Yes. It wasn't long after Dwight Eisenhower was elected president that we started to put it all together."

"The president? Whoa, what's the scoop on that?"

Coleman had come over and put his ear to the phone when he heard Nola say the president.

"We did some checking and it seems that he and Ike were in the military together. Eisenhower must have told him of his plans to run for president one day."

"I'm not following. What does that have to do with the land that my parents owned?"

"You've heard about the plans for the new Interstate Highway System?"

"I think it's been on the news. We've been too busy to pay much attention."

"That new four-lane highway is coming right through all that property south of Bozeman. People that own the land are going to make a killing."

"By people, do you mean you?"

Bruce paused for a few seconds.

"Yes, I'm going to make money on your former property."

Nola could hear concern in his voice.

"Well, good for you. You treated us fairly, and now you'll be rewarded for it. I couldn't be happier."

She laughed, and Bruce laughed nervously in return.

"I have a feeling that none of this would have been possible without some intervention by you and Coleman."

Nola thought about what he had just said.

"If I were you, I would go out and speak with the closest neighbor to our old property. If I'm not mistaken, there may be something you two might have to move before they start digging up the place."

"I'm not following."

"I'm sure the state will have all grave sites moved before they can build the road."

"That's pretty standard. They move cemeteries all the time. Your parents' graves will be moved outside of the property. I'm sure you can request where you want them relocated."

"I'm not so concerned where they end up. I'm more concerned where you and the neighbor might end up if they discover the third body."

Bruce couldn't wait to get off the phone to make a trip out to his property. When Nola hung up, she smiled.

"I'll bet Bruce breaks all speed records getting back to the mine."

Coleman laughed. It was as if a weight had been lifted from his body. Nola was back. At least she would be for a while.

21

Fat's schooling had been easy for him. When he got into high school, he started spending more time away from the bar. His easy-going personality helped him make friends. People liked to be around him. Nola didn't seem to care what he did, and Coleman encouraged his time away from the bar. He wanted his son to have some of the experiences he never had.

Everyone called him Fats. Most people in Whitefish no longer remembered his real name. It was fine with Fats. He never really liked the name Roland much. He still found time to sharpen his pool-shooting abilities after school hours. Many of his friends came into the Icehouse to have Fats teach them how to better their skills. Knowing the game of pool made him an excellent teacher, and he never took advantage of his students. He would set up tournaments on the weekends not ever participating, because he would be the rule judge.

Coleman smiled at his marketing strategy. Fats had his players come to the Icehouse after the lunch crowd had left. For a few hours, the bar would stay busy selling sodas and snacks to the teens, when it would otherwise be slow.

No money ever changed hands, but the first two places in the tourney would win a free soda and candy bar courtesy of Coleman. It was the least he could do. Fats thought so as well. He suggested that he be allowed a percentage of the business he brought into the Icehouse. Coleman just laughed and told him he would cover his living expenses.

Like everything else, the pool tournaments started to wane as the teens got older. There were too many other distractions. Sports took a great deal of time for many. Others found that their love of cars took most of their time. Fats went out for most of the activities the school had to offer, but he wasn't much of an athlete. He might have scored well on the debate team if he had been motivated to do the research. He wasn't.

Fats decided to spend most of his time on women. He was good at that activity. For some reason the females were attracted to Fats. They didn't really want to date him. They just wanted to be around him because his personality was infectious. Fats also made them laugh. It was an interesting phenomenon. Surrounded by girls most of his high school days, Fats never had a date with any of them. If it bothered him, he never really let on.

Before he graduated, Fats decided on a college. He had a good grade point, so he hadn't been concerned about whether he could get into the school of his choice. His concern was finding the school of his choice. He couldn't find anything that had a pool shooting major.

Nola had shown some interest in helping find a school that would fit. College had always been high on her list. She knew it was a way out of a life for many of the disadvantaged. She included herself on that list. Roland would also be on the list because of his lineage.

Lately she had been feeling like she had fallen back into that category. She didn't know why. The Icehouse was extremely successful, and Coleman had always meant more to her than anyone else in her entire life. It was true that they weren't married, but that was by Nola's choice. Heaven knows, Coleman had asked her a thousand times.

There was just something missing in her life, but she couldn't put her finger on what it was. It made her frustrated, and she became more and more withdrawn. When she tried to figure out what was wrong, she would get angry. Mostly, the anger was directed right back to herself. She knew frustration and anger served very little purpose in maintaining her relationships with Coleman and her son. She was powerless to climb out of her little prison, however.

Fats finally decided on the University of Montana at Missoula. They seemed to have a good business school, and Fats was interested in making money. He thought he might have a head for it.

~

A few weeks before graduation, the last of four life-changing events reared its head. It was a Saturday afternoon, and there were only a few patrons in the bar. School was in session, with Fats busy teaching a group of young ladies how to hold the pool stick and shoot the ball without a miscue.

Suddenly, the front door opened and two Native Americans stood in the doorway and looked around.

"Come on in. The Icehouse is open to everyone," Coleman said.

The men said nothing, but nodded toward Nola behind the bar. Nola nodded back, and the two left.

"What was that all about?" Coleman asked Nola.

"I really don't know. They are men from my tribe." Nola started to make her way from behind the bar, when the door opened again.

The two men entered again pushing someone in a wicker-backed wheel chair. Coleman looked closely, but didn't recognize the shriveled-up woman in the chair.

Nola stood for a moment, and then rushed to toward the chair. She buried her head in the lap of the woman. Coleman let his eyes adjust to the scene, and then realized that the woman was Nola's aunt, Moon Flower.

"Moon Flower, I never expected to see you again. You make my face smile, and I've needed that for a long time," Nola gushed.

It seemed out of character for Nola to say things like that, and Coleman wondered what she meant. Lately, he had thought things were getting back to some semblance of normal. He decided to greet her and began to come from behind the bar.

Moon Flower noticed his movement and put up her hand to stop him. He did so immediately. Then she pointed to a table, and Nola and Moon Flower took places opposite each other. One of the men removed a chair and wheeled Moon Flower closer to the table. Then the two men turned their backs to the women and peered out over the bar. Coleman thought it looked like they were on guard.

Both Moon Flower and Nola were in discussion. There hadn't been any pleasantries or warmth. This was strictly a business negotiation. Coleman wondered what it was all about, and he watched from his perch behind the bar. He couldn't make out what they were saying, and the two guards made sure no one came close to their table.

Fats had completed his Saturday lesson and wondered who was speaking with his mother. He started to approach their table when he noticed Coleman waving him over to the bar.

"Who's talking to mom?"

"That's her aunt, Moon Flower. Your mother was basically raised by her when your grandmother left," Coleman said, and realized he hadn't given much in way of family history to his son.

"What's going on? It looks serious." Fats was concerned.

"You tell me. I'm just as much in the dark as you."

"Why don't we just go over and find out?" Fats asked.

"It isn't their way. We would have to be invited, and you can see that just hasn't happened." Coleman was resigned.

Nola had been animated, and her gestures had been big. Moon Flower had very little movement in their conversation by contrast.

"Whatever that woman said to mom has got her pretty worked up," Fats said, putting his head on the bar and resting his chin on his hands.

The conversation went on for over an hour. Coleman went about his business, but Fats remained at the bar just eyeing the two women. Nola looked over at her son and motioned him over. Fats sat up, surprised.

He stumbled over to the table.

"Sit," Nola commanded.

Fats did as he was told and kept his mouth shut.

"This is Roland Sinning, my son."

"Skinny," Moon Flower said.

"Some people call me Fats," Fats said, smiling at the old woman.

"Too much Anglo," Moon Flower said, and then pushed herself away from the table.

The two men moved, and as quickly as they had come into the bar, they left.

"How rude was that?" Fats asked Nola.

"She liked you," Nola answered.

"Strange way of showing it, don't you think?"

"You just aren't familiar with the Indian ways."

"Well, lucky for me I'm mostly white," Fats said.

He knew he had misspoken. He could see hurt in Nola's face, and it was the first time he had seen any emotion in his mother.

"I'm sorry. That was insensitive. I didn't mean it."

"Never apologize for what you said. If you didn't mean it, you would not have said it. My people are always truthful and say what they believe. If you didn't mean it, you should have never said it." Nola stood, and went back to the bar.

Fats stayed at the table trying to process what his mother had just said. He knew he had some of her characteristics and was sure his blurting out whatever was on his mind was one of them. It didn't mean he had to like what had just happened. He would need to figure out how to use some kind of filter before he blurted out things that might hurt people close to him. It was one of the first of many introspective life lessons that would serve to shape Fat's future.

22

Coleman watched Nola, as she made her way back to the bar. He knew something was wrong immediately.

"What's wrong? Did something happen?" Coleman asked, after Nola had poured herself a cup of coffee.

Nola chose not to say anything and went into the kitchen. Coleman knew it was her little cue to let him know that she didn't want to talk in front of her son.

"Keep an eye on things," he said to Fats.

He followed Nola into the kitchen.

Fats found a place behind the bar as close to the swinging doors as possible. He could hear Nola's voice but couldn't make out what she was saying. She was doing most of the talking, and Fats supposed when it got quiet that his father was responding to something she said. He thought about putting a glass up to the door to try and listen to what was being said, but he thought he would look stupid if he got caught. He didn't know if that really worked anyway.

Fats helped a few customers with some tap beer. He probably was too young to be serving alcohol, but no one seemed to mind. He kept his eye on the kitchen door wondering what was going on.

Finally, what had seemed like forever to Fats, his parents emerged and went about their business like nothing had happened.

"What's going on?" Fats asked his father.

"Don't know much yet. I'll let you know when I find out more," Coleman said.

Fats thought his father looked distressed, however. He hated secrets. When he was in school, a lot of the girls whispered secrets to each other. It drove Fats nuts. He would make fun of the perpetrators by mimicking them. He got laughs from the bystanders and embarrassed the students' pettiness. He couldn't try that same arrangement with his parents. He would have to wait until his father was ready to share their conversation. He knew it would be almost impossible for Nola to share anything with him. He wasn't sad or angry at her behavior toward him. He had learned to accept it without much feeling. His mother had always been a puzzle with many of the pieces missing. Fats couldn't be bothered with things he couldn't control.

The summer seemed to plod along sluggishly for Fats. He had made his decision to attend college, and he wanted to get on with it. He worked at the Icehouse, and Coleman paid him enough for spending money. When he had time off, his friends would take him to other towns and watch Fats hustle his pool game. It was the major source of his income that summer. It was a little fact he decided not to share with Coleman. His father had decided to pay for Fats' college as long as he agreed to help out at the Icehouse during vacations and summer months. Fats agreed immediately. He could see a good deal when it fell into his lap. Coleman never shared the fact that Bella had set up a college fund for Roland, and there would be more than enough money to cover the costs. Everyone needed to have his or her secret it seemed.

There were two more visits from Moon Flower and her two attendees that summer. The second meeting seemed calmer than the first, and Nola spent some time looking at some papers Moon Flower had shared with her.

Once again Nola spoke to Coleman away from Fats. This time when they emerged, Nola seemed more at ease. Coleman, however, was visibly shaken and wouldn't talk to anyone the rest of the day. Fats saw that he was thinking about his options. It didn't look at all promising to Fats. The entire concealment was making Fats somewhat resentful. He had a feeling he was no longer commanding a place in the family hierarchy. Some might have been depressed at such treatment by their parents. It just served to piss Fats off. He needed to get to college and get away from this noxious environment. But school didn't start until September, and it was only the first part of August.

Fats' friends were all getting ready to go their own way. Not many were going on to school. College was still a luxury that many couldn't afford. Nursing and teaching were the careers most colleges offered to the women. Many decided to go to beauty school as a way to mark time until they got married. The men had more options, which was the accepted norm. Most of his friends found jobs to match their skill sets. It made Fats depressed. He couldn't fathom going to work at eighteen or nineteen for the rest of his life. There was a big world out there, and he was determined to be a part of it.

The final visit from Moon Flower came just before the Labor Day holiday weekend. Fats went about getting his gear together to start his life as a college student. When he went up to the loft to organize his things, he saw two suitcases next to the door that led to the steps. Thinking that maybe Nola had packed some things for him, he looked into the first case. It held nothing but female clothing. It was his mother's things.

He went down to the bar taking two steps at a time. Moon Flower, Nola and her two goons were already sitting at the usual table. The only difference being that Coleman was now included in the little parlay. Fats knew he needed to stay calm. Lately he had begun to resent his mother, and he didn't know how to handle the feeling. He was afraid he might say or do something he would regret.

Fats took a spot behind the bar and tried to listen in. As usual the dialogue was hushed, and Fats couldn't make out what was being said. He realized later that he didn't really need to hear the conversation. Coleman's face told Fats everything he needed to know.

Coleman saw Fats standing behind the bar and motioned toward him. Nola turned around and got up moving to the bar.

"I guess you are leaving," Fats said.

"The tribe needs me," Nola said, not looking into Fats eyes.

"They need you more than your family?"

This time Nola looked right at Fats.

"You have never needed me, Roland."

The comment stunned Fats. He looked over at his father and could see the pain in his eyes.

"What about my father? Doesn't Coleman count for anything?"

"I'm not leaving forever. There is some business the Crow nation needs me to handle. It was why I went to college, and I need to follow this through."

"I don't understand. You have this place. You and Coleman have made a successful business. Why do you need more?"

"It's who I am. My spirit is restless and needs to move on to something else. I'm afraid it is one of the few things that I gave to you as well."

Fats thought about what she had just said. It was true. He always felt a bit of restlessness, and he wanted to try other things. But he wasn't married, and he didn't have commitments.

"I thought you and Coleman loved each other."

Nola's temper flared for a moment, and then she calmed herself down.

"I love your father, and you'd be foolish to ever doubt that. He has been my rock and without him, this opportunity would never have presented itself."

"You have a funny way of showing your love for this family."

Nola knew what he was saying.

"I'm sorry I haven't been more of a mother to you all these years. You were such a skinny little kid. I thought it was best to make you strong so you could deal with life. It is the Crow way."

"I always thought it was weird the way all my friends called their parents mom and dad. I can't ever remember you wanting me to call you anything but Nola."

"It makes you stronger."

"No, all it did was make me resent you." Fats said, angrily.

Nola stood. She moved toward Fats and put her arms around him. It was a half-hearted hug to be sure, and Fats decided not to return it.

"I hope you do well in college. You have Crow blood coursing through your veins. Maybe you can help out the Crow people yourself someday."

Fats looked away. He had no idea how to respond to Nola's sudden interest in him. It was something he always needed, but now it just made him angry.

Nola went up to the loft without saying another word. One of the Moon Flower's goons went up with her and came back carrying the two suitcases. He went out the front door followed by Moon Flower and the second goon. Neither said anything to Fats or Coleman.

Nola came down from the loft and walked toward the front door. She looked around taking what Fats thought might be her last view of the Icehouse. She opened the door, turned and looked right at Coleman. Coleman returned her gaze and smiled. She smiled back. Fats seemed to be at a loss for words. The door closed, and Nola was gone.

Coleman remained at the table and seemed deep in thought. Fats decided to join his father at this table.

"Would you mind telling me what the hell is going on?" Fats asked.

"Language. Please don't talk like that," Coleman said, still in a fog.

"I'm angry, and you and Nola just don't get it."

Coleman turned quickly, "Don't think for a moment that your mother and I don't understand."

"She's never been much of a mother to me."

Coleman's eyes gave away some of his pain.

"Not in the traditional sense. That's for sure. But Nola has never been much of a traditionalist. She would never have been with me if she had been."

"Why didn't you ever get married?"

"It wasn't important to either of us. We were committed to each other and that was enough."

"And now she's gone."

"For awhile. Not forever."

"You can tell yourself that, but we both know the truth. She's not coming back."

Coleman said nothing, and that told Fats everything he needed to know. They both sat at the table not saying anything to each other. Coleman was at a loss for words, while Fats tried to get a handle on his anger.

Finally, Coleman broke the silence.

"Are you still set on going away to college? I could probably use some help at the Icehouse, now more than ever."

"Funny you should say now more than ever. That's what I'm feeling right now. I can't be stuck here for the rest of my life."

Coleman showed a rueful smile. The mother's son was quite evident, even if Fats couldn't see it.

"I can't say that I blame you. This must be difficult for you to understand."

"I don't get any of it. I don't know what makes anyone do anything. Would you mind telling me what is going on? I think I deserve an explanation."

"You do. Nola wanted me to wait until she left to explain things. The Crow tribe has obtained permission to build a hotel on the reservation."

"What's that got to do with Nola?" Fats had never called her "mother", and he wasn't about to start now.

"It's going to mean quite a bit to the Crow people. It will help to bring more tourists to the Little Big Horn area."

"Anyone can build a hotel."

"True. But not everyone has the wherewithal to deal with the government when planning a casino on an Indian Reservation. First they will build a hotel, and then after a bunch of hoops, they will complete a gambling casino called the Little Big Horn Casino. It will mean a windfall for the Crow. It will bring them out of a subsistence living standard. It will breathe new life into Nola's tribe. She couldn't pass up the chance to do something this big for her people."

"How long will this take?" Fats asked, more subdued.

"That's the unknown. Dealing with the Feds is always a crap shoot."

Nola's comments about Fats' college degree somehow helping the Crow people began making sense. She was telling him what she wanted him to do with his life. It was subtle to be sure, but that's the way she operated.

He wasn't sure he could follow her wishes. He was still angry, and if she had wanted him to care about the Crow, why hadn't she treated him differently all these years? It was confusing to Fats and his head hurt.

"How could you just let her go?"

Coleman thought about what Fats had just asked him.

"It's never that easy. I was lucky to have Nola in my life for as long as I did. She is a free spirit, and I knew I could never keep her. She needed to find her own way. It is called destiny, I guess. I don't understand it all, but I did understand your mother and her needs. Most people never experience a passion as deep and long as the one we had. It is enough and will sustain me."

Fats left his father at the table. He was confused. He decided to finish packing and get out of this perplexing situation. It was something he would never be able to eliminate from his mind.

23

It was set. Fats would leave for college the very next week. The Memorial holiday was a busy weekend at the Icehouse. He was somewhat amazed at how hard he had worked trying to keep up with the demands of the holiday. He realized how hard Nola had worked and how much Coleman had relied on her. All it did was serve to make Fats angrier with Nola.

Coleman had taken him aside after a busy evening, and they sat at the bar.

"I want you to think about something. Have you thought about staying and partnering with me in the Icehouse? I only ask you this because of Nola's sudden departure. I wanted to make the offer if you are interested."

"I would be lying if I told you it hadn't crossed my mind. I don't think you are going to be handle everything without some help."

"Help is easy to come by. A college education isn't, and I don't think you should jeopardize your future by staying. Staying here without exploring other walks of life would only serve to make you deeply unhappy. Please listen to what I'm telling you. I speak from experience. This place was my dream, but I know it isn't yours. I think everyone needs to find his or her own way. If you find that after you've explored other things that you want to return here, then I'll welcome you back with open arms. It has to be your decision, however."

"It's something to think about," Fats said.

"Thinking is over. You are going to college as planned. As of next week I am firing you from employment at the Icehouse."

Fats smiled and finally realized what his father was telling him. He felt like a huge burden had been lifted from his shoulders. He then did something totally out of character. Fats went over to his father and gave him a huge bear hug.

Coleman returned the hug, until they both started feeling uncomfortable. Coleman broke it off first.

"I'm firing you next week, but right now, we've got to get this place back into shape." Coleman eased himself off the barstool and went behind the bar.

It was late and almost time to close for the evening. Mandatory closing for bars in the area was 1:00 a.m. It was close to that time, so Fats went over to lock the front door. Just as he reached for the latch the door opened.

A group of five men entered the Icehouse pushing Fats to the side. The group looked around and finally settled on a table that would accommodate their number. They were wearing some kind of denim jacket with the sleeves removed. There was writing on the back that Fats couldn't make out. It was obvious that these were members of some motorcycle gang. Fats had heard about the Hell's Angels but had never encountered anyone from the gangs. He knew the Angels were the worst of the worst, and he hoped this wasn't a group of them.

Fats looked helplessly over at Coleman, but then decided to handle the situation himself. Coleman looked on with interest.

"I'm sorry guys but we close at 1:00," Fats said.

"It's not 1:00 yet." A voice from the group growled.

"We don't serve any alcohol fifteen minutes before close. You couldn't finish it, and we'd be forced to take it away."

"Try us." Another voice from the group was heard.

"That's not policy, and we aren't going to change it for you." Fats' ears were turning red. He didn't like being put in this position, and he didn't care for their attitude.

These guys were all huge. Fats thought they looked like they each weighed 250 to 300 pounds. Fats' 150 pounds hardly came to half their weight. He knew he couldn't get into a pissing match with any one of them. He smiled at the thought. Maybe he could get into an actual pissing match because these guys were so big they might not be able to find their junk very well. Fats knew he could.

One of the bikers saw Fats smile.

"What the hell are you smiling about, Skinny?"

"That would be Fats to you."

The speaker was obviously confused. Fats smiled again. The speaker thought he was being made fun of and jumped up and went immediately over to where Fats was standing. He raised his fist and took a wicked shot at Fats' head. Fats saw it coming and leaned away and turned his head. The blow missed the bulk of his head but caught Fats' right shoulder and turned him around. Fats lost his balance and fell to the floor on his back.

The bikers were amused and were trying to get the biker to finish the job on Fats. When he took a step toward Fats, Coleman hollered out.

"That's enough."

All the heads turned toward the bar. Coleman had a double barrel shotgun on the bar pointed at the group of bikers. The barrel was a shortened version. Fats thought it had been sawed off, and he was confused. He had never noticed the shotgun behind the bar in the past.

"We can do this the easy way, or we can do it the hard way. The easy way is that you all walk out that door and leave. We'll call it a draw. The hard way will end up with some of you dead. The choice is yours." Coleman's voice was strong.

The leader of the group spoke out immediately.

"You've only got two barrels. You can't get us all."

Coleman moved the shotgun and pointed it at the leader.

"You're right, of course. I'll just start with you, and I might get two of you by the time the pattern spreads. Then the second barrel might get two more. That would leave one of you, and between my son and me, I believe we could survive."

The leader glared at Coleman and for a minute or two it looked like there was going to be a confrontation. The others began to move away from their leader. It was apparent Coleman's bluff made an impact on what little good judgment they might have. The leader saw his strength in numbers take a turn for the worse. He stood, raised his hands and moved toward the door. The rest of the bikers preceded him out the door. As the leader got to the door, he turned and looked at Coleman.

"You won the first round. You might not be so lucky the next time." He left the building. Fats thought that he was no Elvis Presley.

Fats jumped up and went over and locked the door.

"I didn't like the odds there for a moment," Fats said to Coleman.

"Bunch of punks. That's all."

"Big bunch of punks. 300 pounds most of them, I think."

"The bigger they are, the harder they fall."

"Said the man with the shotgun. Where did you get that thing anyway?"

Coleman placed the gun behind the bar in the place where he had found it.

"Freddy gave it to me. He said that it was for any problems that turned up when he wasn't around."

"It solved this problem tonight."

Coleman smiled, "Yeah, and it wasn't even loaded."

Fats looked up at his father, exasperated.

"Are you kidding me? We could have been killed."

"Sometimes, it's not what you have but what others think you have, that makes all the difference. Having said that, I think I'll keep it loaded from now on."

~

Fats felt that he had blinked twice, and the time for him to leave for college had arrived. Coleman had helped him load the pickup, and on Sunday Fats would move into the dorm. He had assumed that his father would be going along and dropping him off. However, when the time came, Coleman tossed over keys to the truck.

"You want me to drive?" Fats asked.

"No, I want you to take the pickup, and go to school."

"I thought you would drop me off. How will I get the pickup back to you?"

"You don't. I want you to have it. That way, you can come back and help out, whenever you have the time. What am I going to need transportation for around here? I live in the bar, and delivery solves any other issues. Besides, I don't think I could handle just dropping you off and leaving. It would feel like I've lost the rest of my family, and losing Nola has been hard enough."

Fats knew his father was hurting, and he wished he could do something to ease his pain. He also knew that sending him to college was the hardest decision of Coleman's life. That's what made him a great father. Fats' needs and wants always came before Coleman's own. It still made Fats sad.

He took the keys but went back over to Coleman and gave him a hug. They parted quickly to avoid the tears that were sure to follow.

The drive down to Missoula wasn't all that far, but it seemed like a lifetime away from Whitefish. Maybe it was. Fats settled into his dorm and found the parking lot for the pickup. He wasn't worried like the other students who were concerned about their vehicles. It was old and looked terrible. No college student, or anyone else for that matter, would be caught dead driving something like that around.

Fats' roommate showed up the day after. He was short, slight, and puny. Fats liked him immediately. They had nothing in common. While Fats was planning on majoring in business management, Kenny was going to pursue something with music. They would be going to orientation for the rest of the week. There would be a few mixers inserted in the evenings to get the new students to better know each other. Kenny wasn't all that excited to go, but Fats dragged him along anyway. Fats had the gift of gab, and the new students couldn't help enjoying his company. Even the assholes liked him, and there were quite a few of those. He worked extra hard on them. Most of the time, they didn't even know they were being set up or perhaps they didn't care. Fats had never been a threat to anyone, so he was accepted or tolerated, whatever the case might be. He became well known on campus for his pool-shooting abilities at the student union. He cleaned up on quite a few students. Most still thought they were pool shooters before they even knew what hit them. He did it with style and grace, so no one ever held it against him.

Fats liked the fact that the worst people he met at college were the assholes with the biggest egos. They weren't mean-spirited or violent people, they were just assholes. He could deal with the assholes, or he could ignore them. The outcome was usually the same.

After the first week, Fats decided that business management was dull and wasn't for him. He switched most of his classes and decided to try a potpourri of offerings just to see what would stick. His schedule was somewhat unusual for a freshman, but he figured life was too short not to try a bit of everything. He finally settled into Intro to Music, Intro to Theatre, Intro to Sociology, Intro to Psychology, and Intro to Philosophy. He signed up for three other courses, but they made him stop at 18 hours.

Fats never really had to study much in high school, and he found that his course load forced him to change that behavior. It seemed to him that most of these introduction courses relied on rote memorization, and he wasn't a big fan. His disdain stopped with the philosophy class. He was absolutely mesmerized. The professor enjoyed dressing up in costume of whatever philosopher they happened to be studying. It made for interesting class time. Fats thought the guy had been a former beatnik, and that made him someone he wished to study.

There was no doubt; philosophy was on Fats' front burner. Psychology and sociology almost fit in the same genre, and he liked them as well. The rest he could take or leave. He managed a three-point grade point average at the end of the semester without cracking very many books. He decided to change his schedule again and concentrate on becoming a philosophy major. His advisor told him to take some of the required general education courses, but Fats just ignored the advice. It was all or nothing for him, and college just became a whole lot more meaningful in his estimation.

He was still mulling everything over in his mind, as he made the trip back to Whitefish in Coleman's pickup. The trip back didn't seem as long as it did when he had driven down for the first time.

Fats didn't know the trip would last a lifetime.

24

Coleman missed his son. He missed his work ethic, but more importantly, he missed having him around. He had hired both a day and night bartender, and they had been working out quite well. Being a bartender in a place like the Icehouse wasn't all that tough, and they weren't afraid of doing things around the place that needed to be done. Neither was afraid of work. Coleman liked his no-nonsense employees. It also gave him time to himself. That wasn't necessarily a good thing, because he sat around thinking about Nola and feeling sorry for himself.

He had also started drinking again. It started slowly at first and picked up steadily, until he was drinking every day. Sometimes he drank more and sometimes less, but it always served to numb his broken spirit. He hadn't totally given up on life, but he was close. He needed his son back to feel like he had family once more.

Fats could see the change in his father, when he walked into the Icehouse. It was Christmastime, but the bar didn't have anything to suggest it. Fats knew that had been Nola's role, but she was gone and someone had to step up.

"Where's the Christmas tree?" Fats asked.

Coleman shook off his stupor.

"Hey, it's nice to see you, too. Welcome back."

Fats took a seat beside his father at the end of the bar.

"It's a little early for that, don't you think?" He motioned to the drink in front of his father.

"Maybe for some folks." Coleman looked at his drink.

"What's going on? I never saw you take a drink until after work. Then you only ever had one."

"Slipping back into a bad habit, I guess."

Fats took his father's drink, went behind the bar and poured it down the sink. He looked at the bartender and shook his head. The bartender nodded. Fats smiled at him. It was a classmate from high school. They had always gotten along, so Fats knew he could trust him to do what he wanted. He went back to Coleman.

"You need to show me where the Christmas stuff is stored. We need to decorate this place. It looks bleak and twice as depressing."

Coleman looked at Fats and smiled.

"It's good to have you back."

"You need to come back as well. Get off your dead ass, and get things done. Nola is gone. Face the fact, and get on with life. Feeling sorry for yourself won't help anyone."

Coleman got up immediately and went toward the storage area in the back. Fats followed and winked at the bartender as he passed by. The bartender raised his thumb in response. Apparently, the employees were concerned about his father as well.

Coleman and Fats spent most of the rest of the afternoon decorating the bar. They finished just before five with the Christmas tree. It was one of those silver things with a rotating color wheel that shined multiple colors. It had always fascinated Fats. Coleman never cared much for it. He was more of a traditional tree man. He disliked artificial things. It had been Nola's purchase, so he tolerated the aluminum thing. Now he didn't have the heart to throw it out. In the back of his mind he had hoped that Nola would come back for Christmas, but he hadn't heard anything from her and his hopes were diminishing.

"Do you think she'll come home for Christmas?" Coleman asked

Fats, as he was putting the last aluminum branch into the tree pole.

"Don't know. Don't really care," Fats said, casually.

Coleman looked at him.

"Don't say that. She's still your mother."

"I'm not so sure. I don't know if she was ever much of a mother to me. I was thinking that you played both roles. I'm surprised I don't have some deep-seated neurosis because of her behavior." It was an attempt by Fats to show off a bit of his psychology coursework.

Coleman put his arm around Fats' shoulders.

"It was something she hadn't planned on. She didn't know how to handle it. Try not to hate her for her lack of understanding."

Fats thought about it.

"I don't think I really hate her. I am just so disappointed in her behavior, that I'm frustrated. Mostly I'm frustrated for you. I see what it has done to you."

Coleman dropped his arm and sat down at the nearest table.

"You're right. I've been drinking again."

"Again? You never drank before."

"I did. Before I met your mother. I quit when I met her, and we started seeing each other."

Fats sat beside his father.

"I didn't know anything about all that."

"I wasn't very proud of it. I was in a dead-end job, and I wasn't very happy. No, I was miserable. Then I met your mother and everything changed."

"Can we agree to just call her Nola? I'm not comfortable calling her mother any longer."

Coleman looked at his son for a moment. What he said broke his heart, but he couldn't argue the point. He nodded in agreement.

They sat at the table together but not saying anything. Each was thinking about Nola. Coleman couldn't bear the thought of not having her close to him. Fats couldn't bear the thought of being near her. Both would need to discover some kind of a separate peace concerning Nola.

Fats got up from the table and went to the storage area. He found a ladder and some tinsel and was busy placing it around the front door. He needed people to see that the Icehouse was back to normal even without Nola's touch.

When he came back into the bar his father was gone. He put away the ladder and sat down at the bar.

"Where's Coleman?" He asked the bartender whose name was Ned.

"He went up to the residence. He said he had to take a shower. It was good you came back. He hadn't been doing much with his personal hygiene lately."

"Yeah, I could tell. Maybe this was his wake-up call."

"I hope so. Business hasn't been that good lately."

"What do you mean?" Fats asked, alarmed.

"We just aren't getting the families in here like before. The place is getting kinda greasy, if you get my meaning."

Fats understood immediately. The element that Coleman and Nola had tried to keep out had found it's way into the Icehouse. Fats knew he had to get to work if he was going to change this ebb in the bar business. He only had a few weeks to turn things around before he had to go back to college.

"We need to go to the newspaper office and start running ads for the Icehouse. Maybe we should hit the radio station in Kalispell as well."

"You write up what you want, and I'll drop it off tomorrow before I come to work."

"That's not in your job description, Ned. You don't have to do that for us. I'll do it myself."

"No, you need to be here for your dad. If he's going to get off the sauce, it will be because of you. You're all he's got now," Ned said.

The statement hit Fats like a shot to the head. He hadn't thought about how alone his father actually felt. Suddenly, he was very sad for his father's existence. Fats' life was just beginning, but Coleman felt his life was over.

Fats found a notebook behind the bar and started to write some copy for both the newspaper and the radio station. He was almost finished, when Coleman came back down. He looked better. In fact, Fats thought he almost looked normal. Whatever that meant.

"What are you doing?"

Fats explained his idea and showed him his copy. He asked Coleman for whatever input he thought they should include.

"I kind of let the place go," Coleman said, after reviewing Fats' work.

"Just kinda?"

"I didn't care much when you left. I was so alone. I just tried to drown it out with the booze."

"How did that work?"

"Not well, as you can see. But it's going to be better now. I decided to quit the drinking."

"That's a good start," Fats said. "But you've got to do something to get rid of the low-life."

Coleman stopped and thought.

"It might be worse than that."

"What does that mean?" Fats sat up.

"The biker gang has been back a few times."

"What the hell?" The anger in Fats voice was unmistakable.

"They didn't cause much trouble," Coleman said, trying hard to minimalize the bikers' intrusion in the Icehouse.

Ned was violently shaking his head.

"Ned, is that true?"

"They are the reason we've lost business. They intimidate the customers with their loud and aggressive behavior. People are afraid of them, and they don't want to come back if they think they might be here." Ned looked at Coleman. "Sorry man. I just thought Fats needed to know the truth."

Coleman didn't argue. He couldn't have even if he wanted to. He was just too fragile.

Fats stood up immediately.

"I've got to run an errand. I should be right back." He put his hand on Coleman's wrist. "Do you think you can manage without me for a while?"

Coleman knew he was making light of the entire situation, and he actually laughed out loud.

Fats smiled, pointed to a bar glass and drew his figure across his throat. Both Coleman and Ned got the message.

Fats left the Icehouse and went to the sheriff's office. Freddy was still in his office, although he was thinking about leaving for the day. Fats pushed right past the receptionist and burst into Freddy's office.

"Do you know what's going on with Coleman and the bar?" Fats asked, louder than he had originally intended.

Freddy looked up to see who had just invaded his space. When he saw Fats his face relaxed and he stood.

"Good gosh, Fats. It's mighty good to see you."

Fats immediately settled down.

"Thanks Freddy. Sorry about bursting in here like that. It's just that I'm a little frustrated right now."

"Just a little? Seems just a bit more than a little if you ask me. Sit down."

Fats sat quickly. He and Freddy had a fine history together. When he was little and was still called Roland, he had spent a lot of time with Freddy. Freddy let him ride along in his sheriff's vehicle, and he allowed him to play in the jail from time to time. Roland had even thought he wanted to go into law enforcement for a time. Freddy spent a lot of time at the Icehouse during his off hours. Coleman had always said he was good for business.

"Why don't you tell me what brings you to my office?"

Fats explained what had been going on. Freddy nodded as he told the story. He already seemed to know all about the problem. When he was finished, Fats sat back in the chair.

"I'm worried about all this."

"You should be. We all are. I've spent as much time there as I could. These bikers never come in the place when I'm around. It is a little puzzling because I've never had any dealings with any of them. I don't know where they come from. I've called around to neighboring communities, but no one seems to know much about them."

"But yet they seem to know you?"

"Exactly. They must have someone doing some reconnaissance. At first Coleman would call, and by the time I would get to the bar, they would be gone. Lately he just quit calling."

"I think we may have to handle this problem quickly," Fats replied.

"I'm very glad you're back. Coleman needs you."

"I know. I didn't realize things had gotten this bad. I would have come back sooner."

"I wanted to call you, but Coleman wouldn't hear of it. He made me promise not to involve you. Your college education is very important to him. In retrospect, I should have broken the promise and called you anyway."

"What can I do to solve this?" Fats asked.

"I've thought about it. I think confrontation is the only solution. If I could put someone in the bar, I would. We've got just a three-man department, and I just don't have the resources for something like that."

"I understand. Coleman told me about the shotgun you gave him. So that's something."

Freddy looked out the window.

"He doesn't have it anymore. He gave it back."

"Why would he do that, for God's sake?"

"I've thought about it, and I figure he didn't trust himself with it. He was hitting the bottle pretty hard and judgments can be compromised under the influence. Besides, your father is not a violent man. He's a pure spirit, and that's why Nola's departure was so hard on him."

The sheriff seemed to know everything about what had been going on. It was a relief for Fats not having to explain.

"What are we going to do about this?"

Freddy liked the fact that Fats used the word "we." He stood and went to his gun cabinet and pulled out the sawed-off twelve-gauge shotgun. He handed it to Fats along with a box of shells. Fats knew it was the same gun he had seen in the Icehouse previously.

"Be careful with this thing. Since it is sawed-off, the pattern will spread almost immediately. You don't want any collateral damage, so be sure no innocents are close to where you are aiming."

"I don't think I'd be able to get to the shotgun if things got weird. Maybe I'll let Ned handle it."

"Great. Ned knows his way around firearms. Also, if these assholes show up, someone needs to call me immediately, and I'll be over in just a few minutes. I'm not planning to leave the office much over the next few weeks unless there is an emergency."

"I guess it's about all we can do right now. Hopefully nothing will come of it."

"No. Something will have to come of it, or it will just go on and on until there is no longer a business to run. I've seen things go wrong like this before. If you don't grab the bull by the horns, it will maul you to death."

Fats thought about what Freddy had said on his way back to the Icehouse. He knew he was right.

25

Fats ran into people he knew on his way back to the bar. He would stop and talk, and everyone he saw would tell him how good it was to see him back. Fats didn't miss the opportunity to invite them to the bar that evening. Some seemed hesitant, until Fats told them the sheriff would be joining them as well.

Since he had walked over to the sheriff's office, they both thought it would be better for Freddy to drop the shotgun off later that evening rather than having Fats flashing the thing around on the street.

When Fats got back to the Icehouse, there were a few end-of-the-workday men having their favorite libation before they went home to face their families. Fats noticed that the early diners were absent. There was a heavyset guy at the center of the bar that Fats hadn't seen around the place in the past. He wondered if he could be the leak. He didn't have any colors on to identify him as a member of the group, but that didn't mean much.

Fats decided to check out his suspicion.

"I was just over to the sheriff's office. He's coming over to spend some time with us this evening."

Fats spoke loud enough for everyone in the bar to hear. The

stranger pushed his half empty beer away and stood. He stretched, turned, and left the bar quickly.

Fats' suspicions were confirmed.

"That's the mole for the biker gang," he said to Ned. "You need to keep an eye on him when he comes in."

"I would feel a little more comfortable if I had something besides just my dick in hand."

Fats laughed. "Yeah, especially with the size of your little pistol. You probably couldn't hit anything with it anyway."

"Very funny," Ned said, but he wasn't at all upset.

"Sorry, just couldn't help myself. Actually, Freddy's bringing back the sawed-off shotgun. He said you could handle it."

"Great. I hope it's got 04 loads with lead shot instead of steel."

Fats had no idea what he was talking about, but his apparent knowledge of guns made Fats feel somewhat relieved.

A short time later, Freddy walked in with the shotgun and put it and a box of shells on the bar. Ned quickly placed both underneath the bar behind the beer cooler. Coleman watched from his stool at the end of the bar. He was shaking his head.

"What's the matter? You got the palsy or something?" Freddy asked Coleman.

"Thanks for not saying the DTs," Coleman replied.

"We've had this discussion, Coleman. You've got to have some fire power in here, just in case."

"It makes me nervous. I don't want any innocent bystanders hurt over all this."

"That ship has sailed. You let the situation get out of hand, so you need to take it back. You've got help now." Freddy indicated both Fats and Ned.

Coleman didn't respond. He knew the sheriff was right. This whole thing was his fault, and now he had to rely on those closest to him to bail him out. He knew it, but he didn't have to like it.

Freddy went to the door and made a motioning signal toward the parking lot. A moment later some of the locals starting entering the bar. Within a half hour the place was full, and people were ordering drinks and food. Kids were playing pinball, and a few of the older teens were shooting pool. Fats went to help behind the bar, and Coleman had gone into the kitchen to help the cook get the food out.

The Icehouse had returned to its former glory. The bar stayed busy most of the evening. Everyone felt comfortable with Freddy in attendance. Fats hadn't worked so hard in a long time and neither had Coleman.

Coleman closed the kitchen at 9:30 and helped behind the bar. The patrons began to thin after 10:00, and by 11:00, only a few people remained. Freddy sat at the bar and ordered his first beer.

"What kind of beer?" Ned asked.

"I don't care, it all comes from the same Clydesdale."

"Funny," Ned said, he had heard it all before. He ran him a Miller tap.

"Thanks, Freddy," Fats said, "I know you had something to do with all this."

"Small towns and phone trees can put many things in motion," Freddy said.

"Well, whatever you did, Coleman and I thank you. Maybe we can turn this thing around by Christmas. That's my goal."

"I'll stop in as much as possible, but this is going to be on your shoulders," Freddy said to Fats.

"Hey, I'm involved in this. It is my place after all," Coleman said, a little louder than he had intended.

"I'm here as well," Ned said.

Freddy looked at the three.

"Prove it."

He stood and then walked right out the front door. The three watched him go.

"He's got a point," Ned said and looked over at Coleman.

"I'm back. I'm done with the bottle," Coleman said, and took a drink from his bottle of Coke.

I like what I'm hearing here," Fats said. "But one night doesn't turn things around. We've got to be in it for the long haul. You need to have a handle on things by the time I leave to go back to school. I can be back in May, but if this place is going to survive, it will have to do so until I come back."

Coleman took comfort from what he had just heard coming from his son. It would mean he would be coming back for the summer and not finding a job around campus like so many other students seemed to do.

"I'm tired. Let's lock up. Ned, you go home and get some sleep. I want everyone back here by 8:00 so we can clean this place up. I've let it go too long, and I'm not happy how things look."

Ned took off his apron and threw it on the bar. He walked to the kitchen and out the back door to his car. Coleman locked the back door, and Fats began turning out the lights. He decided to leave the color wheel pointed toward the Christmas tree lit. It gave the place a warm feeling.

Both Coleman and Fats slept well that night.

~

The newspaper ads and radio spots seemed to be working. The Icehouse was a busy place, and Coleman had put both Ned and the other bartender on full-time duty for the rest of the holiday season.

Fats saw the same man at the bar a few times but he never stayed long. The place probably seemed too busy for his biker group, and the random visits by the sheriff added to his reluctance, Fats figured.

Things were finally feeling comfortable at the Icehouse for everyone. Coleman was his old self again, and there was a light-hearted atmosphere back in the air that had been missing for quite some time.

Coleman hung a sign up on the door telling everyone that the Icehouse would be closed on Christmas Day and also closing by 3:00 on Christmas Eve. There was still no communication from Nola. Coleman and Fats realized that she wouldn't be coming back to see them. Neither had thought about how they were going to spend Christmas; they had been just too busy.

"What should we do for Christmas?" Coleman asked Fats.

"Maybe we could just relax and cook dinner together. We've been going non-stop pretty much the entire month of December," Fats replied.

Coleman liked the idea, but he felt a little pang of regret at not showing a little more Christmas spirit for his son. He had an idea two days before Christmas and left the bar in the afternoon.

"I'll be gone for a few hours. Think you can handle the place by yourself?" Coleman was returning Fats' previous joke.

"Funny man. Where are you off to?" Fats asked.

"It will be a surprise." Coleman left the building.

The second bartender had already gone to his other job, which left Fats and Ned to hold down the fort.

The noon rush had come and gone, and Fats and Ned were busy cleaning up when that same big guy took a place at the bar. Ned went over to help him.

"What can I get for you?" Ned asked.

"Beer. Tap. I don't care what kind it is."

Ned drew out the least popular beer from the tap.

"Not very busy today," the big guy said.

"Between shifts," Ned said. He figured if the guy couldn't use full sentences, he didn't have to either.

The guy grunted and then drank his beer. Ned went about his business. Fats emerged from in the kitchen, saw the guy and became immediately pissed.

"You aren't fooling anyone here. We know you are the eyes for those bikers we kicked out of here."

"I don't know what you mean," the guy said, playing dumb.

That made Fats even madder. He swept up his partially consumed beer and poured it down the drain. Then he reached in the register and pulled out a dollar and placed it on the bar next to where the beer had been resting.

"That was your last drink in this place. In fact, you're never going to set foot in the Icehouse again."

"You can't do that." The guy was incensed.

Fats went over to the place Ned had hidden the shotgun and

placed it on the bar. Then he turned it until the barrel was pointing at the overweight guy.

"This says I can, and if it doesn't, then my friend the sheriff says so."

The spy didn't like the odds, it seemed, and stood up to leave. When he got to the door, he turned around.

"You just made this a whole lot worse for everyone here."

Fats picked up the shotgun and put it to his shoulder. He turned quickly, and it appeared that he was ready to pull the trigger. They guy almost ran out the door through the glass.

Fats put the shotgun back where he had found it. Ned went over and retrieved it.

"You know it wasn't loaded, right?"

Fats looked at Ned.

"What the hell does everyone have against loading a gun around here?" He sat on a stool quickly.

"It's a mistake I plan to remedy immediately," Ned said, and then found the box of shells, took two out and put them in the two barrels.

"You probably better find another place for the gun where we can put our hands on it easily."

"What's wrong with this place?" Ned asked.

"They know where it is hidden now, don't they? I don't want to be rushed some day and they pull out our shotgun and leave you with your dick in your hand."

"Duly noted," Ned said smiling. "I wouldn't like that either."

"I should hope not, or I'm going to have to find a new bartender."

They both laughed, but Fats knew things were coming to a head. He didn't like the odds. He knew they would show up when there were the least amount of witnesses, and that bothered him. It would be in the afternoon where they would be most vulnerable. Those few hours after the lunch crowd and the 5:00 bunch would be where they could do the most damage.

Fats knew they would all have to be vigilant in order to keep things under control. Quite honestly, the fact that Freddy couldn't find out anything about them made him more nervous than ever. It could be they were after more than doing damage to the bar itself. It could be that they wanted to cause some bodily harm to both he and Coleman and anyone else who got in their way.

He was still thinking about their predicament, when Coleman snuck in from the back with a package under his arm. He went up to the loft. Fats heard him come in but didn't see anything. He was hoping that Coleman hadn't been sneaking around and drinking at another establishment.

26

The rest of the week turned up nothing unusual. The Icehouse had been busy, but the downtime Fats had been worried about never materialized. He had shared his concerns with Ned and Coleman, and they all agreed that they had to be more vigilant.

Freddy hadn't been able to spend a great deal of time with them, but between the three of them on the force, they tried to stop in briefly each hour in the afternoons. It took some of the pressure off Fats.

They agreed to place the shotgun right under the tappers, and Fats once again reiterated how important it was to keep the damn thing loaded. The closer it got to Christmas, the spirits seem to lift and less attention was paid to the bikers. It proved to be a mistake and one Fats would regret for the rest of his life.

Christmas Eve day saw a busy lunch. Most of the customers had left the Icehouse by 1:30. People were busy getting ready for whatever traditions they followed. Even the non-Christians followed the gift-giving and festivities of the season.

At 2:00, Fats decided to practice some of his trick shots on the pool table. Coleman helped the cook clean up the kitchen with another motive in mind. She would help him roast the turkey he had bought and thawed the day before. She left him a note with all the steps he should follow before she left for the Christmas Holidays. Coleman was grateful and slipped her a crisp hundred in an envelope for all her trouble.

Ned was wiping down the bar. Coleman came back from the kitchen and handed a similar envelope to him as well and told him to go home.

"Just as soon as I'm finished here. If I go home too soon my parents will put me to work. I'd just as soon hang out where I actually get paid," Ned said.

"You are always welcome here. You know that," Coleman said.

Ned nodded and continued to clean the bar.

"Hey Pops, want to shoot some pool with your number one son?" Fats said, as he racked the balls.

Coleman thought for a moment and then started for the pool table. He got almost halfway, when the front door opened and six members of the biker gang stormed into the bar.

"It's time to answer for your sins," the leader said, as the six men fanned out.

Coleman did a quick survey and saw that they weren't carrying firearms. Just as he was feeling a little relief, they brought out their knives. The blades appeared to be six inches or more. Coleman couldn't be sure.

Ned had slipped into the kitchen and was on the phone to Freddy. His message was short and sweet, and he came back into the bar. One of the bikers moved toward the end of the bar where they had kept the shotgun previously. Ned noticed it was the spy they had dealt with previously. His dress had changed, and he was wearing his biker colors as well as some chains hanging from his belt. He pulled the end of the chain away from his body and cracked it on the bar.

"Stay away from the shotgun," he barked at Ned.

Ned immediately moved to the taps and put his hands on the shotgun. He would wait for the opportune time.

The group had been focusing their attention on Coleman and Fats. The leader sat down at a table and faced Fats.

"Hey, tough guy. Come over here."

Fats stood his ground. He lowered his pool cue and kept his right hand near the tip.

"I don't think I will. I'm pretty comfortable right where I am," Fats said, and tried to smile.

The leader motioned to two of his men to get Fats and bring him over. The men started for Fats. Coleman blocked their way.

"Stop this. We don't need to have anyone get hurt. We can talk this over and settle it." Coleman knew they wouldn't listen, but he was trying to buy some time. It didn't work.

One of the men struck Coleman just under his left eye, and Coleman went down to the floor. Fats immediately raised his pool cue and swung it over his head. He built up momentum until finally he brought the barrel of the cue on the other guy's head. He caught him just above the temple. A bit lower and the guy would have died immediately. He went down nevertheless, and was bleeding from the side of his head. Fats wasted no time and swung around. He caught the man who had decked Coleman right in the throat. The barrel of the cue caught him full force in the Adam's apple. Fats thought he should remember the move for the future because it was very effective. The big brute went down to his knees immediately. He was clutching his throat trying to say something, but it sounded like he was gargling with mouthwash. Fats knew he had done some real damage and was fine with it.

The spy had taken his attention away from Ned during the exchange. Fats swung the pool cue again and hit the first guy in the same place as he was trying to get to his feet. He went down hard. He wouldn't be getting up again.

The leader got up too slowly to save his two friends. He looked around, two down, four left. His knife had been on the table, and he picked it up. The spy moved to join him with his knife also visible. It was his mistake.

Ned pulled up the shotgun and brought it up to his shoulder. He put both barrels into the spy's back. He had a hole in him about the size a good-sized pie plate. He wouldn't be eating anything from any plate again. Ned smiled at the thought about it. Three down. Tie game.

The leader moved quickly for a big fat guy. He grabbed Coleman by the hair and pulled him up. He backed him up, until they were at the wall. Coleman was in front, and the leader was holding a knife at his throat. Ned couldn't shoot without fear of hitting Coleman. He moved the shotgun, picked out another biker and covered him. He couldn't shoot without the fear that the leader would cut Coleman's throat. The truth was he couldn't shoot at all. He had expended both barrels on the spy.

"Stalemate. Put the gun down," the leader said to Ned.

Ned paid no attention. He was hoping they hadn't realized he had blown both barrels when he shot the spy. It was a mistake he regretted, because the box of ammunition had fallen to the floor earlier and had burst open. The shells went flying in all directions. He couldn't get to any of them in time to load and shoot. All he could really do was to play the game. It was a dangerous game and could mean their lives if he wasn't careful.

"I said lose the gun," the leader said, and put pressure on the knife.

Fats could see a line of blood on Coleman's neck. He yelled at Ned.

"Do what he says. It's not worth Coleman's life." The distance was too great for Fats to make any use of the pool cue. He felt totally helpless.

Ned pushed the gun across the bar. One of the bikers took it. He aimed it at Ned. Ned didn't mind. He was busy trying to figure out what he could use for a weapon before all hell broke loose. He knew it was just a matter of time.

"Lose the pool cue," the leader said to Fats.

Fats placed it on the center of the pool table and took a step back.

"Put your hands on the bar," the leader said to Ned.

Ned followed his instructions. His mind was still racing just trying to come up with some sort of weapon. He noticed a fly swatter lying under the taps where the shotgun had rested. It was one of those fly swatters with a thick wire handle. The actual swatter part was plastic. He knew he could pull it off with his foot resting on the plastic. He would have two sharp wire ends to do some damage, if he was fast enough.

"Keep the gun on him. If he moves, blast him," the leader said, indicating Ned.

Coleman hadn't moved. He was still in a fog from the sucker punch the biker had given him. He couldn't have moved anyway because the knife would have cut his artery. The leader knew what he was doing in that arena. He probably had a wealth of experience.

"Now what?" Fats asked.

"Well, now you die. You have to pay for my men here." He indicated the three bodies on the floor.

Fats knew he had the upper hand as long as he had his father under the knife. His mind raced and wondered what ideas Ned had. He wished they could talk it over.

"So, who's going to be first?"

No one said anything. The other two bikers smirked. Fats hated people who smirked. He wanted to say something to the leader, but there was really nothing to say to change what was going to happen. They needed some kind of diversion if they had any chance of getting out of this alive.

Coleman's fog had lifted, and he saw the problem immediately. He knew the leader wouldn't sacrifice him as a hostage while the other two were alive. He was too much of a coward. That's why these idiots always traveled in packs.

Coleman thought of his life. It was true. In times of extreme stress it flashed right before your eyes. He thought of Nola and his sadness at her departure. He thought of his miserable life before he met her. He thought of Roland and the Icehouse. He knew it was never his son's dream. He had to live his own life, and he knew he wouldn't do that unless Coleman could give him the permission to do so. He knew what he had to do.

"Son, pick up that pool cue. Don't stop until all these bastards are dead. They are just a bunch of cowards anyway," Coleman said, and reached up for the knife at his throat.

Fats picked up the cue in one fluid movement, and everyone remained still. Then Fats saw his father pull the leader's hand and knife blade across his throat. Blood squirted out of his neck immediately.

For a moment everything went into slow motion. No one really understood what had just happened. It couldn't have lasted more than five seconds, but it seemed like an eternity.

The leader was the first to speak.

"Take them out." He let go of Coleman to avoid getting all the blood over his colors. Coleman was dead before he hit the floor. He bled out over the Icehouse floor.

The biker with Ned's shotgun turned to pull the trigger but it just went click. Ned had the plastic off the fly swatter's handle in one quick motion and jumped over the bar. He plunged the wires into the biker's left eye before he had time to realize he needed to drop the shotgun. The wire didn't go deep enough to kill the guy. That bothered Ned, but the biker wouldn't be doing much for a while so he took heart in that. Who knew there would be that much blood? He was still thinking about the blood, when he picked up the shotgun and moved back behind the bar to find some shells to fill it.

The leader paid no attention to the scene behind him. He and the one remaining biker were advancing on Fats with their knives. It would be difficult to take them both with the pool cue. Fats had just witnessed the murder of his father. He was going through the motions, but his gut instinct of self-preservation hadn't really kicked in.

The leader was smiling, because he sensed the confusion in Fats' response. He had a feeling this was going to turn out in his favor. He had lost four men, but that was just collateral damage. It was something you had to weigh when you chose a lifestyle like theirs. The trade-off was worth it as long as he wasn't the collateral damage.

Fats finally cleared his head, and he was angry. Angry wasn't the right word at all, he was enraged. The fury that followed was something he later couldn't even fathom. It took total control, and he was no longer in charge of his actions.

He swung the pool cue toward both men with such rage, that they actually took a step back. Fats hit nothing with all his swinging, but he was beyond making sense of things.

The two bikers circled him, and as Fats would swing at one, the other would thrust his knife. Fats had been skewered a number of times but he wasn't feeling anything. The leader had done a good job of staying away from the barrel of the cue. The other biker wasn't as lucky.

One of Fats' wild swings had caught the biker on the nose and it broke immediately. The blood and the pain slowed him down immediately. Fats saw an opening and concentrated all his effort on the bleeder. Unfortunately, it left him vulnerable to the leader.

Fats' back was turned, and he came at him with the knife raised. The plan was to bury it in Fats' spine just below his head. He might have followed that plan, but the front door was flung open at the same time.

Freddy entered with his service revolver drawn. He saw immediately that Fats was in trouble. He took the shot and put a .38 slug through the leader's head. He wasn't the leader any longer. The pool table would need to be recovered with new felt because of all his blood and brain matter strewn over it. It was beyond cleaning.

Ned had come from behind the bar with both barrels loaded and two extra shells in his hand. He walked over to the biker who was still screaming something about his eye. Ned blew both barrels together and separated his head from the rest of his body.

Looking at the leader's dead body, Fats hadn't been paying attention to the other biker with the nose problem. The biker was getting up and looked like he was trying to place his knife in Fats' stomach.

Freddy raised his pistol but stopped when Ned walked right in front of his target. Ned had placed the remaining two shells into the shotgun and pulled both barrels once again.

Another pie-hole entry and the last biker was dead.

27

Fats dropped to his knees and cradled his father's body. He didn't even notice all the blood. He rocked back and forth like he was putting Coleman to sleep. It broke Freddy's heart.

Freddy and Ned sat at the bar. Neither had any words and watched Fats share his grief. Freddy knew he had to do something about all the bodies lying around the bar, but he wanted Fats to have the time he needed. He and Ned needed the time also.

Eventually though, Freddy got up and went behind the bar and began making calls to his two deputies. He hated to disturb them on New Year's Eve, but he needed their help.

They came immediately and brought members of the local hospital ambulance staff as well. It was a nasty bit of work loading the bodies into one of the deputy's pickups. There were six bikers, and they had to stack them on top of each other. It was heavy work, and the four men had all they could do loading each body.

Freddy told his deputies to take the bodies to the morgue in Kalispell since Whitefish didn't have any facilities. He gave them a name to call when they got there. He figured no one would be around on Christmas Eve.

Freddy was dreading the impending paperwork, but he knew it

would have to wait. Fats would not be in any shape to give an interview for quite a while. He would rely on Ned's account and back it up when Fats was finally able to get past his father's death. Freddy wondered if that was even possible.

Finally, Freddy and Ned went over to Fats. He had stopped rocking and was just staring at the floor. Freddy knelt next to Fats and put his hand on his arm. Slowly, he removed each arm from around Coleman's body. Then he pushed Coleman's body away from Fats' lap. There was so much blood, and the body basically slid away from them.

Freddy stood and picked up Fats by placing his arms around his chest from behind. Fats came along without resistance. Ned had gone into the storage area and came back with a tarp and gently placed it over Coleman's body. He tried to cover most of the blood with it as well.

Together, they brought Fats to the loft and placed him on the couch. They both hoped he would fall asleep, and he did almost immediately.

Freddy went back downstairs. The two hospital workers had left with the deputies. Freddy had wanted them to take Coleman's body to the local funeral home but forgot to give them direction before he and Ned had taken Fats upstairs. He couldn't really blame them. He knew they had a life and family that needed them home on Christmas Eve. He called the local funeral home and after what seemed like an eternity, someone answered the phone. They sounded irritated at being disturbed. Freddy immediately told them who he was and what had happened.

"I need someone to come to the Icehouse to retrieve Coleman's body. The quicker the better, and please listen to me. This has to stay between us. I don't need this to come out and spoil Christmas for people. Do you understand me?"

The person on the other end of the line assured the sheriff that he understood perfectly, and they were always discreet when it came to people's privacy.

"That's good. Now the other thing is that I don't want you coming down here with the hearse. We don't need to be drawing that kind of attention."

Freddy was once again assured they would be discreet and use a station wagon.

"That's great," Freddy said. "Just don't be using a body bag. Blankets only."

Freddy hung up the phone and went back up the stairs to the loft. It seemed like a long way, and Freddy's legs felt like rubber. The day's events had taken a toll.

Freddy and Ned sat at the kitchen table, and Freddy took out a small notebook from his shirt pocket.

"Ned, you need to tell me what happened, and don't leave anything out."

"If I tell you everything, what stops Fats from getting in some kind of trouble over this thing?" Freddy asked.

"You just let me worry about that," Freddy said.

Ned told Freddy everything. He thought carefully, when he relayed the story, trying to be sure not to leave anything out. He figured the best thing to do was to tell the truth and let Freddy work out the details.

Freddy took notes as Ned spoke and almost filled the entire little notebook. When Ned was finished, Freddy got up.

"I need to go and start on the paperwork. You need to stay here. Fats can't be alone tonight."

Ned agreed by nodding his head.

"I'll call my parents and tell them I won't be able to make it for Christmas Eve dinner."

"Be careful what you say. We don't need the gossip mill working overtime on this thing," Freddy warned.

"I'll tell them the basics. They won't share anything if I warn them not to. They've always liked the Sinning family. This will be as hard for them as it is for us."

"Ned, you're a good man," Freddy said, and put his hand on his shoulder.

"Be sure to tell everyone," Ned said, trying for humor, but it just rang out hollow.

It would be a long time before they could get past what had happened on this Christmas Eve.

Freddy moved to leave.

"You'd better come down and lock up after me. Be sure to shut everything down. We don't want any unwanted lookers."

"What about all the blood? I need to clean that up."

"Tomorrow's another day. I don't think the Icehouse will open for some time, do you?"

Ned had to agree, but it didn't mean he wouldn't be cleaning up that very evening. No one needed to start Christmas day seeing the carnage left in the bar.

The sheriff left, and Ned locked the front door and turned out the lights. He waited for the funeral home to pick up Coleman's body. When they arrived, he opened the door and went into the back room. He didn't want to see them load up Coleman's body. It was too heartbreaking for him to handle. When they left, he locked the front door once more.

It was time for Ned to clean up all the blood. The lights from the beer signs, and door glass coolers, would be enough for him to get the job done without drawing attention by putting the bar lights back on.

Ned went back up and sat with Fats until midnight and felt he had finally fallen into a deep sleep. It took Ned until six the next morning to clean the bar to his standards. He had used thirty gallons of hot water in five gallon increments to scrub away most of the blood. Then he used floor cleaner and cleaned the entire floor once more. His final step was to use two gallons of bleach. He wanted to get rid of traces of the blood as well as the smell. He thought he could still smell the tinny residue, but he thought it might be just stuck in his nose.

The entire place smelled like bleach. It wasn't necessarily a clean smell, but it was better than the blood and bodily tissue. He had to throw most of the scrub water out the back away from the building. He didn't dare put it down the drain for many reasons. He didn't want to think about it.

When he was finished, Ned poured himself some bourbon. He didn't even bother with any ice. He needed a jolt. He chugged the first immediately and poured three fingers for his second go-round. He decided to nurse it and finally finished the whiskey as the sun was trying to make an appearance outside.

Ned got up from the table and turned on all the lights. He wanted to see if his work would pass muster to the common eye entering the Icehouse. It looked good. Then he noticed blood spatter on the wall where Coleman had died. Ned was sure it was Coleman's blood, and he retrieved a pail and poured in some bleach until it looked like it was half-and-half. He found some yellow rubber gloves and a scrubbing sponge.

The wall was cleaned in short order. Ned noticed the tarp that had been covering Coleman lying on the floor when they took his body away. He began folding it up, when suddenly; he noticed the bloody cloth on the pool table. He threw the tarp over the table. When and if they opened the Icehouse again, this pool table would be out of order. He made a mental note to call the company where they had purchased the table and have someone come out as soon as possible and recover it.

Ned walked up the stairs to the loft. He was dog-tired. He wanted to just sleep, but he knew he couldn't. He found a chair facing the couch and looked at Fats sleeping. He was in the process of dozing off when he heard Fats stir. Ned tried to shake off his tiredness and sat up. He waited for Fats to regain consciousness. It was a slow process, and Ned knew that his brain hadn't processed everything that had happened yet. That's why his body was able to sleep. Sometimes the mind needs to escape everything that happens to it, and by sheer will it commands the body to sleep. That was Ned's theory anyway, and that's why he thought he was going to have to sleep very soon.

Fats sat up and looked at Ned. It took a few seconds before he remembered what had happened. His puzzled face made Ned drop his eyes.

"What day is it?" Fats asked.

Ned hadn't thought much about hours, days or weeks. He

realized what day it was with a start.

"It's Christmas day."

"Hell of a way to celebrate the birth of Jesus if you ask me." Fats tried to stand up.

"Why don't you stay put for a while," Ned said and realized there were a number of bloody marks on Fats' shirt.

"Hey, are you hurt?" Ned jumped up and went over to the couch.

"The stooges tried to use me as a pincushion I think. They aren't very deep, but it hurts like hell," Fats said, pulling his shirt away from his chest.

"Take that thing off. I'll go get some stuff from the bathroom. If I can't stop the bleeding we'll have to take you to the emergency room." Ned raced toward the bathroom.

Fats took off his shirt and looked at his chest. There were a number of small cuts, but most of them had stopped oozing. He couldn't see his back but thought it might look similar judging from how it felt.

Ned came back with bandages, rubbing alcohol and some antibiotic ointment.

"You are not going to use that alcohol on these punctures," Fats growled.

"Stop being such a pussy. We've got to make sure these wounds don't get infected, or maybe you'd just like to go to the emergency room right now."

Fats didn't want any part of doctors or hospitals, so he put on his brave face. Ned could see that none of the wounds were serious enough for medical care beyond his own expertise, so he went to work. He took his time trying not to stab his rubbing alcohol soaked cotton swabs too far into each wound. He figured there would be enough pain for Fats just with the alcohol finding its way into each wound. They were scratches in reality. Some were deeper than others but none so deep as to cause any real concern.

Ned took his time. He realized the longer he could keep Fats' mind on his condition, the longer it would take to revisit Coleman's death. He tried to make small conversations about nothing, but he could see that Fats had no interest. His mind was far from his place on the couch in the loft.

"Thanks for what you did at the bar yesterday," Fats said, simply.

"I'm so sorry."

"For what?"

"For everything. For your father."

"My God. It wasn't your fault. If you hadn't been there, I would have been dead as well. You are a good friend."

Ned didn't say anything in return. He had no words for what Fats had just said. He knew he might be right, but it didn't change the outcome. He knew Fats had to talk through things just to get his head on straight.

"It's Christmas, Ned. You need to go home, and be with your family."

"No. I won't leave you alone on a day like this. I wouldn't be much of a friend."

"You won't be much of a friend if you stay here, when I want you to leave. I need to be alone for a while."

Ned didn't like it. He was concerned that Fats might do something stupid like harming himself. He heard of people being so depressed, after losing someone they loved, that they tried to kill themselves.

Fats knew what Ned was thinking.

"I'm not going to try and off myself, if that's what you think."

"That's what I was thinking."

"Well, then you have some flawed thinking skills, my friend. I would never do anything like that. There is too much to live for, and I just started."

Ned thought for a moment.

"Okay, I'll go, but you need to understand that I'll be back this evening. I'm not letting you spend Christmas night all by yourself."

Fats knew he was stronger than anyone realized, and he'd be fine without everyone's meddling. Still, he knew that Ned cared about him, so he agreed that Ned could spend the night.

"Better take the keys, and lock the door behind you. I'm not leaving the place today."

"Why don't you come and have Christmas dinner with my family? They would love to have you."

"They would love to feel sorry for me, and fawn all over me, you mean. Besides, I don't want to be very good company today. I want to feel bad and feel sorry for myself. It's Christmas, and I deserve it."

Ned smiled. Fats' sense of humor was brewing just under the surface. It was a start.

Fats walked down the stairs with Ned. He glanced over to where Coleman had died.

"What did they do with my father's body?"

"Freddy had Scripps Funeral Home come and get it. They are expecting direction from you after Christmas," Ned said.

"Thanks. Could you tell Freddy to stop by and see me tomorrow?" Fats asked.

"It's already in the plans."

"Good. Now get out of here, and be with the people who still love you."

The comment bothered Ned. It just proved how everything could fall apart in a matter of minutes. Just when life seemed to be going along so splendidly, it could be taken away without warning.

He knew Fats would be all right. Maybe not right away, but down the line he would get back to being his old self. That's what he kept telling himself, when he left the Icehouse.

28

Fats knew Christmas would be a long day. It started to hit him that he was parentless. He looked around the bar and decided not to spend any time working. There would be plenty of time to decide on things.

He walked up the stairs to the loft and sat down on the couch. He turned on the television just to disturb the quiet. There was some kind of parade with floats and later there would be football. Fats didn't care for either one, but he kept the TV on. He got up and boiled himself a couple of hot dogs. Fats never got the hang of cooking. It was probably because he didn't really try. He thought the notion might have to change now that he was an orphan. The feeling was quite strange, because his mother was still alive. Her body was alive, but Fats considered her spirit to be dead. Maybe that was the Indian part in him.

The hot dogs weren't all that bad when they were doused with both ketchup and mustard. They were the kind with the natural casings, and Fats liked them because of the snap when he bit into them. He always called them snappers.

After he ate, Fats decided to go into his father's bedroom and sort through his things. It might have been too soon for some, but Fats felt that the time to do things was when it presented itself. Besides, he never was much for sentiment.

The closet held Coleman's clothes and shoes and not much of either. Neither Coleman nor Fats had ever been much for fashion. They were functionaries only. They both lived Spartan lives.

Fats decided he would donate everything to Goodwill. There was nothing he really wanted from his father's things. He looked around for something he could use as a keepsake, but he found nothing of interest. He was almost ready to leave the room, when he saw a package standing in the corner beside the bed. Fats went over and picked it up. It was wrapped with Christmas paper. The paper was green with red Santas all over it, and it looked like it was meant for a child.

There was a tag on the top. Fats pulled it close, so he could read what it said. The writing was Coleman's, and it said simply, "For my son." Fats just stared at it. It might have been the last thing his father had ever written, and it was for Fats.

Fats clawed off the paper. He had always done that with presents people gave to him. Nola would tell him to unwrap his things gently so the paper and bows could be used again. Fats told her that the gifts were for him and so was the paper. He didn't want anyone else to have anything that was given to him especially if it was recycled paper. He had won that argument with Nola, one of the few times in his recollection.

It was a plain cardboard box. When he stood it on end, it came up to his waist. It wasn't very big around, and it looked like it was just a bit bigger than one of Fats' hands. Fats milked the unwrapping of the gift. It was the only thing he would ever receive from his father, and he wanted to relish the feeling.

Finally, he opened the top of the box. He had to get a kitchen knife, because the seams were all secured with strapping tape. Fats wondered if the package had come from Sears. He knew they always shipped things with everything securely wrapped.

He looked inside but couldn't see anything, because it was loaded with some kind of loose fill. Fats thought they looked like peanuts. He dumped them out on the kitchen floor and reached into the box.

He pulled out a pool cue that came in two pieces. It was a beautiful piece of work. The wood was dark and inlaid with porcelain diamonds all over the barrel. Fats screwed it together. It fit together like a glove. He placed it on the kitchen counter and rolled it over a few times. It was perfectly straight, and when he ran it through his hands it felt as smooth as a baby's butt.

Fats knew that the cue had cost Coleman plenty. This was a work of art, and Fats had seen very few pool cues that matched this kind of quality. He sat down.

This was the heirloom he had been looking for when he had been in Coleman's bedroom. It was especially meaningful because of Fats' love of the game, but it had even a greater significance. The pool cue had nothing to do with Nola. It was something that was just between his father and him. A warm feeling washed over Fats.

He checked the box once more and found a black case with two gold clasps. It also was inlaid with the white diamond design. Fats took the cue apart and placed it in the case. This was something he would use only on special occasions. Maybe he would use it when he cleaned out some unsuspecting idiot with a bigger-than-life ego. The possibilities could be endless.

Fats knew what he would be doing the rest of the day. He would break in his new cue. He went back down to the bar taking two steps at a time. He stopped when he saw the tarp on top of the far table. He couldn't use that one, but there were two others. The center table was his favorite anyway. He thought it was the best leveled of the three, and the balls rolled true.

Fats racked the pool balls and then sat down and put his cue back together gently. This would be his pride and joy, and he would always be very careful with it. The cue fit into his hands perfectly. It was the right weight for him. He was amazed that his father had paid that much attention to the kind of cue he was using.

Christmas day ended much better for Fats then it had started. He was still shooting with his new stick, when Ned came back through the front door. Fats had turned on all the lights, and a few people had tried the door hoping the bar was open. Fats had ignored them even when they had knocked.

Ned looked over at Fats and noticed his new cue immediately.

"Hey, nice stick."

"The best. It was a Christmas present from Coleman. Too bad he didn't get a chance to see me use it," Fats said.

Ned nodded. He didn't know if Fats was sad or if he was just thinking out loud.

"Hey, have you eaten?" Ned said, changing the subject.

"I had a couple of hot dogs."

"I'm not talking about lunch. Have you had dinner?"

"Why, what time is it?" Fats asked.

"It's 8:30. That's 8:30 p.m. buddy."

Fats had totally lost track of the time. He hadn't been hungry, but when Ned asked him about dinner, he suddenly had hunger pangs.

"I don't know what's here. I think Coleman was going to try and make a turkey, but I'm sure that's in the cooler. There isn't enough time to do dinner, I'm thinking."

"No problem. My mother packed up everything for a great dinner for you."

Ned went back out the door and returned with a wicker basket and something that looked like a cooler but had soft sides. Immediately, Fats had interest and began taking his cue apart.

"What you got there?"

"It's an insulated carrier. Mom packed you turkey, potatoes and gravy, green beans, some kind of lettuce salad, croissant rolls and pumpkin pie. Why don't you sit down, and I'll be your server."

He was sitting before he was even told to do so.

"Just a little hungry, I see," Ned said

He took the food into the kitchen, filled a large plate and put the remainder of the food in the oven on low heat. Ned put the plate in front of Fats, and he never looked up until everything was gone. Ned filled the plate three times that evening, and Fats almost got plate number three halfway gone when he had to stop.

"That was so good I just want to keep eating."

"What's stopping you?" Ned asked.

"My gut. I can't put another forkful into my mouth."

"What about the pie?"

Fats groaned. He hadn't thought about the pie before he entirely filled his big old pie hole. He had never been this gluttonous before. Maybe it was because of what had happened to him less than twenty-four hours ago. Maybe he had needed all the comfort food he could get.

Ned cleared the table while Fats groaned. When everything was finished and put away, Ned brought over two glasses filled with some amber liquid.

"What's this?" Fats wondered.

"It's Benedictine. Made by some monks, I think. It's supposed to aid in digestion."

"I could use that right now." Fats took a sip.

The alcohol was very sweet but rather tasty. Fats took another small sip.

"That's quite good."

"I can't believe you've never tasted it before."

"I've led a sheltered life," Fats said smiling. "Coleman never wanted me to drink."

Ned looked at Fats. His comment puzzled him.

"Ned, you saw what alcohol did to Coleman when he jumped off the wagon. I guess he never wanted that for me."

"Can't say that I blame him, but I've never seen you take more than one or two drinks ever."

"I don't dislike it. It's just that I don't like to lose control. I like to be in charge of my actions even though people don't think I am."

"That's about as true a thing as I've ever heard. You are goofy enough without drinking. I can't even pretend to fathom what you'd be like on the sauce."

"Me either."

They both laughed and sat for another hour just talking about nothing in particular. The Budweiser clock on the wall chimed 10:00, and Ned suggested they turn in.

"You go ahead. I think I'll go for a little walk. I've been cooped up here all day, and I think I need to get all this food to settle." Fats pointed to his stomach.

"Don't go far. It's damn cold out there."

"Why don't you use Coleman's room? There are fresh sheets in the closet."

Ned looked at Fats for a moment.

"I don't think I could do that. It just wouldn't be right. Besides, it would kind of creep me out. I would never want to sleep in his bed. I'll just use the couch if you don't mind."

Fats didn't mind at all. In fact he could understand Ned's apprehension. He was having some of the same feelings, and he was just happy to have Ned around so he wouldn't have to dwell on it.

Fats made sure to bundle up and then took a leisurely walk around the downtown area. Everything was lit up for Christmas but now that it was over, it seemed very sad. There was no one driving around, and Fats assumed everyone had bunked down for the night. He heard Christmas carols playing somewhere in the distance. It was from someone's loudspeaker and the carols were probably playing on a loop. He couldn't really tell where the sounds were coming from, but he was sure it was some business that had forgotten to turn off their system before they left on Christmas Eve. Excitement always prevailed during the Christmas season. It was always about anticipation of something better to come.

Fats thought about his life and what had happened. It seemed like such a random act. He thought about Coleman, and how he had sacrificed himself to save his son. The Sinning family had never been very religious. They had attended church a few times over the years, but nothing seemed to stick. He knew all the stories, because he attended Sunday school until he was ten or eleven. Fats thought about Coleman's sacrifice and it made him think about what Jesus had done for the children of the world. It was the same, wasn't it? He thought it was, but he really didn't know. He liked the thought, because it made him think of his philosophy class at college.

He stopped walking. He had made a decision without ever realizing it.

He wouldn't be returning to college in the fall.

29

Fats and Ned woke up about the same time. It was after 8:00. Both had slept soundly, but Ned was complaining of a stiff neck from his bad position on the couch. Fats had no sympathy.

Ned cooked a breakfast that consisted of eggs and toast. There was no bacon or sausage, and Fats complained about it the entire time. Ned ignored his grousing and just smiled. He knew Fats was a complex character, and he also knew he had more on his proverbial plate than he could handle. He might have an idea that could help, but it would have to be saved until later.

After breakfast, Fats showered first and went down to the bar. By the time Ned arrived, Fats had called the pool table company and explained what had happened. They were understanding and would have someone there to replace the felt by 11:00.

The place was in good shape considering the previous day's events. Ned and Fats worked hard to make it look presentable. There was some damage to the floor from the shotgun blasts, but they even had the wood looking pretty good after they used a great deal of oil soap on it.

The pool table was fixed by noon, and a few guys were shooting on it before the technician even left the building. Things were back to normal, only they never would be normal for Fats. Coleman was gone. The place no longer offered Fats the charm it once had.

Fats had planned to visit the funeral home and make arrangements for his father's remains, but he hadn't been able to make any decisions. His decision to ask Freddy for his guidance seemed like a good one. When things slowed up after lunch, he left Ned in charge of the Icehouse and walked over to Freddy's office.

Freddy was on the phone trying to figure out where the bikers had come from and what he was going to do with the bodies. He seemed frustrated and just motioned for Fats to sit.

When Freddy finished on the phone, he wrote down a few things on a yellow pad he had in front of him. Fats waited patiently. They both had their own set of annoyances.

Finally, Freddy looked up.

"How are you doing today?"

"Getting by, I guess. I figure I don't have much choice."

"You've got the strength of both your parents," Freddy said.

Fats didn't want to hear that and quickly blurted out why he had come.

"I'm not certain what to do with Coleman's remains. I thought maybe you could help me."

Freddy turned in his chair and looked out the window for some time.

"What were you thinking?"

"I don't have the first clue about how to handle this. You knew him better than anyone. What would he want us to do?"

Freddy smiled when he heard Fats say "us."

"Well, you know Coleman wasn't much for religion."

Fats nodded.

"He didn't have roots from his past. He hasn't been here all that long, so I think he wouldn't have wanted a big church-type service," Freddy said.

"I was thinking the same thing, but I want to do something. People around here have been so supportive of the Icehouse. There should be some kind of ending, I think."

"Have you thought of cremation?"

Fats hadn't given that idea a thought.

"Coleman might have liked that," Fats said, and wondered what they would do with the ashes.

Freddy seemed to be reading Fats thoughts.

"You could scatter the ashes at some favorite place of his, or you might just want to keep them in an urn."

"His favorite place was the Icehouse, and I couldn't throw his ashes around there. Keeping them in an urn would just be creepy. I'll have to figure out something."

Fats had a great idea. He decided to keep it to himself, because Freddy might not understand his motives. He decided to press on.

"What about having some kind of celebration at the Icehouse? I think Coleman would like that."

"Seems unusual, so you might be right. I think you might want to call it a memorial rather than a celebration. People around here would think that was weird."

Fats agreed.

"I'm heading to the funeral home after this. I think I'll run all this by them."

"Don't let them try and sell you a bill of goods. You don't need a casket, but they will want you to buy one for his viewing. You also don't need to embalm the remains if you have him cremated right away. That should keep your costs down. You also don't need an urn. A small wooden box would be just fine."

Fats walked out of Freddy's office, happy. He had given him some great advice, and that was important, since Fats had never dealt with death before.

His visit to the funeral home was quick and right to the point. The funeral director knew immediately that Fats had made up his mind, and it was useless to try and change it. He and Fats both agreed that they didn't need to waste any more time on the transaction.

Fats would get the ashes by the end of the week. He chose a simple wooden box with some fancy etching on the lid. There was a place to put an eight by ten photo and Fats hoped he could find one without Nola posing with Coleman.

He had fought the urge to call her after he found her number in Coleman's wallet. Part of him wanted her to know so she would have regrets about leaving them. His other half didn't care.

He had already made the decision to eventually leave Coleman's ashes on her desk. That meant he would have to see Nola once more. He would relish that fact, and any pain he felt at seeing her once more would be alleviated when he would observe the anguish in her face.

Fats found a decent picture of Coleman, but it had Nola in the frame as well. Fats cut her out of the picture. Instead of a 5 by 10 it would be a 5 by 6. It would be just fine. He checked in with Ned, and he assured Fats that he could handle things at the bar until later.

Fats decided to spend the rest of the day going through the Icehouse books. He had no idea if the bar was making or losing money. He thought it was doing well, but he had never paid much attention to finances. Coleman had never shared any of it with him. He wished he had stayed in the business management major at college instead of hopping around with all his hippie friends in the social sciences.

Fats couldn't find much bookwork. He found the checkbook and decided that it was Coleman's entire business plan. There were the daily deposits listed and check payments to the distributors. It didn't appear that there was a personal account, and everything went through the business.

There was a passbook savings account that Coleman had labeled "Roland's College Fund." It was impressive. Fats saw that there was almost ten grand in the account. He hoped Coleman had specified that he could withdraw from the account. He didn't want the money tied up. He wondered if Coleman had left a will. There was a small safe in the back of the closet.

Fats rifled through Coleman's wallet once more and found a card with what looked like the combination. He tried it twice, and it opened on the second time.

There wasn't much in the safe. There was a folder with the bar's insurance policy, an address book, and six plain envelopes. He glanced at the insurance policy and noticed it was up-to-date, so he tossed it aside. The address book looked interesting, but the content was meaningless. He knew he would keep it, because it was a tie to Coleman and someday the people in it might have things to share with him.

He took the six envelopes and looked at them one by one. The first was a letter to Fats. It was short and to the point.

Roland. If you are reading this then I have gone to another place, wherever that might be. There is a letter included that will let you take out the money in the college fund if you so desire. I hope you use it to get your degree, but that will be your decision. My will is also included in one of the envelopes. There is also a copy with the lawyer, so it will need to be followed to the letter. That may not be what you want, but it is what I expect. There is a letter for Freddy Thornton. It is sealed and please deliver it to him that way.

The last two envelopes contain money. It is cash from the bar. I called it my rainy day fund. You are in charge of the money. Only a fool would report all the income from a place that does a cash business. Coleman.

Fats smiled. His father had been skimming from the business. Who would have thought it? He looked into the envelopes and counted twenty thousand total. Add that to his college fund, and he had almost 30 grand at his fingertips. That was a hell of lot of money. He put everything back into the safe but kept the will to see what Coleman had meant. He would be prepared for the worst. He would not be disappointed.

Coleman's will left the bar and contents to Nola. At first, Fats was pissed off. How could his father leave the place to Nola? She had left them without so much as a second thought. He knew she would never leave her tribe and come back to run the Icehouse, and the thought made him just sit and stew. He stopped himself from simply destroying the will, when he remembered Coleman had said the lawyer had a copy. It would have been so easy to fix things without the legal copy. After all, Coleman and Nola had never married. The bar would have gone to him without a will specifying any inheritors.

He kept running it through his mind, and eventually he calmed down. Fats tried to see things from Coleman's point of view. He knew his father loved Nola. He knew he loved her right up to the end of his life. They had put everything into the business, and it had been a total partnership. Fats decided he needed to follow his father's wishes. There was really nothing he could have done about it anyway.

The mind has a way of calming the body if one would let it. Fats felt calmer. He looked at the will once more and put it back into the safe with the rest of the items.

The cash would be his, and no one needed to know about it. He would need to have one more confrontation with Nola, but now that seemed of little consequence. He thought more about the bar and smiled. He hadn't really ever wanted it anyway. He liked being around the place shooting both pool and the breeze, but he never really wanted the shitty life of owning a place like that. He had other things he wanted to do. Both Coleman and Nola never had a life. When other people were finished working for the day, they were still at full throttle. Their free time in the mornings didn't correspond to other people's schedules, so they had few friends outside the people that came into their bar.

When Nola left, the life was sucked right out of his father. Fats made a decision, right there and then, not to ever let that happen to him.

30

By the time Fats went back down to the bar, the place was packed.

"What's going on?" Fats asked Ned.

"People started coming in about 5:00, and they just kept coming in. I called in the second bartender and the cook helped out until they started ordering food."

"Why didn't you call me?" Fats asked.

"Figured you needed some time. Besides, you've got your A-team on duty." Ned smiled.

Fats went right to work. It was busy until after 11:00. The cook wanted to go home at 9:00, but people were still ordering food, and she didn't leave until 10:15. Fats sent the second bartender home at 10:30. Ned stayed, and Fats felt the two of them could handle the remainder of the crowd.

"I wonder what prompted the rush this evening?" Fats was puzzled.

"Don't be so dense. It's the day after Christmas. People would normally be partied out. The fact that they were here tonight tells you what they thought of Coleman. It's their way of paying tribute to him, and in a way, to you as well."

Fats hadn't given much thought to the impact Coleman had on the community. It amazed him that a bar owner would be held in such high regard.

"Now I know I'm going to need to have some kind of memorial for Coleman," Fats said, to himself.

Ned heard his comment and weighed in immediately.

"That's a great idea. Let's do it soon."

"How about Sunday?" Fats asked.

"Well, you can't sell drinks on Sunday. You know that, right?"

"We won't sell drinks. The drinks will be on Coleman. No law says we can't have a private party with free alcohol."

"I'm not so sure about that."

"Well, I'll clear it with Freddy. I think he'll like the idea."

Ned agreed and took off his apron.

"I think I've had enough for one night. I believe I'll head home."

"I've been thinking about your living arrangement. Don't you think it's time you moved out of your parents' place?"

"Can't really afford it."

"How about considering this? You talk to your parents and tell them you have an opportunity to have your own place. Then you move in here. I'll get rid of all of Coleman's stuff tomorrow, and you can move in tomorrow night. You might have to buy a bed, because I'm going to trash the one that's there now."

"How much is this going to cost me?" Ned asked.

"Consider it a perk that comes with the job. It will cost you zero, zilch, nada, aught, naught, nil, zip…"

"Enough. I get it. I'll talk to my parents at breakfast tomorrow. I think you should plan on it, unless you have a change of heart before then."

"I won't. I've got some things running around in the old noggin. If it all works out, you may play an even bigger role around here."

Ned didn't know what Fats meant, but he was just too tired to query him. Fats always had mystery about him, so it wasn't something unexpected. Ned was feeling good about seeing Fats making plans. He realized he was going to be all right. Once they got past the memorial for Coleman, maybe things would get back to normal. Even though the night was cold and the wind was blowing, Ned walked home with a spring in his step. Things were shaping up in his life, and he had Fats to thank for it.

Fats gave six remaining customers the last call at 12:30. He was tired and wanted to go up to bed. The men decided to forgo the last call and finished their drinks. Fats wondered if they realized that he wanted to close early. Maybe they could read the exhaustion on his face. When the last customer left the bar, Fats locked the door behind him. He was asleep as his head hit the pillow. He slept soundly and better than he had in quite some time.

~

Fats woke up just a little before 10:00. He looked at the alarm clock on his nightstand, and after he finally could focus, he realized he had slept for nine hours straight. He hadn't even got up to use the bathroom. That reminded him that he had to piss like a racehorse. He meant to be up by 8:00, because he had a list of things to do. He would have to let Ned run the show by himself for a while.

After he showered, and got himself ready for the day, he began to disassemble Coleman's bedroom. He started with the closet, took all his clothes and put them in the back of his pickup. The brass bed came apart quite easily, and he made three trips to his pickup. He would see if Goodwill would take it along with the clothing. If not, the mattress and box spring would find their way to the dump.

He looked over the bedroom and decided to leave the table and lamp for Ned. Otherwise, everything had been removed. Coleman had lived a simple life. Fats could appreciate not having to go through a lot of stuff. It made things much easier on many levels. Fats decided to get his errands finished as quickly as possible. He opened the safe and took out the contents, looked at everything once more and tossed the insurance policy in the safe along with the money in the envelopes. He removed everything else and put the envelopes in his back pocket.

Ned was busy getting the bar ready for the day. The cook was in the kitchen dreaming up the day's special.

"I have some errands to run. Can I leave you in charge of the place today?" Fats asked Ned.

Ned saluted Fats in affirmation.

"Aye, me Capitan." Ned closed one eye and pretended to be a pirate.

Although Fats would have liked to baffle Ned with bullshit, he wasn't quite ready to let his inner college persona kick in. He needed to be serious for a while. He thought he owed Coleman that much. There would be time for his wiliness after the reminiscences on Sunday. The last thought made him smile to himself, because his mind was still thinking in its usual hipness vigor.

Fats went out to his pickup shaking his head. He needed to get back to trying to sell some sucker a line of bull. There was no doubt that he needed to get back to what he did best.

His first stop was the sheriff's office. He delivered the sealed letter that his father had written to Freddy. Freddy looked at it and placed it on the desk. Fats had hoped the sheriff would open and read it. He was mildly curious about what was in it. He could tell he wasn't going to find out anything at present. He visited with Freddy about Sunday and serving drinks. Freddy didn't see a problem with it, and he would be on hand to help dispel any problems some folks might have with it.

"Just make sure you only serve one drink to each person with no money changing hands. Unless of course that person is me, and then you can give me as much as you want." Freddy winked, and went back to his paperwork. Fats left feeling good about how things were working out.

Fats' second stop was at the bank. He showed the teller the college fund passbook and then the letter from his father. The teller went to show everything to someone with more power to make decisions, and soon Fats had the money in hand. They wanted to give him a cashier's check, but he was having none of that. He wanted it all in cash.

He was planning to stop at the Goodwill store, when he had a better idea. He went to the local furniture store owned by the funeral director. When Fats walked into the business, the director thought he was there for his father's ashes.

"I'm sorry Roland. Your father's remains won't be cremated until this evening. We don't have the facility here and have to take the remains to Missoula. I can personally deliver his remains to you when they arrive tomorrow."

"Thanks, but I'm not here for that. I would like to purchase a bed. I have Coleman's in the back of the pickup. Would you take it if I buy a new queen set from you?"

"Of course. That's part of our service. Let me show you what we have."

Fats looked around and picked out something priced more in the middle-of-the-road. He liked Ned a lot, but he didn't need the best bed in town. The bed would be delivered that same afternoon. Fats liked the fact it would be a surprise for Ned. He picked out a set of sheets and pillows and paid for everything with the cash he was carrying.

His next stop was the Goodwill and he unloaded the remainder of the things out of the back of the pickup. As he was getting back into the old truck, he had a thought. The pickup was an ancient thing that Coleman had kept around long after similar models had expired. Fats needed something newer and more dependable. He was about to make some changes in his life, and the old set of wheels wouldn't take him where he needed to go.

Fats decided to drive the twelve miles to Kalispell and find something better to drive. They had a Chevrolet dealer there, and he wanted to find something that fit his personality. He was almost twenty, and he knew he deserved something better. That's what he told himself anyway. The new 1970 models would be coming out in the spring. He thought he might be able to get a good deal on a 69 model.

He drove to Kalispell slowly. It had snowed overnight, and the roads were a little slippery. The snowplows were out sanding, and Fats took his place in a line of cars following the plow.

He was thinking about what would happen during the next few

weeks, when he realized something. He had never been any further from Whitefish than his first year of college at Missoula. He had spent almost twenty years never going anywhere. That would need to change.

If Fats thought that he would be getting a good deal on a new vehicle, he was badly mistaken. He tried his smooth college lingo on the salesman without any luck. Fats thought that maybe the guy thought he was a bit loony, so he went off by himself to look at something used.

Nothing really stuck out in the car area. There was a Corvette that he considered but then nixed. He figured he probably would have killed himself with something that powerful.

Fats kept winding his way toward the pickups. He had decided earlier that he wasn't going to go in that direction, but they kept jumping out at him as something a little more practical than any of the sedans he was looking at.

He found a red 1966 Chevy pickup with an eight-foot box. He found the salesman, and together they went for a ride to test it out. The mileage was lower than most of the other used trucks, so Fats decided to take it.

The salesman changed his attitude when Fats peeled off twenty five one hundred dollar bills. Cash was king, and it was a lesson that Fats learned quickly. The dealership agreed to deliver the vehicle, after they found that Fats wasn't trading in his old wheels. They hadn't wanted to take it anyway, so the delivery was a great deal for them.

Fats drove back to the Icehouse and parked the old pickup around back. He entered the bar and threw the keys to Ned. Ned looked at him and then the keys.

"What's this for?"

"Your new wheels. Well, not new but new to you. I just bought a new used pickup at Kalispell."

"Why would you do that?"

"Because you're going to need something, when you run the Icehouse after I leave."

31

Ned just looked at Fats. He didn't know what to say, because he had no idea what Fats was even saying. Fats could see the confusion on his face.

"I'm going to be leaving soon, and you're going to be running the Icehouse at least for the near future." Fats had no idea what Nola would want to do with the place. "I'll be talking to Nola soon. Maybe you could purchase the place from her."

Ned was still confused, "What the hell? I thought we would run the place together."

"It's not mine to run," Fats said, and handed Ned the copy of Coleman's will.

Ned read it over trying to understand everything. Finally, he put it down on the bar and pushed it over to Fats.

"That doesn't seem right. I don't know what Coleman was thinking. Nola left you both, and I thought he would leave the business to you."

"Coleman took care of me. I'm not all that upset at how this turned out."

"Why? This is a great business. People like you, and you could do great things here."

"Not really the point. I need to see the country. I've never been anywhere past Missoula. There's a world out there, and I want to experience it."

"It's pretty darn good around here if you ask me," Ned said, almost pouting.

"That's the thing. I'm not asking anyone. This is something I have to figure out on my own. Did you know that I've never really been with a woman? That's something that's just got to change."

Ned was confused again.

"You've had girls around you all through high school."

"That's not the same thing. I said that I've never been with a woman. I have no carnal knowledge. What kind of twenty year old would I be, really, if I couldn't experience the best life has to offer?"

Ned thought about it for a moment and then smiled.

"Maybe you swing the other way."

"I'll drop you like an elk if you ever say that again." Fats pretended to be angry.

Ned saw through it immediately.

"Maybe I'll just call you swishy."

Fats feigned a right hook, and they both grinned. Fats realized he would miss Ned. He would do his best to try and convince Nola to sell the place to him. He knew he wouldn't have much leverage, however. Nola was smart, and if he could show how this would be beneficial to her, she just might agree.

Ned held up a poster he had been working on. It surprised Fats at how professional it looked.

"Hey you've got some talent there. I didn't know you could draw."

"Took a lot of art in high school. I've always liked it, but there isn't much call for it around here."

Fats thought he should tell Ned to get out of the area. He decided against it. People needed to find their own way. It was harder to reconcile when those people were his friends. Fats would always struggle with the feeling.

Fats looked at the poster. It was all about Coleman's memorial.

Fats had seen similar artwork back in the late sixties advertising musical groups. He could remember seeing one from a Jefferson Airplane concert. There had also been a lot of them at the time of the Monterey Pop Festival. Fats had always wished he could have gone to see it. But he was stuck in Montana, where the groups just flew over on their way to either coast. Coleman and Nola wouldn't have let him go anyway. He was about to remedy that previous shortcoming in his life.

"I'm going to put copies of these posters around town. The banks and the post office for sure. Can you think of anyplace else?" Ned asked.

"How about the hardware store and the café?"

"Good idea. That should be enough. We only have so much room around here. I don't know what we would do if the whole town showed up."

"A problem to be sure. We couldn't put them outside. It's way too cold, and that's just another reason for me to move on. This cold just keeps getting into my bones. There's got be other places where it's not winter nine months of the year," Fats said.

Ned suddenly got serious.

"When are you leaving?"

"Monday, after the memorial service."

"Where are you going?"

"Haven't given that much thought yet, but the first thing is to look up Nola. It's time she found out about Coleman," Fats said.

"That might be a difficult meeting for you," Ned replied.

"I don't think so. She's out of my life. This will be just a meeting to tie up some loose ends."

"You can tell yourself that, but some of us know better," Ned said.

The comment puzzled Fats for a moment, and he was about to say something, when the door opened and the deliverymen came into the bar with Ned's new bed.

"Where do you want this?"

"Upstairs in the vacant bedroom."

"Naturally," one of the men grumbled.

"What's this? I thought you were leaving," Ned said.

"It's not for me, you idiot. You're going to need something to sleep on if you are going to be staying here."

"I thought that would be my responsibility."

"Well, you thought wrong. Now get those posters finished and hung around town." Fats followed the deliverymen up the stairs making sure they found the right room.

Ned knew that Fats would miss being in charge. It was in his nature. He supposed he got that trait from his parents.

~

Sunday came, and by 12:30, the entire bar was packed. People were standing around the perimeter of the room and behind the bar. Ned opened the back storage area for the overflow.

Coleman's ashes were front and center on the bar in the wooden box Fats had picked out.

Freddy had come early and set up a portable speaker and mike. Fats had been trying to think of something to say. He was relieved when Freddy told him he would be doing the eulogy.

"It was what Coleman put in the letter to me. He thought it might be too much for you to handle," Freddy explained.

"Is that all he said?" Fats asked.

"He was a man of few words, you know that, right?"

Fats agreed, but he couldn't help feeling that Freddy might be leaving something out.

The memorial started precisely at 1:00. Fats knew it was really a celebration, however. Freddy talked for fifteen minutes about how he had met Coleman, and how they had become best friends. Fats noticed he was being careful not to mention Nola. That was just fine with him.

Some woman, who Fats didn't know, sang the Beatles tune "A Long and Winding Road." Fats thought it was totally appropriate. The hardware man spoke about Coleman's ties to the community. It was short and to the point, and that was the end of the ceremony. Fats stood and thanked everyone for coming.

"This is something Coleman would have wanted. I am quite sure wherever he is right now, he's happy. Now the bar is open, and Coleman would like to provide you one more drink." Fats looked at Freddy. "Well, maybe more than just one."

Freddy shook his head and just smiled at Fats. He had expected as much, and he wouldn't be standing in the way of a celebration, no matter what it was called.

The Icehouse went through a great deal of beer and served a number of drinks as well. By 4:00 things had pretty much settled down, and Freddy told Fats that it would be a good time to send the remaining folks on their way. There were quite a few barflies that shouldn't be behind the wheel. They would need rides, and Freddy and his deputies would see to that.

Fats shook Freddy's hand, and Freddy responded by putting him in a huge bear hug.

"Try not to forget about us here," Freddy said.

Fats thought he noticed some water at the corner of Freddy's eyes.

"I won't," Fats said, but he knew he would never return.

"This will have to be goodbye then," Freddy said. "We have a state officers meeting in Great Falls tomorrow. We're driving there tonight, so I won't get to see you off tomorrow."

"No one will know I'm gone except Ned. That's the way I want it. I hate goodbyes."

"Better get used to them," Freddy said, and went out the door.

Fats wondered what he had meant by that. Oh well, he had no time to dwell on anything. He needed to help Ned clean the bar, and then he had to pack. It was time to move on down the line. He still didn't know what he was going to say to Nola, but he would have time to get it straight in his mind while he was driving.

It was difficult for Fats not to just leave immediately. He was anxious to get behind the wheel of his new wheels even though they were a few years old, but it was better than anything he had ever driven before.

The pair had cleaned up after the all the people in the bar, and

Ned had actually helped Fats with his packing. They were finished before 8:00 and each realized that they hadn't eaten anything all day.

Neither appeared to want to cook, so Ned suggested they go out for dinner. There wasn't much open on Sundays in the area.

"What are you thinking for food?" Ned asked.

"I don't really care. What's open?"

"I know of a pizza place in Kalispell. I think they are able to serve 3.2 beer even though it's Sunday."

"Sounds like that's the place we need to be," Fats said.

"I'll drive. You look like you are beat."

"I am. Thanks. We can take my pickup."

"I should say not. I have wheels now. I might as well get used to using them."

Fats couldn't argue, so he didn't. They were the only people in the place, and the waitress seemed happy to have someone to break the boredom. The pizza was good, and the beer was better. Fats didn't even know what kind it was, but it didn't matter. Beer always went down good with pizza, and they had ordered a giant pie with everything that was available in the restaurant.

Neither spoke on the trip back to Whitefish. Ned was thinking about the Icehouse and how he was going to handle everything without Fats. Fats, already dreading his Nola visit, thought about what he was going to say.

When they got back to the Icehouse, both went straight to bed. Ned called out to Fats telling him that he liked his knew bed. He was sure he would be quite comfortable in it.

Fats hardly heard it and fell asleep almost instantly. He was overtired, and his sleep was filled with dreams, most of them bad.

He was up and showered before Ned even woke the next morning. Fats rattled around in the kitchen making toast with peanut butter for breakfast, when Ned walked in.

"What time is it?" Ned asked.

"Time for me to leave. It's after 6:00, and you'd better get cracking if you want to make this bar successful."

Ned nodded and went into the bathroom to shower. Fats took the opportunity to make a quick exit. He took his peanut butter toast with him and would pick up some coffee at the service station when he got gas.

He needed to get going, and he knew if he stayed Ned would find a way to detain him unnecessarily. It wasn't something he wanted to do, but he knew he needed to do it.

By the time Ned was showered and dressed, Fats had gassed up his new vehicle, got his coffee and was meandering down highway 93 toward Missoula.

Later, he would realize what a mistake it had been not to say goodbye to Ned. It gnawed at him.

32

Fats took his time on the way to Crow Agency. He was in no hurry and wanted to take in all the sights. He decided to do a scenic route and took in Great Falls. Then he went straight down to Bozeman and Livingston. In truth, he was just stalling for time. He had no idea how he was going to confront Nola, and he wanted time to figure it out.

There was a little bar off the beaten path in Livingston, and he stopped in to have a beer. There was a pool table, and soon he had a game of bait and switch. It wasn't high stakes, so nobody got very upset when he cleaned the table on a double-or-nothing bet.

Fats decided that it would be better to exit, before the locals decided they no longer wanted to tolerate his pool shooting abilities. There was a cheap motel down the road from the bar, and he checked in. He made sure Coleman's ashes were safely hidden under the seat of his pickup.

Fats threw the comforter off the bed and fell into it. He hadn't realized how tired he actually felt. He hadn't eaten since lunch and thought he probably should find someplace close, but that was the last thing he thought about. He closed his eyes and when he opened them, it was 7:30 the next morning. He had slept over twelve hours and hadn't moved a muscle. He was still in his clothes and had to piss once again like a racehorse.

After his shower and a change of clothes, Fats decided to ease down the road before he found breakfast. He thought Billings just might be the place. Coleman had told him stories about his life there, and he wanted to see it for himself.

He found fuel and food at a truck stop on the west edge of town. He looked around the city and understood why Coleman wanted out. He stopped at the refinery's office to let them know of Coleman's death. No one there had any idea who Coleman was and most of his coworkers were long gone or dead. It wasn't a place where many spent their entire life. Working for a company where the conditions were dangerous was just too difficult for most.

Fats decided he was delighted that Coleman had found satisfaction away from this place. He had seen enough to know this would have never been a place for anyone to flourish. It would be very difficult to just exist.

Fats checked his map and found the next stop in the road was the Crow Agency. He was shocked, because he hadn't really given his confrontation with Nola enough thought. Somewhere between Billings and the reservation he pulled off the highway onto a little turnout. He cut the pickup's engine and cracked his window a bit. The thermometer was hovering around zero. Fats needed the cold air to help him think. It didn't take very long for him to realize that it was damn cold in the pickup. He rolled up the window and started the engine to get a bit of heat. He was dreading the confrontation, and he didn't know why. He was the one with the righteous indignation, and he should have been all geared up to let Nola have both barrels. The thought of Nola made him nuts, and yet he still had something nagging in his head. Then he realized that the only way he was ever going to get past this thing with Nola was to have the confrontation immediately. He had to get everything behind him.

Fats put the pickup into gear and pulled out onto the highway. Ten minutes later he was at the Crow Agency. He noticed a small welcome center as he pulled into the community, and he drove in. He found someone with a card that said "information and assistance" and he sat down at the young Crow woman's desk.

"Can I help you?" she asked smiling.

Fats smiled back.

"I'm looking for a person from your tribe."

"Certainly, that's why I'm here," she said, and took out what looked like a directory.

Fats waited for her to get situated and finally decided to take another tack.

"The woman's name is Moon Flower."

There wasn't even a moment's hesitation, and the woman didn't appear to need the registry.

"I'm sorry to have to tell you that we lost Moon Flower on Christmas Day."

Fats felt nothing at the news of Moon Flower's death. He said nothing but waited for the woman to continue.

"Moon Flower lived a good long life. No one really knew for sure, but we believe she was well into the century mark."

Fats didn't think that was true, but he didn't really know for sure.

"She was definitely old, that's for sure. Does she have any living relatives around here?" Fats asked, knowing full well that no one on the reservation would have any knowledge of his existence.

"Yes, she has a niece who is planning our new hotel and eventually a casino."

"Can you tell me where I can find her?"

The woman was immediately suspicious.

"I'll need to know what you want with her before I can give out that information."

Fats thought about his response for a moment.

"I don't know if you knew a man called Coleman Sinning, but he and a woman named Enola McGuire were together for many years."

"Yes, I'm aware of the name."

"I'm Coleman's son. My name is Roland Sinning, but everyone calls me Fats."

As Fats expected, his name had no meaning to the woman.

"I am unsure what you are asking me to do."

"I'd just like to speak with her. Coleman is dead, and I thought she'd want to know. I also have his will, which has her as a beneficiary."

The woman was immediately interested.

"Really? What did he leave her?"

Fats smiled. "I don't think that's something I wish to share with anyone other than Enola."

The woman was immediately embarrassed. She understood she had overstepped her role. Fats knew that her knowledge of Coleman's death, and the mistake she just made, would keep her from contacting Nola before he could find her.

After exchanging some information, the woman told Fats where she could be located. Fats drove immediately to the site of the new hotel. There were all kinds of people working around the area. It looked like they were pouring the foundation, because Fats followed cement trucks into the building site. There was dust in the air, and everything looked like it had previously been caked in mud. Fats couldn't imagine what the place would be like in the spring when the ground became frost-free once again.

Fats watched the activity from his pickup's window for quite some time. There were tarps all over the ground, and when a cement truck dropped its load, the workers scrambled to cover the fresh concrete so it wouldn't freeze. Others were building a tent-like structure and wheeling in portable heaters to keep the cold from the concrete as it cured. Fats thought everything looked quite professional.

Finally, he looked around and saw a trailer with a sign that read "clerk" near the entrance door. The woman had told Fats that it was Nola's office. He drove the pickup toward the trailer. The ground was rough, and he was jostled around.

Fats parked the pickup near the entrance and shut off the engine. He could hear the tinkling of the lifters from the motor as they cooled. He reached under the seat and found Coleman's ashes. He looked at the ornate box with Coleman's picture attached.

"I'll say my goodbyes here, Coleman. It's time Nola took some responsibility for the time you two spent together. Thank you for what you gave to me. I just wanted you to know that I'll be fine, and I'll always be grateful for what you have done for me."

It surprised Fats that he wasn't emotional when he said the words to Coleman. It was a fitting way to say farewell. He sat a few more minutes just looking at Coleman's box of ashes. Finally, he opened the door and climbed the metal steps to the trailer door. He thought about knocking but then decided against it. He opened the door and stepped inside.

There was a desk for a receptionist just inside, but it wasn't being manned. Fats looked around. The trailer was a nondescript place divided into two rooms. There was an artist's conception of the hotel on one wall and a mock-up of the future casino on the other. Fats looked them both over briefly. He heard what sounded like someone on a telephone in the second room. The door was open, and he walked over and looked in.

Nola was sitting in a leather office chair looking out of the back window with the phone in her hand. Fats thought that she might have been talking with a contractor or supplier. She was definitely in charge, and the tone in her voice told him she was not very happy.

There were two chairs in front of the desk. Nola, feeling the presence of someone in the room, motioned toward the chairs. Fats took it as an invitation to sit. He slid quietly into the left plastic chair.

Fats looked around, while Nola continued her phone conversation. The walls were barren. Her desk had some paperwork on the top, but other than that there was nothing to see. Fats wondered what he had expected. Maybe he thought there would be pictures of the family. The thought actually made him smile. He was still smiling when Nola finished her call and turned around in the chair.

Her eyes met Fats, and she almost dropped the phone. Fats thought he could see panic in her eyes just for a moment. It was fleeting, and Nola seemed to recover almost immediately. She stared at Fats for a minute or two. Fats wondered if she was trying to find something to say.

Finally, after Fats just looked back and said nothing, Nola decided to speak.

"Roland," she said as a greeting.

"Nobody calls me that. I go by Fats these days."

"Well, what can I do for you, Fats?"

Fats looked around at the surroundings.

"I would have expected something a bit more inviting. Not much of a welcoming environment for any hotel investors."

"Where do you think you are, anyway? This is the reservation. We function by a bootstrap. This new hotel will be a shot in the arm for the entire reservation. We're not going to squander anything on a temporary clerk's office."

Fats, in agreement with what she was saying, hated it when his ideas and Nola's were similar. Nola had always been practical, and from time-to-time, had kept Coleman in check from unnecessary spending.

He knew he had to get back on his agenda, or he would lose his edge.

"We missed you at Christmas."

Nola said nothing but didn't lose eye contact with Fats.

"We had an exciting time at the Icehouse over the holidays."

"They usually are," Nola replied.

"Probably not what you are thinking, however."

Nola appeared to have had enough.

"Why are you here?"

The comment took Fats off guard. If he thought she would be showing any remorse at leaving her family, he was badly mistaken.

"I was wondering what in God's name possessed you to leave us? I'm not even thinking about myself, but you left the man who loved you. You were his whole life, and you just walked out on him without a word."

"Like mother, like daughter I guess."

Fats had heard the story about his grandparents, and he wasn't going to let Nola off the hook that easily.

"One major difference, don't you think?"

"What would that be?"

"Your mother didn't leave the man who loved her."

"No, she just left me."

"So, you decide to take it one step further. You not only left your child, but you left the man who loved you."

"He wasn't my husband."

"Common law says he was, but it's no longer worth pondering, I guess."

Nola sat forward.

"What's that supposed to mean?"

Fats leaned, took the wooden box from inside his coat and placed it on Nola's desk.

"Say goodbye to Coleman."

33

Nola's eyes grew large. She looked from the box to Fats. He knew right then, that she had never been as vulnerable. He liked what he saw. She wasn't totally without some feeling. Maybe she had a soul hidden somewhere after all. He got what he had come for and it was enough.

"Here is a copy of his will. He left the Icehouse to you." Fats threw the paper on her desk.

Nola picked it up and looked at it briefly.

"I don't want it," she said, and slid the document back toward Fats.

"That's a shame, because it's yours."

"I'm giving it back to you."

"Mighty magnanimous of you. Sorry, but the place is legally yours, and I don't want it," Fats said.

"I'm confused. You don't want a thriving business?"

"How would you even know that? You haven't been around to know what's going on."

"I have eyes on everything. Don't think for a moment that I don't know about what happens with the Icehouse."

Fats looked at the wooden box.

"And yet you had no idea about Coleman."

"Maybe it was too difficult for my eyes to tell me."

Fats knew that her eyes had to be Freddy.

"Freddy gave a nice tribute at Coleman's memorial. I suppose he was too busy to explain things."

Nola looked away.

"How did it happen?"

Fats gave Nola a detailed description of the events that led to Coleman's death. He spared no detail and was especially graphic when it came to all the blood on the pool table.

Nola listened without speaking. Her stoicism was a mask for what was really going on inside. She had become schooled in the art of concealing her emotions. It was a trait that served her well in the business world predominately run by men.

Nola was good, but Fats wasn't buying any of it. He knew that she had always loved Coleman, and this was the biggest blow in her life. Bigger even than having been left by her mother. When he finished the gruesome tale, Fats sat back in the chair just waiting for Nola's response.

Nola sat for a bit just trying to wrap her head around all the information that had just been dumped on her. She decided to try a different tack with Fats.

"What do you suggest we do about the Icehouse? I assume you closed it up," Nola said, and her tone of voice had softened considerably.

"Your assumption would be comprehensively amiss." Fats said, using his college-developed hippie-speak.

"I suppose you need to speak like that because you are becoming college- educated."

"An event of former times. Auld Lang Syne and history of yore."

Nola sat up quickly and looked right at Fats.

"That's something Coleman and I wanted you to complete. Why would you throw it away?"

"I don't know. Why would you throw us away?"

"It is hard to explain the way of the Crow," Nola said.

"Bullshit to that notion. It is the way of the Nola, methinks."

"I suppose we could go on with this banter all day, but it doesn't beg the question does it?"

"A conundrum for query. A solution may be forthcoming, if you'd care to take notice and be guided by my advice."

Nola rolled her eyes.

"I'll prick up my ears."

"I have a collaborator that goes by the moniker Ned Kendall. He's aces and has done admirably for Coleman in the past. Sell the place to him if you want. Better yet, give it to him, since you expressed resentment at having inherited the watering hole."

"I'll take that under advisement."

"Remember, you don't have to take my word for anything. You can always check with Freddy." Fats noticed just a little embarrassment on Nola's part when he brought up Freddy.

Fats wondered if there was something going on between the two of them. Then he stopped himself. Freddy was true blue to Coleman. His communication with Nola was probably just trying to get the two of them back together. That was an item of the past, however. It really didn't matter any longer, because Coleman was gone, and soon he would be as well.

"Where will you go from here?" Nola asked, realizing the double meaning after she said it.

"I will be a free spirit. I will move wherever the winds blow me," Fats said, and stood up.

"Why don't you stay for a while, and see what's going on around here. You have a quarter of Crow blood running around in your veins. There might be a place for someone like you in the big mix."

"You are kidding of course. Who would mistake a blue-eyed, sandy-haired white boy for a Crow Indian?"

"Everyone would, if I told them."

"No thank you, dear mother. I believe it is time for me to spread those proverbial wings of mine and leave you forever. I can't say I'll miss you, because it would be a misrepresentation."

Fats moved toward the door and turned around to face Nola.

"I sincerely hope you discover what it is you have been looking for all these years. Since it apparently wasn't me, I'll bid you adieu." Fats walked out her office, past the receptionist's desk and out the door. He never turned around to look back.

Nola rolled her desk chair to the window and watched as Fats climbed into his pickup. She didn't move until after he was down the road and out of sight. Then she rolled back to her desk. Nola was extremely tired and wanted to lay her head down on the desk and sleep. The meeting with Roland had taken everything out of her. She knew she had handled it poorly, and she tried to tell herself that he would come back when he tired of being a vagabond. She knew it wasn't true. In her heart, she knew she would never see her boy again.

Nola felt powerless. The only meaningful relationship she ever had was Coleman, and she had screwed that up. Now she had made an enemy out of her only son. Not having the first clue how to fix anything so monumental, Nola went back to work.

34

Fats moved on down the road. It felt like someone had just removed an anvil from his neck. He had no idea where he was going, but it didn't really matter. Any place away from Nola was fine with him.

His pickup was heading east, so Fats decided to follow it wherever it decided to go. He had never been anywhere, so anywhere would be an adventure no matter where it was.

He saw a sign that pointed to Devil's Tower National Monument. He followed the signs and saw a rock formation that rose right out of the prairie. Fats had never seen anything like it and went to the ranger station to get some information. He found that the tower was 867 feet from the base to the summit and was considered to be part of the Black Hills even though it was in Wyoming rather than South Dakota. Many of the Indian tribes considered it a sacred place. Fats could see why. The stone was amazing, and there were all kinds of lore surrounding how it was formed. It didn't matter to Fats how it came to be. He was happy just looking at it.

There were a number of people at the base path looking up and pointing at something. Fats walked over to find out what was going on. It didn't take him long to notice two small specks about three-fourths of the way up the monument.

"What's going on?" Fats asked the nearest bystander.

"Couple of climbers. Looks like the woman got cold feet, and she's not moving. The guy looks to be trying to help her."

"Wow man, that's something crazy," Fats said.

"You said it. I wouldn't go up there for a million bucks."

"For a million I might have to consider it," Fats said, smiling.

"Not me. I like the view just fine from right here."

"I believe you might be correct in that assumption." Fats looked away. The couple made him nervous.

"You want to get in on the bet?"

"What bet would that be?" Fats asked.

"We're betting who can call the closest time to her fall."

"What if she doesn't fall? What if she makes it down?" That type of bet bothered Fats.

"Oh, she'll fall all right. They are free climbing and don't have any equipment. She's lost her nerve, and there's only one way down."

"No thanks, man. That's too ghoulish for me. Does this kind of thing happen frequently?"

"All the time. People are stupid."

Fats couldn't really argue the point, but he didn't have to stand around waiting for the outcome. He was sorry to go. He had wanted to walk around the monument and get a view from all the sides. He hustled back to his pickup and got back on the road as quickly as possible. He didn't need to be a witness to shit like this. It was bad karma.

Fats decided to spend some time in the Black Hills, since it was just down the highway from Devil's Tower. He would come in from the north, and the first town was called Spearfish, gateway to the Black Hills gold rush of 1876.

Spearfish became the supply town for so many of the camps all along the Spearfish Canyon. Fats enjoyed learning the history of an area. He knew about Montana, at least the western part, but he hadn't been around geographically to learn about other places.

He learned that Spearfish held the world record for the fastest recorded temperature change. On January 22,1943 at about 7:30 a.m., the temperature was-4 degrees F. The Chinook wind picked up speed rapidly, and two minutes later the temperature was a +45 F. The 49 degrees rise in two minutes set a world record. By 9:00 a.m., the temperature had further risen to 54 degrees F. Suddenly, the Chinook wind died down, and the temperature tumbled back to-4 degrees. The drop took only 27 minutes. The sudden change in temperature caused glass windows to crack and windshields to instantly frost over.

Fats liked the fact that Spearfish was in a transitional zone between the subtropical and continental. So, January generally bounced around between 40 and 60 degrees. That was much better than any Whitefish January he had ever experienced.

Today was no different. The high was predicted to be 48 degrees. Realizing he was overdressed for temps like that, Fats thought he might be able to survive.

Fats found a cheap little hotel on the outskirts of town and checked in for the night. He found a service station and filled the pickup's tank. They had a few free maps of the area, so Fats took one. There was a pizza joint just down the street, and they served beer. It wasn't a family place by any means, and Fats decided it fit him like a glove. He ordered a pizza and shot a friendly game of pool with one of the locals until his pie came. He ordered a beer and studied the map while he finished eating.

He wanted to see Mt. Rushmore, so he decided to take his time the next day, taking in as much as possible before he got there. It was winter, so he didn't worry too much about a lot of people getting in his way.

He finished the pizza and beer and was almost ready to call it a night, when someone asked him to play doubles for money. Fats never passed up the chance to make some money and put some pool players in their place.

"You looked like you knew what you were doing when we played a while ago," the young man said, whom Fats had played previously.

"I've been around a few games, I guess. What's the deal?" Fats asked.

"Just a couple of assholes who need to be put in their place. They think they can't be beat."

"Whoa, now. I don't want to get in the middle of some beef with a bunch of locals." Fats said.

"They don't have any friends. They just have each other. They're assholes and nobody likes 'em."

"Okay, but let's keep the stakes reasonable. Nothing goes south faster than a game where people lose a bundle." Fats tried to be firm.

"Sounds about right. I don't want to lose a bundle either."

"I've seen you play. If you can hold your own with these guys, we won't lose," Fats said.

"I'll set it up then." He walked to the back, and Fats saw him talking to two wide-bodies.

He thought about going out to his pickup for his good pool stick but nixed that idea immediately. He didn't want to scare the two marks off right from the start, and he didn't want to damage his cue if he needed it to bean either one of these guys.

The young guy came back over to Fats.

"It's a game."

"Sounds like a good way to spend an evening and make an occasion out of it," Fats said, smiling.

The young man didn't know quite what to make of Fats.

"I guess so, but they want to make this for more money than you'd probably like. I don't like it for sure."

"If we're going to play together, first I need to know your name. Then I need to know how much money," Fats said.

"My name is Ryan, and they want to play for a hundred a game."

"Well Ryan, that's too much money. Nothing good would come of it when we would win. They will be angry and try to take it back. Then I'll have to do something I might be sorry for later."

Ryan just looked at Fats.

"Let me go over and reason with these hombres," Fats said, finally.

He walked over to the table the two men were occupying.

"Ryan over there tells me you want to play for a hundred a game. That might be a little rich for just a friendly game."

"Who said it was a friendly game? If you want to play, those are the stakes," one of the men said.

"Sorry, but I'm going to have to pass," Fats replied, and turned to leave.

"You probably don't have a hair on your ass either."

Fats turned back, took out his billfold and put two fifties on the pool table.

"Money on the table, boys. We don't play until we see the color of your green." He was instantly sorry he let them goad him into taking the bait.

"We're good for it," the bigger of the two said.

Fats picked his money back up.

"Not good enough. I don't know you. Maybe you're not gentlemen of reputation. Would you play me without seeing the money up front?"

"Ask around, people will tell you."

"I did. Some say you are assholes." Fats realized he had just turned the tables on these two. Now they would have to play or lose what little honor they had.

Fats walked back to his table and sat down.

"What do you think they'll do?" Ryan asked.

"Watch and wait. They'll leave and come back with the money. It will be done quickly as well. They don't want to lose us as marks."

"I don't know about all of this. Did I bite off more than we can chew?" Ryan asked nervously.

"You didn't. I did. Don't worry about the hundred. I'll put it up."

"Thanks. I don't have more than a ten on me."

Fats smiled and decided to give the duo ten minutes. If they didn't return by then, he would go back to the motel and settle in for the night.

He only had to wait seven minutes. The two assholes were back with a hundred on the table and two cues being sprinkled with talc.

"Let's go, pussy boys. The game is waiting."

Fats put his hundred back on the table.

"Who's going to hold the money?"

"I think Frank should hold it. He owns this place," Ryan said, and picked out his cue.

"Sounds fair," Fats said, and delivered the money to Frank behind the bar.

He found a cue to his liking. It had some weight to it in the barrel end. It would be helpful if he needed to use it for self-defense. Fats thought it might be a strong possibility with this pair.

"Who breaks?" One of the two asked.

"Let's let Frank do the coin toss. One of you call it in the air." Fats tossed a quarter to Frank and he flipped it into the air.

"Tails."

"Tails it is," Frank said.

Fats didn't know if it was Frick or Frack who broke. It really didn't matter. A striped ball fell into a side pocket. Fats and Ryan would have the solids. Frick or Frack took the second shot and put a ball nicely in the corner pocket. Fats could see these guys were pretty fair at the game.

Frick had almost run the balls out when he scratched on the one remaining 15 ball. Ryan retrieved the cue ball and found a comfortable place in the kitchen to make his shot. He was nervous, however, and missed a thin cut to the side pocket. He redeemed himself by snookering Frick or Frack from making the 15 and possibly the 8.

Fats ran the table. There was only the black 8 game ball left. Unfortunately, it was about two inches behind the 15 ball. Had there been no ball in front, Fats could have easily put the ball away in the corner pocket. Fats looked over the situation. There was really only one thing to do.

"Well boys, it doesn't look like I have much choice. I am going to jump the 15 and put the 8 in the corner pocket. Any problem with that?"

Frick and Frack started laughing.

"Good luck with that," they said, almost in unison.

Fats aimed carefully at the bottom of the cue ball and sent it flying over the 15. It hit almost perfectly on the 8 sending it toward the corner pocket. It bounced off the end of both cushions and then fell into the pocket.

Fats looked for a moment, and then turned toward Ryan.

"Sorry, man. It seems I need a little practice. That was just not a very good shot."

Ryan was smiling. He didn't care. Frick and Frack were not so benevolent.

"What are you, some kind of con man?"

"Nope, just a good pool shooter."

Ryan already had the money. He took out fifty and gave the hundred and fifty to Fats.

"Not a bad night's work," Ryan said.

"Put that money on the table. We're not finished."

"Oh, I think you're finished unless you want to go double or nothing," Fats said.

"Done," Frack said.

"Not so fast. Put the two hundred on the table." Fats said.

They both looked at each other.

"We don't have that kind of money on us. But we're good for it."

"I thought we had this conversation previously. No money no game."

"How about we just take it all back from you right now?" Frick and Frack stood.

Fats wondered if he possessed one of those personalities where people immediately disliked him. It seemed he was always in some kind of altercation even when he was trying not to involve himself. He had even dropped his hippie-speak so as not to provoke these two. On the other hand, he never ran away from an altercation and he wasn't about to start now.

"Frank, you might be wise beyond your years if you would call the local constable at this moment."

Frank moved to a phone on the wall and began to dial. It didn't seem to faze either Frick or Frack. They started to circle Fats and Ryan. Fats stepped in front of Ryan and moved him backwards.

Fats knew it was always better to be the first out of the gate. He twirled the pool cue in his right hand above his head and took a step. He cracked Frick right over the top of his head. Frick staggered but didn't go down. It was a surprise. He must have had a harder head than Fats imagined.

Frack tried to land a punch, but Fats was too quick. He moved out of the way and drove the tip of the pool cue right into his solar plexus. Fats had never used that move before and found it to be an effective one. Frack went down immediately and was grabbing at his chest. Fats wondered if he had broken his clavicle, but it was no matter because he still had Frick to still deal with.

Frick had recovered somewhat and grabbed a folding chair. He was swinging it menacingly at Fats. About that time, an officer stormed in with his .38 special drawn.

"Drop your weapons."

Fats could see that this was no Barney Fife and put his pool cue down immediately while raising his hands. Frick was not so forthcoming and still was advancing on Fats.

"I said put down that chair, or I will shoot you where you stand."

Frick took another step, and the officer shot him in the leg. Frick went down with a roar. Fats thought this was going to end up being a long night filled with questions and accusations. He thought wrong.

"Ryan, you and Mr. Pool Cue get out of here. I'll clean up this mess with the help of Frank." The officer turned to Fats. "If I were you, I'd get away from Spearfish as soon as possible so these two don't continue to be stupid."

"Would early tomorrow morning be quick enough?" Fats asked.

"It would be just perfect," the officer said.

As Fats was leaving the building, he heard the police office call for backup and some first responders.

35

Fats took the advice he had been given the night before and was on the road by 6:00 a.m. He decided to save the stone face presidents for later and check out Sturgis instead.

It was only 30 miles down the road according to his map. Fats had heard of Sturgis, even all the way back in Whitefish. Every year, during the first week of August, the entire place was taken over by motorcycle enthusiasts. The yearly rally had been going strong since 1938. Fats had heard stories about the revelry and participants in various states of undress.

It sounded interesting but something Fats wanted to avoid like the plague. He hated big crowds, and Sturgis boasted tens of thousands bikers descending on the place for weeks on end. Fats had no opposition to seeing naked women, but the cost would be too high in his opinion. That's why he was visiting in the winter. He thought it would be interesting to see the place without the throngs of people. He wasn't disappointed.

Fats didn't know how many people lived in Sturgis, but he put the population between four and five thousand. It was a small town by anybody's standards, and a perfect number in Fats' mind.

The entire place looked more like a ghost town, however. There were a number of bars, but they all were closed. Fats looked at a sign in one window that read, "Opening In March—Weather permitting." Fats had thought about staying and taking in some local color. There didn't seem to be any local color to be had until after March. Having dealt with a few motorcycle toughs, he wasn't enamored with a place that catered to them specifically.

He was back on the road in less than half an hour. His map told him that the small town of Deadwood was just sixteen miles away. He had heard of Deadwood. Travellers had said it was a wide-open town. Fats didn't know what that meant, but he was willing to find out.

Deadwood had been a gold rush town in the 1870's with a population of over 5,000. As Fats drove through the community, he realized that there were probably only 2,000 left. There was history here, but the little town looked like it was going to be relying on tourism. Fats supposed that was about all they had to offer, since the days of mining for gold had long passed.

Fats liked the town. He decided he wouldn't mind spending some time getting to know the area. He could base right out of Deadwood, since it was pretty much in the middle of the Black Hills.

As he was riding through the main drag, he noticed a place called Nuttal and Mann's Saloon. A sign on the building proclaimed that Wild Bill Hickok had been killed on the premises. It piqued his interest, and soon he was talking to the owner about a bartending job. He could start whenever he wanted, so Fats decided to spend a few days looking for a place to stay. The owner told him there were quite a few furnished apartments over the businesses on Main Street that he could find to rent. Apparently, it was off-season, so there were many places available at reasonable prices.

Fats found a place down the street. It wasn't much. The furniture was threadbare, and the bed sagged in the middle. It would be fine for Fats' needs, since he wouldn't be spending much time there, other than to sleep.

Since he had found his apartment quickly, Fats planned to explore the area before he reported for work. Four miles down the road was the town of Lead. When he asked about it, Fats learned quickly that it was pronounced LEED. It was founded in 1876 after the discovery of gold. There was a mining company called the Homestake Mining Company. It was the largest, deepest, and most productive mine in the Western Hemisphere. At least that's what they boasted. At one time the town had 8500 people in the early 1900's. It was nowhere close to that now.

Fats found a bar called The Boar's Nest, which was no surprise. It seemed that whatever community he visited he gravitated to places that served alcohol. It puzzled him somewhat, because he didn't drink all that much. As he thought about it while sipping on some local tap beer, he decided that the reason he sought out the bars was because he met more interesting people in those places. Fats knew he was happiest when he was observing the common man. He needed to know what made people tick. Unfortunately for Fats, when he became involved personally, it generally went badly. He was pondering his bad luck in that respect, when he felt someone sit down next to him.

He glanced over and saw it was a woman. She was quite striking, and it made Fats nervous. He decided to keep quiet and mind his own business, even though he wanted to strike up a conversation. He knew this woman was out of his league, and nothing would come of inserting himself into her business.

He took a long pull from his tap beer, draining it. He set the glass down on the bar napkin and was deciding whether he wanted another, when the woman picked up his glass and lifted it to show the bartender.

Fats looked over at her not knowing what to say and not understanding what was happening. The bartender presented a fresh glass of tap beer and set it in front of him. Fats reached for his wallet in an effort to pay for the drink. The woman put her hand over Fats' hand and wallet.

"It's on me. Please put away your money."

Fats paused and looked at her. He actually was at a loss for words. The woman smiled.

"My name is Veronica Bullock. My friends just call me Vera," Vera said, and extended her hand.

Fats took her hand, shaking it limply. He said nothing.

"Whoa there, fella. That's quite a grip you've got there."

Fats reddened.

"Can you speak?"

Fats wondered what was wrong with him. He usually was the one to run off at the mouth. This woman had some kind of aura about her that he couldn't penetrate. He would need to rely on his hippie-speak.

"Merely thunderstruck at your exquisiteness."

Vera smiled. "Do you have a name?"

"Please disregard my discourtesy. Roland Sinning is the moniker, however the pseudonym for your indulgence would be Fats."

"You are a strange one."

"Indeed and you are most sublime. Makes me into a blubbering buffoon."

Vera laughed long and hard.

"I genuinely like you, and Baby Boomers ought to stick together."

"No comprehendo." Fats looked puzzled.

"Seriously? What rock did you crawl out from under?"

"Glacier National Park."

"That would explain it then. Baby Boomer is the name they have given to our generation."

"Still nothing to report."

"Well, it is the name given to the children born between 1946 and 1964."

"How did you ascertain that I fit that designation?"

"The length of your hair for one. The way you speak as well."

"Duly noted, and I thank you for your perceptiveness."

"Now, can we just drop a bit of the college hippie talk? It's making my head hurt."

"It is who I am. If I beckoned for you to stop being magnificent and become grotesque, would it even be achievable?"

"How can anyone answer a question like that without sounding stuck up?"

"I apologize and will try to be more conversational."

"Thank you."

"I am intrigued by your last name. I've read some of the history of the area, and it seems the name Bullock has played a prominent role."

"That was three or four generations ago."

"Let's see, I think the name I can remember was Seth Bullock. It was said that he was a sheriff and an entrepreneur."

"That's about all I know as well, unless you consider starting a hardware store in the middle of a gold rush to be entrepreneurial."

"He probably made a lot of money. Was he a relative?"

"Maybe a great-grandfather or a great-great-grandfather. I never bothered to find out."

"Not a student of history?"

"Not family history. I'm just trying to forget about being a Bullock and concentrate on finding out who I am and where I belong."

"Kindred spirits. I'm trying to experience the very same life-changing pathway."

"What are you doing in Lead?"

"Just exploring. I actually have a job at a bar in Deadwood."

"Really? What bar?"

"I have forgotten the name, but it has a sign on the outside that says Wild Bill Hickok was killed on the premises. I just got the job today as a matter-of-fact."

Vera tried to hide a smile.

"What did I say? Have I misspoken?"

"No. It's just that the bar is owned by my family."

"Do you believe in coincidences?"

"Sure. They happen all the time. We were supposed to meet, or we wouldn't be sitting here together at this time in history."

"So, why are you sitting here when your family owns the bar in Deadwood?"

"I get tired of the notoriety. Even though Lead is just a few miles down the road, I can almost get lost here."

Fats had been intrigued with the beautiful woman sitting on his right. He had taken the opportunity to really look at her to see what flaws she might have. It was Fats' experience that some of the beauties he had encountered weren't quite so perfect on reexamination.

He couldn't find one thing he would even call a blemish. Vera had white skin that made her look like a China doll. She wore eye make up, but he could detect little else. She didn't need anything.

Fats measured 5 foot 10 inches in his shoes. He hadn't seen Vera stand since she sat down next to him, but she appeared to be quite tall. Fats liked that in a woman. She was dressed in a long-sleeved shirt with blue jeans and cowboy boots. She had on a coat that came almost to the floor. She looked like she might be ready to herd cattle on some trail drive. Fats couldn't tell what kind of figure she had, because her clothing masked everything from the neck down.

"Looks like you're just missing your cowboy hat to be in full regalia."

Vera motioned to the wall. Fats saw a hat rack with a number of hats on it.

"Second from the left."

Fats smiled.

"It's not what you think. I hate wearing this stuff. It just happens to be the costume of the locals who cater to the tourists. You'll be wearing something similar quite soon."

Fats tried to picture himself as a cowboy. He wasn't seeing it.

"Nobody told me about that."

"Probably thought you could figure it out on your own."

"Hardly. I'm not very intuitive."

"I don't know, you seemed to have summed me up pretty well," Vera said, and her brown eyes danced a bit.

Fats thought it was as provocative an action as he had ever seen. Of course he knew he was infatuated with the woman's beauty, so his feeling didn't count for much.

"I suppose I'm going to have to do some shopping before I report for work. I need some help. Would you help me pick something out?"

"How long are you planning to stay working in the bar?"

"Remains to be seen," Fats said.

Vera looked him over.

"Stand up."

She stood alongside of Fats. First she ran her hand along his inseam, another provocative act. Then she grabbed his shoulders and ran her hand down his back.

"I don't think you'll have to buy anything. I've got some things that will fit you back at my place. Even got the boots."

Fats looked at her wondering why she would have men's clothing. Vera caught his question immediately.

"Don't ask. Bad relationship."

Fats shrugged his shoulders and sat back down.

"Finish your beer. I'm taking you to my place and get you out of your tourist clothes."

Fats couldn't help but smile. Vera noticed immediately.

"Down, boy. Let's take it easy," she said, trying to look serious.

Fats didn't mind. It was something he was good at.

36

Fats followed Vera back to Deadwood, and they stopped at a Western outfitter shop not far from Fats' apartment. They parked in front of the shop, and Vera got out of her vehicle first. She started to walk up the sidewalk to the front door.

"I thought we were going to your place," Fats said.

"We are. I own it. My quarters are upstairs."

Fats followed her up the walk, and Vera opened up the front door and took out a ring of keys. Just inside the door was a staircase that Fats assumed led to the second story apartment. She unlocked the door and pushed Fats inside.

"Go on up and open us a couple of beers," Vera said.

Fats took the steps two at a time and found the light switch at the top of the stairs. Fats hated the dark and went around turning on as many lights as he could. He noticed the apartment was well appointed, and it looked like Vera had expensive tastes.

He went over to the refrigerator and opened it. To his surprise, all he could see were beer bottles. It appeared that Vera had a taste for Pabst Blue Ribbon. He took out two bottles and found a church key in a nearby drawer and opened both. He put the bottles on the counter and opened the freezer side of the appliance. There was nothing but bags of ice inside.

"I don't cook," Vera said, as she entered the room with a large bag.

"Sorry. I was surprised by just the beer in the fridge," Fats said.

Vera handed the bag over to Fats.

"You need to try on this stuff, and see if it fits. If it does, it's yours."

Fats looked inside and pulled out a large cowboy hat. It was stamped with the word Stetson on the inside. There were a number of shirts with tabs on the collar and a few pair of jeans. At the bottom of the bag Fats found a pair of cowboy boots. It looked like they were alligator skin. They were beautiful, and Fats kicked off his shoes and tried them on immediately. They might have been just a little big for his feet, but he decided that it was nothing that couldn't be fixed with extra pairs of socks.

"How do they feel?" Vera asked.

"Great," Fats said, while admiring his new footwear.

"Well, try on the rest of the stuff," Vera said, and sat on a chair at her table.

"Where's the bathroom?" Fats asked, looking around.

Vera grabbed one of the beers.

"Uh-uh. You try it on in front of me."

Generally, Fats wasn't all that shy. There was something about Vera that unnerved him, however.

"Where did this stuff come from?"

"Did you see the store when you came in?" Vera asked sarcastically.

"This stuff looks used. I don't think you sell well-worn items."

"They came from a guy I used to live with. He took off one night and didn't have time to take his clothes."

Fats wondered if she would share the backstory with him. It sounded somewhat sinister. He would need to keep his eyes open and rely on his extra-sensory perception.

"Let's go. Your beer might be getting warm."

Fats began taking off his clothes. He took off his shirt and was going to try on one of tabbed shirts from the bag.

"No. Take off your pants first. I want to see the merchandise."

"Can I leave on my underwear?" Fats asked.

"Depends. You wear briefs or boxers?"

"Tightee whitees."

"Leave 'em on. I can get a pretty good idea about the size of your junk."

Fats wondered what he had stumbled into. This woman had some issues, but it appeared that he might get laid if he played his cards right. He stripped down to his skivvies and paused for Vera to get a good look.

She nodded, and Fats wondered if it was in appreciation or disdain. He couldn't tell. He knew he didn't like being on display like this, so he quickly tried on the jeans. They were western-cut with tapered legs and some number on the leather patch. Fats heard that if they had a red thread running on the seam at the bottom of each leg, they might be worth something. He would check that later.

Next, he put on the one of the shirts, and while it wasn't skin-tight like the cowboys liked to wear, it fit pretty well. Fats didn't like things tight anyway.

"I thought the things might fit. He was close to your size," Vera said.

"Want to tell me what happened to him?" Fats asked.

"No. Why don't you join me and drink your beer?"

Fats pulled on the boots again. They were the best part of the outfit as far as he was concerned.

"Try on the hat," Vera said.

Fats reached over and picked up the Stetson. He could tell it was expensive. Between the boots and the hat, Fats wondered how much money it would take to buy new. He put on the hat.

Vera went into fits of laughter. The hat settled over Fats' eyes and ears. The last owner, it seemed, had an extra large melon.

"Hey, who turned out the lights?" Fats asked, playing along.

Vera hooted even louder. Fats played his blind man routine and tried to feel his way over to the table.

Finally, Vera got control of herself.

"Take that damn thing off. I'll get you something that fits later."

Fats took off the hat and flipped it over to the couch. He went over and sat across from Vera and downed half his beer before he put the bottle back down.

"Thirsty work."

Vera looked over at Fats.

"You are a strange one."

"Said the spider to the fly."

Fats thought he noticed a flash in Vera's eyes. As quickly as he noticed it, it was gone. She was the strangest woman he had ever met for sure. He didn't know what to make of her. He hoped she wasn't dangerous.

They sat at the table for most of the rest of the evening. Fats got up, now and then, to get rid of the beer they had been consuming. Fats had the reputation of holding his beer for someone so skinny. Vera outdid him, however. They traded beer for beer for a count of ten each. Fats didn't see Vera use the bathroom once during that time. Of course, she might have had another bathroom someplace and used it while Fats was busy getting rid of all his beer.

The clock on the stove said 11:00 when Vera finally stood up.

"I've got to open the store at 9:00 tomorrow morning, so I'm going to bed."

Fats looked at her questioning what he should do.

"You can go back to your place or sleep on the couch."

Vera went into the bedroom and came back with a pillow and sheets.

"There's a blanket below the end table if you need it." Vera said, and then turned around and went back into the bedroom slamming the door.

Fats just sat at the table deciding what he should do. He didn't think he wanted to spend the night on a couch, when he had a bed waiting for him just down the street. He decided to pick up the place and then quietly make his exit.

He found an empty case for the beer bottles and put them near the door. He placed the pillow and sheets on the couch and turned to look around to see if he missed anything. As he moved toward the staircase, he heard the door open.

"Are you coming to bed or what?" Vera asked, through a crack in the door.

Fats stopped and thought about what Vera said. "Or what" seemed like maybe the right choice at first consideration. Fats might have been too inquisitive to pay much heed to that little warning voice in his head.

"I guess I'm coming to bed," Fats said.

The door opened fully and Fats stepped through to the bedroom. Vera was standing in front of the bed stark naked. Fats took in all the sights.

It had been hard to discern what kind of body Vera had when she was dressed in her entire regalia. Fats thought that she might have been somewhat coarse throughout the middle. He didn't think she was heavy but maybe just big boned. What he saw was nothing short of amazing.

Vera was slender with small hips and thin legs. She had a flat stomach and broader shoulders. Fats decided her shoulders had to be broad because of the size of her breasts. They were the reason he thought she might have been coarser built.

Fats didn't think he had ever seen bigger breasts on a normal sized woman. He had seen the old calendars with the huge women with gigantic breasts but never anything close to the size that Vera was sporting. He was without words for once in his life.

Vera put up with his ogling, until she could no longer stand it.

"Are you getting enough of an eyeful? Remember, I only got to see you in your jockeys."

In less than 30 seconds, Fats was out of his cowboy duds and nuzzling Vera's tremendous breasts. He tried to put his arms around her but he couldn't until he lowered them to embrace her around the waist. Fats thought he might have died and gone to heaven. He had always been a breast man.

"You are the chestiest woman I have ever seen." Fats, said hoping he wasn't drooling.

"Like the ta-ta's, I see. Look them over. They are all natural. Nothing manmade up here," Vera said, pointing her index fingers at her chest.

Fats could only stare. She was right. They were as natural as anything he had ever seen. He had no Playboy experience, but he had seen enough women to know.

It was Vera's turn.

"I see your jockey shorts didn't really do justice to what was hiding in them."

Fats didn't know if she was making fun of him, or if she really thought he was large in the nether region. He didn't really care at the moment. His body was on autopilot.

Vera could see that she had teased him almost to the point of no return.

"Well, it's bedtime. I have a lot to do tomorrow so make up your mind. Are you staying or are you leaving?"

"I guess I'm staying. I can't leave this way."

"You should be back to normal by morning if you can sleep on it," Vera said.

"It would have to be on my back, or I'll poke a hole in your mattress. I don't know if I'll have enough skin left to be able to close my eyelids to get any sleep."

"You'd better hope so. There will be no sex between us. I may sleep with someone I just met, but I don't have to screw them." Vera moved over to the side of the bed and slipped under the sheets and covers.

As fast as Fats had been aroused, he became flaccid. Who was this woman? He had never met a woman who needed to be totally in charge of every aspect of her life. Fats decided he wanted to try and understand more about her. He would put up with her antics as long as he could. Besides, he wanted as much access to her breasts as humanly possible.

Fats turned out the light, and by the time he got into bed, he could hear Vera breathing heavily. She had fallen asleep. He was totally crestfallen. Fats had thought that maybe she was just playing around and things might actually happen once they got into bed.

Like so many times in his life, he was frustrated once again.

37

Fats finally fell asleep sometime in the early morning hours. His rest was fitful, because he kept dreaming about having sex with Vera. When he finally woke up, it was light outside. He looked over at the alarm and saw it was 9:30. Vera was nowhere to be seen.

He jumped out of bed and pulled on the clothes that Vera had given him. He was hoping she had left the apartment, because he didn't want to talk to her after the night's debacle.

He knew there wouldn't be anything to eat unless he considered beer some type of breakfast. He went over to retrieve the bag he had put his clothes into and saw a new hat placed right on top. He couldn't have missed it if he tried. He tried it on, and it fit perfectly. It would take a bit of wearing to break it in correctly, but he liked how it fit immediately.

Fats looked around, and the Beatles' song "Norwegian Wood" came to mind. "And when I awoke I was alone, this bird had flown." He left the apartment the same zway he had entered the night before. The Western wear shop was dark. He saw that the sign on the door said open at 10:00. He pulled the stairway door closed and made sure it was locked before he made a dash to his pickup.

He thought about going to the bar, but he knew it didn't open until 11:00. Fats realized he had one more day until he had to report for work. He decided to go and see the presidents and take in the rest of the area. He had heard there was some kind of mammoth dig around Hot Springs. Maybe he would check that out as well.

Fats decided he was hungry and knew he needed to eat something, but he wanted to get out of Deadwood before he found a café. He didn't want to risk running into Vera. He wouldn't know what to say to her, so he would eat later. The events of the previous night had him totally confused, and he didn't like the feeling.

Mt. Rushmore was not a disappointment. Fats sat for a long time just marveling at the sheer will it must have taken to carve the images out of stone. After he had his fill, he traveled south. Keystone didn't seem like much of a town. The sign said "population 300", and it looked like they were in the process of catering to the tourist trade. He did make a stop at the National Presidential Wax Museum. It featured wax sculptures of every president in US history and several of the Sioux chiefs.

Custer was bigger than Keystone by maybe 500 more people. The sign coming into town said they had the widest Main Street in the United States. Supposedly, it was to accommodate teams of oxen pulling wagons so they could turn around. It was one the first places in the Black Hills where gold was discovered. There was quite a bit of history, and Fats made sure to find the welcome center to get a full measure.

His last stop for the day was Hot Springs. He looked at the springs and had a desire to participate but didn't have a swimsuit with him. Steam was rising from the springs, and it looked quite inviting. The people in the springs seemed to be enjoying it anyway. His main reason for going this far south was to view the mammoth site. Fats found that it was an active paleontological dig site.

After he paid the entrance fee, he watched as one of the workers tried to unearth more remains. It was painful. The sign said the sinkhole boasted the largest concentration of mammoth remains in the world. Fats liked all the biggest and best tales the Black Hills seemed to be known for but wondered how much exaggeration was really involved. The day melted away, and after two hours, he decided to return to Deadwood.

On the way back, Fats realized he was hungry. He hadn't eaten, and it was after 7:00. He was coming into a town called Hill City, and the street was lined with bars. He chose one that looked like it served food and went in. It wasn't long before he heard about "Sue" the most complete skeleton of a Tyrannosaurus Rex ever discovered. Fats hid a smile. Once again the Black Hills had the most and best of everything. It seemed that for a community of under a thousand, this place had a lot to offer. Fats made a commitment to return and do some further exploration.

The drive back to Deadwood took almost an hour. It wasn't all that far, but Fats decided to take it slow. He arrived after 9:30 and decided not to go back to his apartment until he had a drink. He headed straight to Nuttal and Mann's Saloon. He wanted to touch base and see what was happening. He had to go to work the following day and didn't want to just show up without getting some background from the bartender.

The place wasn't busy, and there were only a few people sitting at the bar. Fats didn't want to make conversation with any strangers, so he found a section of empty barstools and sat on one that didn't wobble. The bartender came over immediately and looked Fats over.

"Nice duds. You know you don't have to dress up for the tourists unless you want to."

"I thought it might be fun. It might coax a few more tips. Besides, I might be meant to sport such vestments." Fats brought back his inner hippie.

"I don't know, you seem more like a dude to me."

"Duly noted." Fats enjoyed jawing with anyone who would listen to him.

"Wait." The bartended reached across the bar and touched Fats' shirt.

"Hey man, I only swing one way." Fats pulled back.

"Sorry. It's just that the western wear you are sporting looks familiar. Where did you get it?"

"Some woman with the nom de guerre of Vera."

"It's what I thought. You know she's nuts, right?"

"In regards to what, may I ask?"

"Those are the same clothes she gave to the last guy who worked here. Well, not the hat. She must want something from you with a gift like that. The hat alone would cost over two hundred."

Fats tried not to show that he was impressed.

"What transpired with the former owner of these fine raiments?"

"No one really knows. He just disappeared. There's a lot of speculation. It was strange that he left his clothes, don't you think?"

Fats pondered his question for a bit.

"What's your take on this puzzle?"

"Couldn't say, myself. I try to stay away from her. I can only tell you what some are saying."

"Which is what?"

"Vera got tired of him. He was living with her. Maybe she just got rid of him, or he got scared and left."

"What do you think happened?"

"Couldn't say. The family owns this place, so I'm not free to give an opinion."

Red flares exploded in Fats' head. He ordered a beer, and the bartender turned to tend to his request. Fats decided he would need to proceed with extreme caution. He had to agree with his bartender friend, she was quite nuts.

He had finished the top half of the pint, when he felt someone sit next to him. It was Vera. It took Fats by surprise, and he almost coughed up the beer he had consumed.

"I don't generally have such an effect on men in a bar," Vera said, smiling.

"I'm not fond of anyone inserting themselves and purloining my space."

"You didn't seem to mind last night," Vera said, and looked straight ahead into the bar's mirror.

"Last night was very strange. You weirded me out. Then I wake up in the morning, and you were absent-without-leave."

"I don't answer to anyone. I do what I do, and that's the extent of it. Besides, I don't screw men I just meet."

"When do you screw them?" Fats asked, with just a hint of sarcasm in his voice.

"When I'm good and damn ready, Mr. Employee."

"I see." Fats could tell she was pissed. He decided to change direction. "By the way, thanks for the homburg."

"You are a strange one. But you are welcome. It seems to fit you quite well."

"Since I hail from Montana, it would make sense that this fedora would be a natural on me." Fats took another sip of his beer for something to break the awkwardness.

Vera turned and stared at Fats for an uncomfortably long time. Women generally didn't rattle Fats, but this Vera was exasperating. He pretended not to notice her scrutiny.

"So, now what?" Vera asked.

"I don't understand the interrogatory." Fats said, trying hard not to play into her hand.

"I mean, where do we go from here?"

"Once again, I don't comprehend the inquisition."

"Will it be your place or mine?"

The question took Fats completely off guard. He tried to clear his mind. He didn't want her at his apartment.

"I would suppose that would depend what you have in your cerebrum."

"It all depends. Since you apparently don't see the need to ask me to your place, I'll see you at mine."

"I'll consider the invitation," Fats said. "After I finish my beer."

Vera stood, and Fats looked at her. Damn it all, she was an attractive woman, and he couldn't help being infatuated.

"Don't wait too long. You might miss out on all of this." Vera ran her hands from her breasts to her knees as she turned around.

Fats watched her walk out the door. He chugged the remaining beer in his glass. He didn't want to give in but she possessed some sort of witchy shit, and he couldn't stop himself. He was almost ready to follow her out the door when the bartender came over and put his hand on his shoulder. Fats sat back down.

"Do you want some advice?"

"You seem like a trustworthy gentleman, so go ahead." Fats wondered what he had in mind.

"Run like hell." The bartender turned and walked away.

Fats knew he had launched himself into an irrational conundrum.

38

Fats' pickup seemed to want to ride past Vera's shop and loft. Together they rode past almost a dozen times. Finally, Fats had enough. He steered himself toward his apartment, fully considering not leaving until the next morning. Curiosity got the best of him, however.

He went over to Vera's loft just as he knew he would from the beginning. He decided to walk and before he left, Fats stuffed a grocery bag with his clothes. He would leave the bag on her steps, and if things started going haywire, he would get the hell out of there and leave her clothes in the bag. Well, maybe not the hat. He liked it and knew he deserved it.

On his slow walk to Vera's, something told him in the back of his head that he would be leaving sooner than he had anticipated. He climbed her stairs and carefully placed his bag of clothes where he thought it would be out of Vera's vision. He knocked on the door.

"Come in," Vera shouted from somewhere deep in another room.

Fats walked in and looked around. There was a pizza box on the counter that hadn't been opened. He walked over and noticed it was from a local place and had everything on it. He took a slice and went to the refrigerator for a beer. When he found what he was looking for and shut the door, Vera was standing next to him naked.

"I was going to tell you to help yourself, but I see you already have."

Fats looked her over. He liked what he saw.

"Well, I haven't participated in all you have to proffer from what I can behold." Fats seemed to lose interest in his pizza and beer.

"You going to eat that or just hold it and stare at me?"

"The latter, if you don't mind."

"I do. I need a slice myself. Get me a beer."

Vera went over to the pizza box, removed a slice and sat down on the couch. Fats grabbed another beer for her and moved over to sit with her. He handed her the beer and wondered if she usually sat on the couch naked. Luckily, it was leather and could be cleaned easily. The thought had a negative effect on his libido, and he tried to put it out of his mind.

Vera was almost finished with her slice of pizza before Fats even thought of taking a bite. He crammed most of it into his mouth and tried to wash it down with some beer. He almost choked.

"Easy there, cowboy, small bites and small swallows are the way to go." Vera turned and switched on the television with the remote.

Fats wasn't interested in what was on. His show was right in front of him, and he needed to decide how to proceed. It was apparent that Vera was baiting him. Unfortunately, he knew it was working.

"So, what's the blueprint here? I mean, what are we planning to choreograph this evenfall?"

"That would be entirely up to you," Vera said, while taking a sip of her beer.

Fats could see that her nakedness didn't seem to bother Vera in the least.

"Why am I getting the receptivity that there will be some type of exploitation enfolding?"

"It's always tit for tat in this life." Vera said, knowing full well what she had said.

Fats knew it as well. The TV was blaring, and it was a huge irritant for Fats.

"Can you perhaps avert that entity to an inactive status? It's having some adverse agitation on my personal psyche." It would have been easier for Fats to say the volume was so loud he couldn't think clearly. He didn't roll that way, however. He loved his little word games. Fats liked irritating Vera, since she was so versed in irritating him.

This whole posturing was going nowhere for either of them.

Shit or get off the pot, Fats thought, and hoped he didn't say it out loud.

Just when he was ready to push Vera into doing something, she stood up. Fats couldn't help but notice she looked fabulous. Everything was in the right place. She wasn't a skinny woman by any means, but she was proportioned exactly how Fats thought a woman should be.

"You're probably the most attractive woman in the entire Black Hills," Fats said, trying not to drool.

"Why stop there? It's a big country, and I doubt you could find someone less inhibited with this to offer." Vera turned around holding her arms out.

Before he knew what was happening, Fats was standing both physically and figuratively. Vera took a step in his direction and put her arms around his waist. Her ample breasts felt soft and full on his chest. He liked the feeling and chose not to move. Vera backed up, to his dismay. She began to remove his clothing starting with his hat and moving down. Soon enough Fats stood in front of her in his underwear. She pulled them down, and he stepped out of them. It was Vera's turn to ogle.

"Relish what you perceive?" Fats asked.

"It will have to do."

Vera led him into the bedroom. The move surprised Fats, because he just assumed that they would be having sex in some unconventional place to satisfy Vera's eerie and eccentric behavior.

Vera was probably thinking the same thoughts concerning Fats. Either way, he followed her into the bedroom, willingly.

Vera was insatiable. Fats thought she might be killing him with her sexual appetite. He was helpless to stop himself, because he knew she was some kind of witch. It was the only way to explain his numerous arousals and ability to satisfy her every desire. Fats had never gone to the end zone with a woman before. His closest experience had been a strong stand-up third base, so nothing even closely compared to his experience with Vera.

That's when Fats knew he had to leave, and it would need to be soon.

39

Sometime in the middle of the night, Vera finally fell asleep. Fats thanked his lucky stars for the chance to escape Vera's sexual marathon, but he was far too wired to even close his eyes. She had fallen asleep on his chest, and Fats waited until he figured she was in a deep sleep before he tried to move her. She rolled over on her side with a little prompting and didn't seem to stir in the least. It was good news for Fats.

He moved as slowly as possible from the bed and picked up his clothes where Vera had left them in the living room. He closed the bedroom door quietly and retrieved his bag of clothes from the staircase. After dressing and putting the western wear into the bag, he placed it on the counter. He wondered if the hat was going to be an issue. It didn't matter, because he was going to keep it.

He let himself out of the apartment and moved quickly to his own place. He picked up everything and put it into the pickup. He realized that traveling light was a good thing. When everything was loaded, Fats left a note and wedged it in the door for the landlord. He was sorry to have wasted the month's rent on the apartment, but he needed to leave. Vera was the first woman that had ever scared him.

Fats hated to leave without letting the bartender know he wasn't coming to work. He knew he didn't want to leave any hints about where he was going, and that was just as well because he had no idea.

He decided to head south on 385 and see where it would take him. Dawn was upon him as he drove past the sign that told him Lead was one mile. It looked like it would be a clear day, but Fats wouldn't see any sun for quite a while because of the hills. He was driving in a valley, and he thought it would be strange living someplace where you only got direct sunlight mid-morning when the sun finally cleared the mountaintops, and then lose it again mid-afternoon when it went behind the western range.

He wouldn't like it, but it didn't matter, because he wasn't staying. He passed through Hill City and noticed the small community was coming to life. He was feeling good about his decision to leave secretly. He didn't really want to hurt anyone, and this felt like the right thing to do.

Somewhere between Hill City and Custer, a car came up on his pickup's rear end too quickly to suit Fats. The headlights were on, and Fats couldn't really make out the vehicle. It was a smaller passenger car and it looked sporty. Fats decided that he would find the first turnout and let the person pass. He or she was probably late for work in Custer.

The road was curvy and Fats couldn't see anywhere to turn out, so he proceeded at the appointed speed limit. The car was riding his ass, and he was starting to feel slightly irritated. The road began to straighten out, so Fats thought he would slow down and let the car pass him.

He took his foot off the gas and let the pickup coast for a bit. The car took the hint and moved to pass. When it was right next to him, the car slowed and seemed to only keep pace. Fats braked slightly, but the car stayed right next to him.

The horn honked, and Fats turned to look. It was a black Chevy Nova Super Sport. It looked like it had some horsepower. Fats thought it looked like a very nice car, and he was puzzled why someone would honk at him when he was trying to give them the entire road.

He looked closer and saw it was Vera in the driver's seat. She was still naked from the night before. The realization shook Fats to his core. She had followed him from Deadwood.

Vera was smiling while giving him her middle finger. Then she grabbed the wheel with both hands and turned the Nova right into the side of the pickup. It was mesmerizing, and Fats didn't react until she hit him again. The side of her car was trashed, and Fats could see she had done some minor damage to his driver's side as well. He wondered what she was thinking. The Nova was no match for his solid old pickup. Then he realized that she was trying to make him lose control. She was trying to kill him.

Vera was a competent driver and matched his speed no matter what he did to try to shake her. They were starting to descend a small hill with a large sweeping curve. Fats knew he had to make a move, or this would end badly for him. There was a small drop off at the edge of the road that emptied into a large ditch. A small stream cut through a meadow just to the right of the ditch. He knew Vera would try to force him off the road right at that spot. He made a decision.

When Vera started to make her move to run into him again, Fats hit his brakes hard. He might have gone through the windshield had he not been holding onto the steering wheel with all his strength.

As Vera cranked her steering wheel to try to hit Fats, the front end of her Nova found nothing but air. She started to skid in front of Fats' pickup. Fats could see her eyes were wide open, and there was a puzzled look on her face. Fats hit the accelerator and caught her passenger door with his bumper. It wasn't much of a bump, but it was enough to get the Nova's tires to catch the pavement and the car flipped over nicely.

Fats hit his brakes and watched as the car slide sideways down the pavement. It finally hit the shoulder and flipped over again and landed in the ditch on its top. The momentum didn't carry the car into the creek, and Fats was happy about that. He didn't need anyone drowning. He went slowly past the upside-down vehicle and tried to see inside. The car was too low, and there was no sign of Vera. He hoped she had her seat belt fastened, or she might have been thrown from the vehicle.

He almost pulled over on the shoulder after he passed the car. Then he realized it would have been a bad decision. He needed to get away from Vera as quickly as possible. He hoped she wasn't killed in the accident, but he wasn't feeling all that much remorse. She had started the whole thing, after all. He was happy no one had witnessed what had happened. He knew it wouldn't have turned out well for him. Vera had a presence in the Hills, and he was a newcomer and drifter. He knew who would be believed.

Fats stepped on the accelerator and got up to speed. He would follow the speed limit to avoid any unwanted attention. He drove south and didn't relax until he passed through Hot Springs. He stayed on 385 until it changed to 26. Fats had no destination, so he followed 26 until it became 30 and finally ran right into Paxton, Nebraska. He pulled into a place named Ole's Big Game Bar.

It was his kind of place and didn't take a lot of convincing before he had himself a job. It was a good place to hide out for a while. If Vera had survived the rollover, he knew she would never find him down here in Nebraska. Fats figured it was where people went when they didn't want to be found. It would work well for him.

~

Fats didn't know how long he stayed at Ole's Big Game Bar. It didn't matter much, because he liked the place. He enjoyed everything about bartending. One of his favorite duties was calling out the numbers for Keno. Late afternoons and weekends, the Keno players were fast and furious. Fats sat behind the bar in a small cutout area and called the numbers as they randomly appeared on some of the balls that he drew out of a rolling cage. It was great fun, and he got to meet the winners. They always seemed to be in a generous mood after they won and tipped him accordingly.

One particular Saturday, he was almost ready to call it a night when he noticed someone taking a seat on his left. When he was finished with the game, he looked over and nodded to the newcomer.

Fats stopped short. It was Vera filling out a Keno slip. She completed her series of numbers and handed the paper to Fats.

Vera was wearing a low cut top and when Fats looked over she pulled it down exposing both breasts. He was startled and yet confused, because he liked what he saw.

"A stunning and decadent perversion of the human condition. In the gaming arena, we would tell you to breast those babies," Fats said, trying to sound nonchalant.

"Take a good look, you asshole. You left me to die on the highway, and I've come to settle up."

"Seems you were the perpetrator, and myself the innocent traveler in that adventure."

"All depends upon one's perspective. I don't happen to share yours."

"You are persistent, I'll give you that. How did you find my location?"

"I know many people and have a huge network of folks who are happy to do me favors."

Fats realized she more than likely took down his license number. It was something he hadn't considered. He should have known better when dealing with a narcissist.

"What persuaded you to imprint my footsteps?"

Fats knew nothing he said would ever bring Vera to admit she was the one in the wrong. He needed to buy some time to find out her intentions.

"It's quite simple, really. I'm going to kill you," Vera said, without the smallest bit of malice in her voice.

If it scared Fats, he wasn't about to give her that satisfaction.

"Have you plotted my demise, or will this be something a bit more impromptu?"

"It will be a surprise. You'll never see it coming."

Vera got up and pulled down her top once more.

"You could have had all of this, so now you get nothing." Vera walked out of the Ole's.

Fats shut off the Keno machine and sat still for a time. He was trying to think what he needed to do. He would probably have to leave, but he was concerned about who Vera might have hired to have him watched. There was one thing for certain, he wasn't going off half-cocked. The last view of Vera's breasts jolted his brain. He had been full-cocked to get involved with her in the first place, but some things just happened, and Fats had no control. He needed to work on not letting his penis do the thinking.

Two days passed and any decision concerning Vera was taken out of the equation.

It was the day Zander walked into Ole's, and Fats' life took a right turn.

Epilogue

In het land der blinden is eenoog koning
Among the blind, the one-eyed is king.
--Dutch Proverb

Still thinking about his past, Fats was snapped back into the present when Fran made her presence known.

"Ground control to Major Fats, commencing countdown." Fran liked to get into Fats' head with variations of song lyrics.

Fats always liked the David Bowie tune, "Space Oddity." He wasn't happy being rousted from his reverie by that particular tune. It didn't help that his last thoughts were of Vera. He wondered what happened to her.

When he had moved to Colorado with Zander, he had changed his license plates and tossed the old Montana tags in the garbage. He was certain that Vera couldn't find him that way. He just didn't know what other resources she might have. He could never let his guard down.

"So, what has you off on some ethereal plane today?" Fran asked.

Fats decided to level with her and told her the whole story involving Vera and the Black Hills. When he was finished, Fran just starred at him.

"Just when I think I know all there is to know about you, you throw out something like this. Where does it all end?"

"It never ends. I'm like peeling a brussels sprout. Once you start, where does it all end, man?"

Fran just shook her head, clearly frustrated.

"It makes for some interesting times. People should maintain some suspense and intrigue or relationships go stale," Fats said, trying to justify his secrets that he kept from Fran.

"Why did you tell me this?" Fran asked.

"I wanted to prepare you for the possibility that this insane woman might somehow insert herself into our lives."

"Thanks so much for the heads-up. Don't you think you should do something to try and protect yourself?" Fran asked.

"I pondered it, but the woman is a total nut job. I don't know how she would come at me. Seems like an impossibility trying to second-guess the different scenarios. There are just too many."

"You've got those two pistols from those bikers under the bar. Maybe you should start carrying."

"I don't trust myself with a firearm. Someone might get hurt, and that someone could be me."

"She threatened your life. If someone told me they were going to kill me, I might take it a bit more seriously."

"She's got to ascertain my present location before she can inflict any harm to my person," Fats said, trying to lighten things up with his little hippie diatribe.

"Cut the crap, Fats. This sounds serious. You need to be vigilant and not let yourself be lulled into your usual fog. I imagine somehow, I'll have to bail your butt out of this mess like every other."

Fats smiled broadly. "That's my woman."

"It won't be for very long if you let this woman kill you."

"I have no intention of letting that happen, my dear."

Fats thought about it for a moment and realized he had no idea what he was going to do about Vera. Fran knew it as well.

Jayne Grafton woke up early. Something was wrong, but she was still half asleep, and couldn't grasp what it was. Something didn't feel right. She sat up in bed. At first she thought she had wet the bed, but then it hit her. Her water had broken. She was in labor. She called out for her Aunt Millie.

Millie appeared almost instantly.

"What's wrong girl?"

Jayne flung the sheet away, and Millie started to smile.

"I don't think it's funny. I'm having a baby, and it shouldn't be here for another month."

"I know, dear. Why don't you put something on, and we'll get you to the hospital," Millie said, trying to ease Jayne's anxiety.

"Something's wrong, I know it."

"Nonsense. Stop talking that way. All the babies in our family come early. That included you." Millie wasn't sure there was any truth in the statement, but it sounded good. She would say anything to get Jayne's mind off any negative thoughts.

On the way to the hospital, Jayne felt her first contraction. It was a strong one, and it hurt like hell. She muttered something under her breath. Unfortunately, it was a loud utterance, and Millie couldn't help but hear it.

"This isn't just his fault my dear. It takes two to make a baby," Millie said, smiling.

Jayne hated her at that moment. She hated everything because she knew Millie was right.

Most of all, she hated herself for getting into this predicament. Her alter ego, Sara Jane, kept rearing her ugly head try as she might to have killed her off.

~

Zander and Aubrey had seen the "USA in their Chevrolet" only it was in Zander's Ford pickup. Zander had found his way back to the Midwest when the weather started to show some promise that winter was over and spring was taking its place.

The two had looked Iowa over, and Zander had no idea what Aubrey thought about his home state. She wasn't sharing.

When they finally found their way to Hospers, Zander couldn't believe his eyes. The place looked like a ghost town. His father's shop was closed and boarded up. Things had changed. He wondered what happened to Juan Alvarez. He hadn't expected his father's shop to be abandoned.

They drove past his childhood home, and Zander decided to stop and find out if Juan's family still lived there. He knocked on the front door and waited. Finally, after a series of banging, the door opened. Zander didn't know the woman who was standing in front of him. But she knew him.

"Well, my stars, Sander Van Zee. I haven't seen you in, well, forever."

"Call me Zander, and I'm afraid you have the advantage. I'm sorry but I just don't recognize you."

"I don't doubt it one bit. I'm Danny Bloemendaal's little sister, Betsy. I always had a crush on you growing up. You just never knew I even existed."

Zander was embarrassed to have never paid attention to his best friend Danny's family.

"I'm so sorry, I feel like quite the fool."

"Oh, don't be hard on yourself. Boys don't pay much attention to little girls, especially when there is over ten years between them."

Betsy's comment made Zander feel a little better.

"I'm surprised that Juan Alvarez doesn't live here. I sold him the house before I left."

"I know. He sold it to my husband and me. That was a long time ago, Zander. A lot of things have changed around here."

"I know, I drove through town before I stopped here. I hardly recognize the place."

"It's so sad, but where are my manners? Come in and have a look at your old place and see what we've done with it."

"I've got someone with me," Zander said, and pointed at the pickup.

Betsy looked over. "Well, go get her. I'll call Danny and Ingrid. We'll have a reunion."

As Zander walked back to the pickup, he thought he might have to explain a few things to Aubrey concerning his past relationship with Ingrid.

~

Fats hustled around the bar making sure everything was ready before he opened the front door. Things seemed to be in order, and he walked over and unlocked the deadbolt. It was 10:00 a.m. and the regulars wouldn't be coming in until 11:00, so Fats took his usual place behind the bar and decided to read the newspaper. The rag came from Denver, and it was only on time when the roads were passable. Today was one of those times.

All the news was bad. It always was. Fats figured that nobody wanted to read about the good things in life. Everyone wanted to feel better about his or her own personal lives, and that happened when others around them had a shitty one. Fats hated the idea but read the paper anyway.

He was almost ready to turn to the sports section when he heard the front door chime. It would be the day's first customer. Fats put down the paper and moved toward the occupied table to take the very first order of the day. He stopped short about halfway there.

It was Vera. She had found him. The idea of the whole thing pissed Fats off.

"So, your little minions have given you my location. What's your next reposition?" Fats asked, trying not to sound alarmed.

"I told you before, I'm going to kill you."

Fats walked over to the table trying not to let Vera see that his hands were shaking. He sat down.

"Maybe we could have a conversation about that decision. I'm sure we could come to a mutually advantageous conclusion," Fats said, trying to defuse her anger with his words.

She wasn't buying it. Vera stood and reached into her bag. Fats could see Vera pulling out a pistol, as she moved with her back to the bar.

"How's this for a conversation, you stupid fuck?"

Fats hated that word. It was harsh and guttural, but he decided not to take issue with her usage at the moment. He could see that the pistol was a small caliber. It looked like a .22 center fire, which made him feel a little better. Some said was easier to survive a shot from a .22 than any other caliber. Vera was awfully close, so it might not matter.

"What can I do to help settle this matter peacefully?" Fats asked. He was starting to get a hopeless feeling in his gut.

"You can die. Nobody ever takes advantage of me and lives to tell about it."

"Is that what happened to the guy whose clothes you gave me?"

Fats could see he hit a nerve, and Vera seemed stunned for a moment. Then she started to smile.

"I was going to ask you how you knew that, but it won't matter. Dead men tell no tales."

"Ain't it the truth? What did you do with that poor bartender's body?"

"You shut your mouth. It doesn't matter."

"I think it matters. If I know what you did, how do you think I found out about it? There are others who have your number." Fats dropped his elegant speech to try to concentrate on the problem at hand.

"Do you think I care? You'll be dead. I'll deal with anyone else when that time comes."

"Damn woman, I've never seen a bigger narcissist. All things must be paid to the universe eventually."

"What the hell does that mean?" Vera was hot.

"Simply put, we all have to pay for our sins. Some sooner than others."

"If that's the case, you'll be one of the sooners." Vera raised the pistol.

Fats braced for the shot. He hoped she wouldn't shoot him in the face. He needed to try to keep whatever beauty he had left.

The shot rang out.

Vera's face exploded and covered Fats with blood and brain matter. Vera went down, and Fats saw Fran holding the Colt 45 pearl handle pistol from under the bar in her hands.

Fats wondered how he was going to clean up the huge mess Vera had left on the floor.

View other Black Rose Writing titles at www.blackrosewriting.com/books and use promo code **PRINT** to receive a **20% discount** when purchasing.

BLACK ROSE writing™

www.ingramcontent.com/pod-product-compliance
Lightning Source LLC
Chambersburg PA
CBHW010442100726
47904CB00008B/2454